Josephine l

The Formica co
dings and scrat
a stack of telephone books sat under a wall phone. The extralong cord dangled an inch above the floor. She envisioned JD pacing the room during yesterday's call from her, wishing the cord were her neck as he twisted the coils around his fingers.

All in all, the kitchen was…well, exactly what she'd expected after seeing the outside of the house. Shabby.

But beneath the room's run-down appearance, Josephine sensed warmth, love and security—things she couldn't see or touch, but that enveloped her in an invisible hug.

She could guarantee that her nephew, Bobby, would get the best of everything if he lived with his grandparents in their Chicago mansion.

Everything except the warmth and love.

Dear Reader,

Daddy by Choice is my second book in Harlequin American Romance's FATHERHOOD series. Nothing melts my heart more than the sight of a daddy taking care of his children. Isn't it fun to watch a five-year-old work his or her father over in the cereal aisle at the grocery store? How come when Dad gets home from the store there's enough junk food and treats to last a month, but Mom can't find anything in the bags to make a meal with?

And what would we do without the thousands of fathers who volunteer to coach their children's sports teams every year, haul tables and chairs around for the school PTO fund-raisers and agree to "keep the kids busy" while Mom finishes her bubble bath? Fatherhood is a blessing that my hero, JD, discovers when the son he didn't know he had is delivered to his doorstep. JD never expected fatherhood to be so difficult, but his determination to love Bobby and do what's in the boy's best interest at any cost makes him a real hero in my heart—and in Josephine Delaney's, too.

JD can't deny that the presence of his son's bossy, opinionated and sexy-as-all-get-out aunt helps smooth the road between father and son. It isn't long before Josephine has JD wishing for things that can never be. Then the truth comes out and JD's perfect world is thrown into chaos.

Can two people from different backgrounds come together to make a loving family and home for the sake of a young boy? I hope you enjoy finding out!

Please visit my Web site at www.marinthomas.com, or drop me a note at marin@marinthomas.com. I love to hear from readers!

Happy reading!

Marin Thomas

DADDY BY CHOICE

Marin Thomas

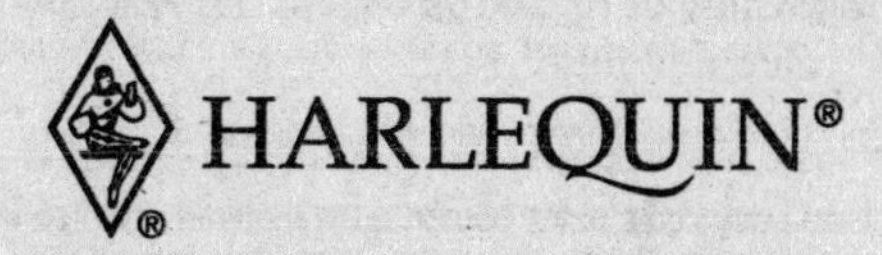

TORONTO • NEW YORK • LONDON
AMSTERDAM • PARIS • SYDNEY • HAMBURG
STOCKHOLM • ATHENS • TOKYO • MILAN • MADRID
PRAGUE • WARSAW • BUDAPEST • AUCKLAND

ISBN 0-373-75054-4

DADDY BY CHOICE

This edition published by arrangement with Harlequin Books S.A.

www.eHarlequin.com

Printed in U.S.A.

ABOUT THE AUTHOR

Marin Thomas hails from the Dairy State—Wisconsin. She played basketball at the University of Arizona and earned a bachelor of arts in radio-television. She is married to her college sweetheart and has two children. She loves writing about cowboys. Good thing home is now Texas, where there's never a shortage of cowboys for inspiration.

Books by Marin Thomas

HARLEQUIN AMERICAN ROMANCE

1024—THE COWBOY AND THE BRIDE
1050—DADDY BY CHOICE

To my husband, Kevin, for all the kids' sports teams you've coached over the years, the father-son days on the golf course, the daddy-daughter days at Six Flags and the hundreds of basketball games in the pool.

To my father, James Milton Smith, for all the years you spent putting together "Santa toys" on Christmas Eve, for playing "Bear" at bedtime and for not blowing up when I got in a fender bender at the Frost Top drive-in the first time I drove the car after getting my license.

And to my brother, Brett. Remember that fatherhood is like a roller-coaster ride…fast and furious, with steep drops, tight turns and sometimes even zipping through dark tunnels. Hang on tight.
Eventually the ride has to end…doesn't it?

Prologue

JD wasn't sure if it was the bright sunlight bouncing off the petite blonde or off the sparkling-clean silver rental car that blinded him as he swung his black Ford truck into a parking space outside Lovie's café. Whichever, both the lady and the car looked out of place among the dusty, battered ranch vehicles lined up and down Main Street in Brandt's Corner.

Because of the oppressive West Texas heat wave, he shifted into Park and left the engine running to keep the air-conditioning on. Without it, the temperature inside his truck would spike to a hundred degrees in sixty seconds flat, and he was in no hurry to get out.

He had some lookin' to do first.

A suit in the middle of July? He shook his head at the blonde's outfit. Pinstripe, no less. She wore her honey-colored hair in a fancy twist at the back of her neck, revealing a clean profile. Evidently, she got her haughty air from the high cheekbones.

The slight bump in the middle of her narrow nose created an interesting contrast with the too-delectable-for-kissing pink mouth. Sunglasses concealed her eyes, but he imagined them a cool hazel or gray. His attention shifted south. Petite, yes, but by no means boyish. The suit showed off her ample attributes to perfection. Wondering if his mirrored sunglasses distorted the mouthwatering curves, he slid the rims down and peered over his nose.

Nope. The lady was a looker.

A couple of local ranch hands strolled by, tipping their hats in greeting. Instead of the customary smile or nod, she lifted her chin and turned away, tapping the toe of one expensive leather pump against the pavement.

Uppity little thing.

All of her, from her wardrobe to her demeanor, boasted a privileged life. Privileged meant money. Money meant trouble.

His gut twisted. Since yesterday's phone call from this woman, his insides had festered as if he'd swallowed a handful of rusty fence nails.

Fear.

Fear of the unknown—the worst kind. He'd rather sit on the back of a rank rodeo bull than go head to head with *her.* Too bad he didn't have that option.

He shut off the ignition, left the truck and headed toward the enemy. His right boot slid across a patch of gravel, and she turned at the scratchy sound. He stopped a few feet away. Up close, he noticed several streaks of burnished gold running through her hair. He'd never seen so many shades of blond on one head.

Showing no surprise at his appearance, none of the nervousness choking his airways, she straightened her shoulders and tugged the bottom of the suit jacket. The stuffy outfit shouted *attitude* a mile away. Fine with him. Ms. Corporation would discover soon enough he had his own share of attitude and then some.

She removed her sunglasses and the air whooshed from his lungs. Blue. Brilliant blue. Eyes the exact color as… He pushed the thought aside and focused on the light brown eyebrows scrunching to create an intriguing wrinkle across the bridge of her nose.

"Usually when someone hangs up on you, it's a hint they're not interested in anything you have to say. What part of my hangin'-up business didn't you understand, lady?"

Perching her fists on her hips, she glared. "Isn't hanging up on a person a little immature for someone your age?"

The purr of her husky voice gut-kicked him. Exactly one hour after he'd slammed the receiver down, cutting this woman off in midsentence, she'd called again. The second time, she'd left a message on the answering machine, stating her intention to meet with him and supplying every damn detail of her travel itinerary.

Like he'd send out a search party if her plane went down?

He'd listened to the information on the recorder once before deleting the message but hadn't remembered her voice sounding as intimate as lovers tangling on silk sheets. He took off his sunglasses, crossed his arms over his chest and stared her straight in the eye. "I wasn't interested in anything you had to say yesterday and I'm not interested today. So, you can put your shapely little fanny in that fancy rental and head back to Chicago." He hoped she'd sputter and stomp away at his rudeness. Fat chance.

Flashing a smug smile, she insisted, "Oh, I believe you'll be more than interested in what I have to say." She slipped a white envelope from her purse, stepped forward and shoved her five-foot-nothing right in his face. "I'm not leaving until we discuss *this*." She flicked the paper under his nose.

When the corner of the envelope poked his left nostril, he clenched his jaw to keep from flinching. The afternoon sun was hot enough to burn a hole through his shirt, but if the lady wanted a standoff, then by God, he'd give her one. He smirked and waited for her to melt into a puddle of frustration. He didn't have long to wait.

A soft huff escaped her mouth and she lowered the envelope. He'd won the first round.

Or so he figured....

"Let's start over." She thrust her hand toward him. "I'm Josephine Delaney, Cassandra's younger sister. Nice to meet you."

"I know who the hell you are." Feeling stupid, he squeezed the small-boned fingers gently. "JD. Just...JD."

A spasm clenched his gut as her slender hand gripped his callused palm. He had an uneasy feeling this woman wouldn't go down without a fight.

"Pleasure to meet you, Mr. JD. As I attempted to explain on the phone—"

"Jeez, lady. It's hotter than a mule's ass out here." After ten minutes in the sweltering sun she appeared fresh and perky as a spring daisy, while drops of sweat rolled down his back, dampening the waistband of his Levi's. Irked the hell out of him.

Turning his back to her, he headed for the café. The *thunk-thunk* of her fancy heels on the wooden boardwalk rubbed his nerves raw. He opened the door and stepped back, darn near smashing his nose against the plate glass when her generous curves, two to be exact, plowed into his back.

"Excuse me," she murmured, stepping around him.

A blast of arctic air hit JD square in the face when he stepped inside Lovie's. Good thing, too. Maybe the frigid temperature would smother his rising temper and cool the tips of his fingers, which had caught fire the moment he'd grasped Josephine's hand.

At half past two, the lunch crowd was long gone—except for the seventy-year-old Peanutty triplets. Wouldn't you know the retired schoolteachers would pick today to linger over tea and pecan pie. The trio of blue-haired heads swiveled in his direction.

JD nodded. "Miss LettyLibbyLilly." He ran their names together, hoping they wouldn't notice if he called them out of order. He'd never been able to tell the women apart. Even in old age, their liver-spotted hands, wrinkled faces and permanently puckered lips were identical.

Three gray-stenciled eyebrows lifted as rusty voices rang out, "Good afternoon, JD." Their gazes glued to the tiny woman by his side, the old biddies didn't even pretend to mind their own business.

He didn't blame the women for being curious. Josephine

Delaney was the first female the trio of teachers had seen JD in the company of since he'd escorted Amber Tilldale to the Future Farmers of America dance in seventh grade.

Wouldn't be long before rumors started flying. He could already picture the headline in the next bimonthly issue of the *Corner Post*: Local Loner Dines with Chicago Heiress at Lovie's.

Ignoring the ladies, JD motioned for Josephine Delaney to lead the way, then followed the enticing sway of her hips as she sauntered toward a booth in the back corner. Wishing more than three feet of worn Formica separated them, he slid in across from her. He set his hat on his thigh, then studied her reaction to his long hair, doubting the woman ever socialized with males who wore ponytails. He watched for a sign of disgust—a curling lip, snort or shake of the head. Nothing. Only genuine curiosity brightened her face.

If he stared into her baby blues long enough, he might forget she was hell-bent on wreaking havoc in his life. Caught off guard by the clarity of her blue eyes, he almost missed the silver glint of vulnerability reflected in their glowing depths. He should blink, break the hypnotic hold she had on him, but he didn't care to.

The first to glance away, Josephine fanned her fingers lightly across the table before setting her handbag on the surface. She pursed her pretty, pink lips, and he thought her determined expression awful cute. Which pissed him off. He didn't want to *like* anything about the lady.

"I realize my call was unexpected—"

"Unexpected? I wouldn't have been more surprised if a meteor had crashed through the middle of the barn."

She slid the white envelope across the table. "Before you open this, I'd like to explain—"

"Hold on a minute. I don't care what's in that envelope. You have no right—"

"Mr. JD, do you make a habit of rudely interrupting people, or are you saving all your macho-cowboy charm just for me?"

Embarrassment warmed his neck, but before he could answer her question with an insult of his own, the waitress shuffled toward the table. "Hey, Susie."

"JD." Susie's speculative gaze darted between him and his booth companion as she set two laminated menus on the table. After removing a pencil from behind her ear, she tapped the tip against the order pad. "What can I get y'all to drink?"

"Noth—"

"I'll have a glass of iced tea, please." Josephine smiled at the waitress as though they were best friends. "With lemon if you have it."

"Sure." Susie shifted her generous weight to one side and brushed a strand of mouse-brown hair from her cheek. "Coffee, JD?"

He swallowed a lungful of impatience. "Yeah. Make it black."

"Y'all take a peek at the menu, and I'll be back with the drinks in a jiffy."

As soon as the waitress walked away, he leaned forward, crowding the table, hoping to intimidate Josephine. Not a chance. She held his stare without blinking. The lady had guts; that was for sure. A twinge of admiration pricked him.

With his height, build and dark complexion from his Hispanic ancestry, most men considered JD a formidable foe and steered clear of him.

But not the petite blonde. He questioned whether he'd met his match, then shrugged the idea aside. He hadn't been a world-class bronc rider because he'd backed down when the going got tough. Her no-nonsense stare stretched his nerves taut. He motioned to the envelope. "To heck with whatever that is, you're not seeing the boy."

"Go ahead and play bully, Mr. JD, but I refuse to leave until I get the answers I came for. Answers you owe me and my family."

He hated the way she said his name. Reminded him of the time he'd been in Miss Libby's fifth-grade class and she'd scolded him for speaking Spanish instead of English, when he didn't know the English word for *homework.*

"Lady—"

"'Josephine,' please. 'Lady' sounds—"

"Snooty?"

Only the telltale click of one manicured pink fingernail against the Formica told him he'd gotten to her. *Good.* Because she'd already squirmed her way under his hide.

Hoping to rein in his temper, he breathed deeply through his nose. The scent of her perfume, something rich and sultry, shot straight to his head, saturating his brain and shooting his concentration to hell.

As she rubbed her temple, a small sigh fluttered across the booth and smacked him in the face. For a split second, he felt the urge to apologize for his less-than-welcoming behavior. But a second was as long as the impulse lasted.

The silence between them stretched and JD figured he'd finally gotten through to her. Wishful thinking.

"I understand you don't want me here—"

"Damn right."

Her eyes narrowed. "I have to see for myself my nephew is being properly cared for."

"Why the sudden concern over Bobby…eight months after his mother died?"

A blush spread across Josephine's cheeks. "Until recently, our family wasn't aware Bobby existed."

"The kid's five years old. How could your family *not be* aware of him?"

Stirring uneasily in her seat, Josephine explained, "Cassandra moved away from home after she dropped out of college her freshman year. When her trust fund ran low, she'd show up at the house and stay just long enough to get my father to add money to her bank account. Then she'd disappear again. After a couple of years, phone calls replaced the visits when she required extra funds."

JD folded his arms over his chest. "I'd prefer the short version."

Josephine's eyes slammed shut for a moment before fluttering open. "Cassandra was…flighty. My father and mother assumed she'd eventually return home when she'd seen enough of the world."

"Your parents never went to visit Cassandra? Check up on her?"

"No. They were too busy with their own lives to give their wayward daughter a second thought."

"And you?"

She rubbed the bridge of her nose and JD wondered if the sudden shimmer in her eyes was caused by anger or the threat of tears. "My sister and I were never close. But I did keep in touch by phone every so often."

"And your sister never told you during one of your phone conversations that she was pregnant or had had a baby?"

"No." The choked whisper echoed like a cannon blast in the almost-empty restaurant.

What kind of family had Cassandra come from, anyway? Shoot, for all JD knew, she'd had a good reason for distancing herself from her folks. "Then how did you find out about Bobby?"

"It's complicated."

"I'm all ears." He watched her clench her trembling hands and his chest tightened at the sign of distress. Damn, he refused to feel pity for this woman.

Before Josephine had a chance to continue, the waitress approached the booth. "Have y'all decided yet?"

He handed over the menus. "We're not hungry."

"No problem. Holler if y'all change your mind." With a puzzled frown, Susie returned to the lunch counter and whispered something to the geriatric triplets working on second helpings of dessert.

"Apparently, you're rude to everyone," Josephine snapped.

JD pointed to his watch. "I don't have all day."

As if to prove he couldn't bully her, she reached for her iced tea and drank a long, long swallow. *Slowly.*

His temper flared. "Maybe you're only giving up a Saturday afternoon at the spa, but I'm losing precious daylight hours. In case you weren't aware, ranchers don't get weekends off."

A shadow of annoyance crossed her face. "Like I said, Cassandra never told the family about Bobby."

"Wouldn't the New York City police have mentioned Bobby when they called to inform your family about Cassandra's car accident?"

"No one notified us about the accident."

"What?"

"Cassandra had legally changed her name when she moved to New York."

"Why would she do that?"

Josephine shifted on the seat cushion and JD got the feeling that what she was about to say made her very uncomfortable.

"She changed her name because she'd embarked on a new career."

"A new career?" Jeez. Getting information out of this woman was like trying to milk a dried-up cow.

"Cassandra had always dreamed of being an actress. She moved to New York and signed on with an agency."

"I understand the need for a stage name, but why would she legally change her name?"

"I believe she was trying to protect our family from the negative impact of her career choice."

"Negative impact?"

"Cassandra was making soft-core porn movies."

JD rubbed a hand down his face. His son's mother had been a porn star. Wonderful.

"A week after the accident, I had called my sister to remind her of our mother's upcoming birthday. Her roommate answered the phone and ended up breaking down and telling me about the car accident, but hung up before I could get any details."

Hell. What a way to find out your sister was dead.

"When my father contacted the New York City police for details of the accident they neglected to mention Bobby."

JD frowned and Josephine held up her hand, forestalling his next question.

"Cassandra's roommate tried to take care of Bobby but for whatever reason couldn't manage and arranged for social services to pick him up a week after Cassandra's accident."

"Okay, I'll buy into this explanation. Now, tell me why social services didn't contact your family when Bobby entered the system?"

A deep rose tinged Josephine's cheeks. "Cassandra had used her stage name on Bobby's birth certificate."

"The roommate didn't know Cassandra's real name?"

Josephine shook her head. "My sister told no one her real name."

"That explains why you never knew Bobby existed all these years. But it doesn't explain why you're here now."

"A month ago one of my father's employees rented an old porn movie Cassandra had acted in and recognized her from a photo on my father's desk."

"That must have been a shock."

Josephine nodded. "My father immediately hired a private investigator to find out everything he could about Cassandra's life after she moved to New York. The investigator tracked down my sister's old roommate and she spilled the beans about Bobby. The detective then traced Bobby to your ranch."

Anxiety raced through JD. How could he keep his son if a man with a ton of money and power had decided to fight him for custody? He'd heard enough. He removed a ten from his wallet and tossed the bill onto the table. "Order yourself a muffin or yogurt or whatever women like you eat these days."

"But we're not through discussing—"

"Lady." He slid from the booth, then swiped the Stetson from the seat and jammed it on his head. "We were through discussing the second I hung up on you yesterday, and again the minute you pulled into town today." He tapped his finger against the brim of his hat, spun around and headed for the door. As he reached for the handle, Josephine's husky voice slapped him upside the back of the head.

"JD?"

Clinking coffee cups came to an abrupt halt at the counter. *Aw, hell.* He stared over his shoulder and flinched at the sparks leaping from her sapphire eyes.

Standing beside the booth, arms crossed under her double-breasted bosom, she taunted, "Running won't make this go away."

The heck it won't. With one mighty push, he flung open the door and stepped out into the July inferno. He headed straight for the truck. The sooner he put some miles between him and the pushy, blond broad, the better.

Chapter One

JD started the engine, not bothering to wait until the air conditioner cooled the interior. After backing out of the parking space, he shifted into Drive and sped out of town, as if a rifle-toting father were taking potshots at his Goodyear radials.

Who did Josephine Delaney think she was? And who the heck named their daughter *Josephine* these days? Sounded like a spinster's name.

When JD had driven five miles, the knots in his gut loosened. He fumbled with the radio dial and let up on the gas. He couldn't afford a speeding ticket any more than he could afford a good lawyer. Slamming his fist against the steering wheel, he let fly a mouthful of four-letter words. *One frickin' night* with a woman and his whole damn life had flipped head over heels.

Bobby had arrived at the ranch last December, and after the shock of finding out he'd had a son had worn off some, JD had started to wonder if maybe life threw curveballs for a reason. Bobby had got inside him, to a place he hadn't realized existed. For the first time in his thirty years, JD's life had taken on meaning.

He eased the truck over to the shoulder and took the gravel road leading to the ranch. No way in hell would he let Josephine Delaney bulldoze her way into his life and turn it upside down. Not now. Not when he finally had something worth living for.

The truck bumped along the rutted, dusty path leading to the Rocking R Ranch house. He passed a cluster of grazing longhorns, then veered left at the fork in the road. The pastures were dry. Too dry. The yellow, strawlike grass could use a month's worth of steady rain. But rain in July was considered a luxury in West Texas. Most ranchers hoped for a brief thunderstorm once a week, yet even those were few and far between.

After a quarter mile the road crested a small rise. Off in the distance sat the main house, along with a faded red barn and two large corrals. As of last January, JD and the bank had become half owner of the Rocking R. Blake Sloan, an aging third-generation cattleman, owned the other half.

JD remembered sitting down with Blake that cold January morning and asking if he could buy into the ranch, intending to put down permanent roots, have something meaningful to pass on to Bobby one day. Although Blake had argued the ranch had always been JD's home, JD hadn't felt right about calling the ranch his *home* until he owned half the assets and property. He'd given the bank every cent he'd saved from rodeoing. He'd always believed money in the bank meant security—until he owned a chunk of land, part of a home and a piece of the future.

He stopped the truck and stared out the windshield. From a distance, the place appeared the same as the day a ten-year-old JD had arrived with a group of Mexican migrant workers to help with the fall roundup. Little had he known he wouldn't be going back with the men but staying on with Blake. His eyes didn't see the barn's peeling paint or rotting corral wood or listing front porch—they saw the only real *home* he'd ever had.

Memories of the year he'd turned seventeen flooded his mind. During the summer, he'd helped Blake build an office off the living room. Pounding nails, sawing boards and keeping up with the ranch chores had almost done JD in. But for the first time in his life he'd felt he'd belonged somewhere, and he'd finally let go of the fear Blake might send him packing one day.

He lifted his foot from the brake and drove into the ranch yard and parked in the shade of the oak trees. Blake materialized between the barn doors. The old man clutched a dirty rag in one hand—a signal he'd been tinkering with the old '55 Ford stored inside the barn. The rust bucket held sentimental value for the rancher. Blake had told JD he'd proposed to his wife in the old Ford. Sadly, Mrs. Sloan had passed on before JD had come to live at the ranch.

As JD approached, Blake remained quiet. The man never wasted his breath grilling a person with questions. JD appreciated that. Now more than ever. "Working on the truck?"

"Checking the plugs." Blake shoved the rag into the front pocket of his overalls.

The temptation to spill his guts about the Delaney woman nagged JD, but he held back. A few times over the years he'd shared some personal concerns with the old man. But he wanted to keep Josephine to himself. At least until he figured out what kind of trouble she intended to stir up. "Where's Bobby?"

"Back with the kittens."

The confrontation with Bobby's aunt had shaken JD more than he cared to admit. Being alone with his son would ease some of the tension tangling his insides. "I noticed a sagging section of fence on the way in. Thought I'd see if Bobby wanted to ride along while I go out and tighten the wires."

"Bobby can stay with me. I plan on tinkering till supper."

The invitation was sincere. The boy's arrival at the ranch eight months ago had lifted Blake's spirits. Right away, Bobby had latched on to the old man. And that made JD jealous as hell. Something he wasn't proud to admit.

He and Bobby hadn't gotten off to the best of starts last Christmas when a New York social services worker had flown to Texas with the boy and brought him out to the ranch. A nasty norther had swept through the area days earlier, leaving behind the frozen and bloated carcasses of seventy cattle. He and Blake had been exhausted and hadn't planned on celebrating the holidays.

There hadn't been time to drive into town to buy presents, but Blake had whittled Bobby a miniature bear and two cubs. From Christmas Day on, his son had followed the old rancher around like a lost puppy. The day after Christmas, JD had driven all the way over to Williamsburg, to the big mall, and had purchased a shopping-cartful of toys for the boy. Hadn't made a difference. Bobby had continued to steer clear of JD. "I haven't spent much time with Bobby lately."

Blake nodded, then disappeared inside the barn. JD followed, walking slowly until his eyes adjusted to the dim light. "Bobby?" he called out, heading for the back room, where a mama calico had delivered a litter of kittens two weeks ago.

A warm feeling filled JD when he found his son cuddling a lapful of orange fur balls in the corner of the tack room. "Have you named them all yet?"

Keeping his attention on the kittens, Bobby shook his head.

JD wished his son felt more comfortable around him. After all this time together, things still weren't easy between them. He didn't blame the boy. In truth, JD didn't know one damn thing about being a father, let alone a good one. "How about you give those kittens back to their mama, and we'll go play cowboy."

The little blond head snapped up and Bobby stared at him with eager blue eyes—eyes exactly the same color as Josephine Delaney's.

"What do you say?"

Instead of answering, the boy nodded, and a pang sliced through JD. The social worker had insisted that children who suffered the loss of a parent often stopped talking. She'd assured JD that Bobby would speak when he felt secure. The fact that his son talked mostly to Blake and not his own father bothered JD deeply. He'd tried every way he could think of to make his son feel safe and accepted—not an easy task for a man who'd never experienced those feelings as a child.

He'd hoped buying Bobby a bike to ride around the ranch, one of those handheld electronic games kids played with these days and several boxes of plastic snap-together building sets would show the boy he cared. But Bobby hadn't been interested in toys. Not until Blake had strung up an old tractor tire to the mesquite tree shading the front porch. While Blake puttered around the yard, Bobby would swing for hours.

"We'll take Warrior and ride double."

His son's face brightened. Bobby loved Warrior. At first, JD had been nervous putting a small child up on the back of a cow horse, but after a few hours of instruction the boy had learned to hold his seat. Warrior was gentle and patient with Bobby, as if he sensed the boy's heartache. Even though the stallion and boy had formed a bond, Warrior was big and powerful and Bobby wouldn't stand a chance of keeping his seat if the animal charged after a renegade cow.

JD hefted the stallion's saddle to his shoulder and shortened his stride so the miniature cowboy could keep up. As they neared the corral, he let out a sharp whistle and the big red roan lifted his head. Another whistle and the stallion trotted toward the gate. His tail swished and his sides quivered; he was ready for action.

"Hold on, pardner, while I saddle up." JD sat Bobby on the corral rail, then watched his son stroke Warrior's nose. Once in a while, JD would catch a glimpse of loneliness in Bobby's gaze...the same loneliness *he* saw in the mirror every morning. Somehow he had to find a way to chase the shadows from his son's sad eyes. "Ready?"

Bobby's mouth curved upward. The boy's smiles were rare. But if JD was lucky enough to catch one, like now, he stowed the grin inside him, close to his heart.

He deposited Bobby in the saddle, then led Warrior out of

the corral, latched the gate and mounted. "I'll let you hold the reins until the end of the driveway."

The boy flicked the rawhide and the horse broke into a trot.

As if he didn't have a care in the world, JD lifted his face to the sun and wrapped an arm around Bobby. At that exact moment everything was right and good and meant to be.

When they neared the edge of the driveway, JD tugged on the reins. They left the road, using a shortcut to the north pasture through several hundred feet of scrub brush. Warrior's slow, easy walk lulled JD's mind, and his thoughts drifted back to the night he'd spent with Bobby's mother.

One night. A few hours of uncomplicated, hot, sweaty sex. That part had been a miracle, considering only an hour earlier he'd brawled with a badass bronc named Elvis, who'd tossed him headfirst into the dirt, then stomped him good.

After he'd taken the spill in the Abilene rodeo, he'd run into Cassandra, or Cassy as she'd been called among the rodeo groupies. She'd caught every cowboy's fancy with her sexy body, flashy snakeskin boots and little red sports car. He'd pegged her as a spoiled rich girl, trying to get out from under daddy's thumb. *Guess he'd been right all along.*

She'd been way out of his league. Girls like Cassy didn't waste time on guys like him. Then she'd walked into the first-aid tent, all five foot nine inches of blond bombshell. He'd remembered glancing over his shoulder to see who the lucky cowboy was she'd come to check on. When he'd discovered he'd been alone in the tent, he'd damn near swallowed his tongue.

There hadn't been a need for conversation. The invitation in her eyes had been unmistakable. He'd followed her out of the arena, hoping he hadn't been the butt of some cowboy prank. Then she'd grasped his hand and led him to the cherry-red Corvette parked in a reserved spot by the main entrance.

Due to his national ranking a couple of years in a row, most of the rodeo groupies knew his name. But Cassandra had never spoken it as she'd driven to the edge of town and paid for a room at an interstate motel. He'd stood aside while she'd unlocked the door, feeling uneasy that all she'd wanted from him was sex. But only a fool would have walked away from a chance to be with the siren.

She'd started taking off her clothes before he'd even shut the door and turned the lock. He'd helped her out of the skimpy watermelon-print sundress and matching bra-and-panty set, then he'd grabbed her hand and had tugged her toward the bathroom.

For whatever reason the Fates had smiled on him, he hadn't been about to jump into bed with a perfect ten while smelling like a horse and wearing B.V.D.s filled with arena dirt. They'd made love up against the shower wall as the hot, pulsing water had beaten down on their heads.

Next, they'd landed on the bed, a wet tangle of arms and legs. The second time and his earlier spill from the bronc had taken a toll on him and he'd fallen into an exhausted sleep. He hadn't known how long he'd been conked out when he'd woken and found her watching him from across the room… curled up naked in a chair, smoking a cigarette.

He'd taken the cigarette from her fingers, stubbed it out, then lifted her from the chair and seated himself with her on his lap, and they'd lost themselves in another bout of wild sex.

JD couldn't recall, but didn't think either one of them had spoken a word throughout the night. And there hadn't been too many moans or groans of pleasure, either. He couldn't say for sure he'd even satisfied her.

The next morning she'd driven him back to the arena to get his truck. After hopping out of the Corvette, he'd bent down to ask for her number, but she'd shifted into Drive and sped away without a howdy-do. He'd been nothing more than a good lay to Bobby's mother.

During the following weeks on the circuit, he'd seen Cassy from time to time, but she never acknowledged him in any way. And he sure as hell hadn't gone out of his way to say hello. After a couple of months she'd disappeared. After a year he'd quit thinking about her.

The woman hadn't crossed his mind until eight months ago when Bobby had landed on his doorstep. Now, thanks to Cassandra's little sister, Josephine, JD was dredging up memories best left buried.

He tightened his hold around Bobby. He refused to consider he might lose his son before he even had the chance to get close to him.

Chapter Two

Of all the arrogant...

No one left Josephine Delaney standing like a dope in a café. Least of all an illiterate, redneck cowboy from some... some corner in Texas!

"Excuse me, ma'am. Did you want a refill on your iced tea?"

Startled, Josephine shifted her gaze from the door to the plump waitress standing next to her. "No, thank you."

Susie waitress motioned to the front window, where a big black truck drove past. "He's so dang handsome, ain't he?"

Handsome? JD was certainly not the smarmy, bowlegged, reeking-of-wet-livestock cowboy with a stained hat, a week's worth of beard stubble and a cigarette hanging from the corner of his mouth that she'd pictured hanging up on her yesterday.

"I'd say he's arrogant, stubborn, rude—"

"Yeah, ain't he somethin'?" Eyes glazed over, the waitress shuffled back to the lunch counter.

JD was *something* all right. His dark, chiseled face and long, black hair rattled her nerves and scattered her wits across the great State of Texas. From the top of his Stetson, to the bottom of his worn boots, and every muscled inch in between, he put her senses on heightened alert and tested her composure. She prided herself on her cool, calm demeanor in sticky situations. So why did this *cowboy* blow her self-control to smithereens?

She hadn't reached the age of twenty-nine and worked the past five years slaving over accounts and climbing the ladder of her father's investment firm to be bossed around by a swaggering, full-of-himself Marlboro man. He'd find out soon enough she wasn't a soft-bellied city slicker he could toy with. She'd developed a thick skin over the years—not by choice, by necessity.

But for a woman who handled corporate sharks with ease, she'd really boggled the meeting with JD. And that stung her pride. Why had she allowed the cowboy to walk all over her? She'd come to Brandt's Corner for one reason—her nephew. She intended to convince JD that Bobby was better off living with his grandparents in Chicago than with him in this backwoods hillbilly town.

After experiencing JD's stubbornness firsthand, she was relieved she'd talked her father, William Delaney, into letting her fly to Texas in his place. He'd sworn he had the clout to bring his grandson home, but she suspected clout wasn't something that would impress a man like JD. Had William come on this trip, no doubt he would have landed either in jail for attempting to kidnap his grandson or in the hospital for a broken nose from JD's fist. Either scenario made her shudder.

Before boarding the company plane this morning, she and her father had argued over his insistence that Bobby live with them in Chicago full-time. He'd never said so, but Josephine had a hunch William Delaney was determined to make sure Bobby didn't travel down the same path his mother had.

She recommended contacting a lawyer to establish what, if any, their legal rights were where Bobby was concerned, but her father had insisted on handling matters his own way. In a last-ditch effort she'd suggested a compromise—bringing Bobby back to Chicago for holidays and summer vacation. William had refused to consider partial custody. It was all or nothing with the man.

A bead of perspiration rolled down between her breasts.

She didn't care to contemplate her father's reaction if she returned home without the boy.

Josephine intended to drive out to JD's ranch and show him she didn't scare easily. Aside from being eager to meet her nephew, she'd wanted another shot at convincing the cussed cowboy to allow her to fly his son back to Chicago for a temporary visit. Just long enough to settle her father down and encourage him to contact his lawyer and handle the matter of Bobby's living arrangements in a more sensible way.

She straightened her suit jacket and faced the group of elderly women occupying the lunch counter. "Excuse me, ladies." Three gray heads swiveled toward her. "I'll be needing directions to Mr. JD's ranch."

Three identical wrinkled faces grinned.

JOSEPHINE STARED through the tinted windshield at miles and miles of flat, dried-out grassland fenced in by rusted barbed wire. Trees were scarce, and the ones she saw resembled the gnarled hands of a ninety-year-old woman. Off in the distance, she spotted what appeared to be a low-lying mountain, but as she drove closer, she discovered the land was nothing more than a small hill.

Chicago might not be the most beautiful place on earth, but at least the city had color during the summer months. All this yellow brown for as far as she could see was bleaker than a Midwest gray winter day.

The local chamber of commerce surely faced a challenge encouraging tourists to spend their money in this area...while enjoying the suffocating heat and nondescript landscape. She glanced upward and decided that if the locals promoted the sky they might be able to attract visitors. It went on forever in every direction, clear and blue. She'd never seen this much heaven without a building or billboard marring the view.

The vastness of the region overwhelmed her, making her feel minuscule and insignificant. She pictured a travel brochure with a couple enjoying the afternoon on a picnic blanket, gazing up at the enormous expanse of blue, while horses grazed nearby. An image of JD lying over her on the blanket, his mouth inches from hers, popped into her mind, and she jerked the steering wheel to the right, almost running the rental car off the road. *Good Lord!*

Bobby's father hadn't been at all what she'd expected. Not that she had anything against cowboys. Other than seeing one in a movie or on the cover of a magazine, before she'd come to Texas she'd never spent much time pondering the breed. Had she realized they were earthy, muscle-packed bundles of testosterone, she might have given them a passing thought or two. Or three. What a shame JD's sexy exterior hid such a cantankerous personality.

What would life be like married to the cowboy?

Now, where had that notion come from? JD might be sexy as all get-out, but Josephine couldn't picture herself married to the man. Her fast-paced city life and his same ol' "round 'em up and move 'em out" life would be nothing short of a disaster.

What did it matter if her heart raced a little faster around the man—she wasn't his type. Surely he only valued a woman for her cooking skills or ability to toss hay bales off a tractor, not for her business acumen. As for social skills, she doubted JD even knew the difference between a shrimp fork and a salad fork.

Even if the cowboy had been taught proper etiquette, he wouldn't pass muster with her parents. Their marriage had been arranged—her mother coming from a long line of prominent bankers in Chicago. And the Delaney name had been linked to the Chicago Stock Exchange as far back as 1894, when her great-great-grandfather had gone to work in the newly constructed stock exchange building on La Salle Street.

Josephine had been lectured since puberty that "family names" were everything. She could be mistaken, but she suspected "JD" wasn't synonymous with education, real estate, money or political power. Although she didn't agree with her father's archaic attitude toward marriage, she hoped her father and the man she chose to marry would at least respect each other...something she doubted possible between William Delaney and a man like JD.

Josephine didn't have a whole lot of dating experience. She'd had one serious relationship in college. It had lasted almost a year...until she'd found the jerk in bed with her roommate. Which had stunned her, because the guy hadn't exactly set the sheets on fire with Josephine. For all she'd cared, her roommate had been welcome to the two-timing bastard.

Then there had been the stockbroker she'd dated two years ago. On the surface Gary had seemed like a great guy. Their financial backgrounds had made conversation interesting and he'd been handsome in a prep-school kind of way. Little had she known, Gary had been milking her for information on her clients' portfolios and assets so he could steal them away from her father's firm. In the end, Josephine had admitted Gary had made a better spy than a lover. When it came to men, Josephine certainly didn't have good luck.

Her father felt she'd needed a little help in the find-a-mate department, so he'd strongly encouraged her to socialize with Stephen Rutgers, the forty-two-year-old chief financial officer of Rutgers Railway, the largest privately owned transport company in the Midwest, with hundreds of millions in assets throughout North America. Harvard educated, Stephen Rutgers came from money and his name carried clout in Chicago. To appease her father, she'd gone out on one date with Stephen. The evening had been a disaster.

Conversation had centered solely on financial topics, and every time Josephine had tried to interject personal observations or ask personal questions he'd acted as if he hadn't heard her. When she'd told her father she hadn't cared for Stephen and wouldn't be dating him again, William had insisted she keep trying, as if the reason they hadn't hit it off had been *her* fault! She had no intention of *trying* again with Stephen Rutgers.

Maybe her fantasizing about marrying JD had nothing to do with the man himself and more to do with her recent thoughts of marriage and motherhood. Shortly after turning twenty-nine last March, she'd felt as if her biological clock had started ticking a little faster, a little harder, which surprised her. Her own mother, Regina Delaney, had been far from *motherly,* leaving the day-to-day care of her children in the nanny's hands. Josephine's recent thoughts of motherhood and marriage gave her hope that she hadn't inherited her mother's lack of maternal instinct.

But no matter how hard her biological clock thumped, one thing was sure: a marriage with JD would never work. They were total opposites and had nothing in common—except Bobby's welfare, and that certainly wasn't enough to build a lasting relationship on.

Josephine drove another mile, then turned onto Rural Route 5 and headed south. A few minutes later, she spotted the ranch entrance. The sign across the entrance read Rocking R Ranch, giving no clue to its owner's surname.

She speculated again about JD's last name. The State of New York had listed the father's name on Bobby's birth certificate simply as JD. It wasn't until social services had questioned Cassandra's roommate that the woman mentioned Cassandra had told her Bobby's father had been a rodeo cowboy. With that information, social services had been able to locate JD in Texas through the Professional Rodeo Cowboys Association.

Slowing the car, she turned under the wooden arches and drove over the cattle guard. The narrow gravel road tested the rental's shocks as the tires kicked up a plume of white dust. The car bumped along the rutted path, until she pulled to a stop at the top of a small incline.

Off in the distance, she spotted movement along a stretch of barbed-wire fence. The horse and rider…nothing more than a dark blur against the horizon. The sun edged lower in the sky, casting them farther into the shadows. She couldn't make out any details, save for the gloomy outline of the man and horse.

For one brief second nothing moved—not the rider, the animal, the wind. A moment later, the black dot disappeared into a thicket of scrub brush, making her believe she'd imagined the whole scene.

Lifting her foot off the brake, she turned her attention back to the road. After another mile, a two-story house came into view. As she drove closer, she studied her surroundings. She had nothing against this way of life—eking out a living off the land. But her family could offer Bobby the best of everything: a superior education, social and cultural experiences. The only thing Josephine wasn't confident her parents could offer freely was their love.

Her train of thought shifted gear when she noticed a tire hanging from a large tree. Had JD hung the swing for Bobby, or were other children living in the house? *Oh, my.* She hadn't considered JD might already be married with kids…which made her feel foolish for fantasizing about the man.

Pulling to a stop near the front porch, she waited for someone to greet her. She'd seen enough movies to believe the moment she stepped out of the car a snarling, vicious attack dog would bound around the corner and head straight for her.

There were two corrals, one occupied by a couple of horses, the other empty. Although the weathered barn could use a new coat of red paint, the structure appeared sturdy enough. A storage shed, with a huge dent in the side, sat several yards behind the barn. Farther back, under a group of scraggly trees, rested an ancient mobile home and an old beat-up Chrysler.

The huge snarling watchdog never materialized, so she

turned off the ignition, then shrugged out of her suit jacket and exited the car. The home didn't have the *Country Living Magazine* appearance that came to mind when she pictured a ranch house. Landscaping was nonexistent. No flowerpots, flower beds, flower-anything anywhere. Just a lone swing hanging at the end of the porch. Planters along the porch rail, overflowing with summer blooms and trailing vines, and a few rosebushes would go a long way toward making the place more welcoming.

A movement to her left caught her attention. An elderly man, nondescript and somber, stood in the darkened doorway of the barn. She opened her mouth to introduce herself, but the ground beneath her high heels started jumping, and a squawk escaped instead of her name.

She twirled just as a huge, cinnamon-colored horse exploded through a break in the line of brush near the end of the driveway. The thundering of the animal's hooves startled her and she froze, awed by the sheer power and presence of man, boy and beast.

JD tugged hard on the reins, bringing the animal to a skidding halt five feet in front of her. A lump of panic lodged in her throat as the animal's hot breath pounded her face in moist, forceful blasts of air. The stallion's eyes, round, dark and feral, reminded her of his owner.

Afraid to make any sudden moves, she lifted her gaze to JD, and for a moment she believed the horse might be easier to tame than the man.

At the sight of her nephew nestled against JD's chest, the lump of panic evolved into one of tenderness, swelling in her throat until she couldn't swallow. Not surprisingly, a motherly twinge tugged at her heartstrings.

Josephine ignored the scowl on JD's face and studied her nephew. His complexion was as fair as her sister's had been, not the deeper bronze of JD's. She wasn't sure what blood ran through JD's veins, but the color of his skin hinted at Hispanic genes.

Seeing Bobby in person was like looking at one of Cassandra's childhood pictures. His sweaty, blond hair wasn't quite as light as his mother's had been, but he had the same-shaped face, the same beautifully sculpted mouth. His eyes were blue, a true blue like Josephine's own, leaving her a little awed that she shared something with her nephew.

Considering what the child had gone through since his mother's death made Josephine tremble and wish her sister were alive so she could give her a piece of her mind. How could Cassandra have kept this beautiful boy a secret from the family?

Hat tilted forward, casting a shadow over his face, JD shifted in the saddle, his thick muscular thighs bunching against the animal's heaving sides. The man looked as though he'd stepped off the pages of a Louis L'Amour novel. His jaw clenched beneath the darkly tanned skin, and she sucked in a deep breath, hoping to calm her frazzled nerves.

Oh, for heaven's sake. Pretend he's one of those arrogant, know-it-all investors you work with every day. She attempted a smile. "Hello, JD."

He returned her greeting with a cold stare. So much for niceties.

She turned her attention to her nephew. "Hello, Bobby." The boy averted his gaze and stared down at the reins in JD's hands. *Ouch.* She shouldn't have expected anything more from the child; after all, she was a stranger to him.

Since JD didn't seem inclined to introduce them, she said, "I'm your aunt Josephine. Your mother was my sister." She watched the blank little face, searching for any hint of recognition or emotion. *Nothing.* "I'm sorry about your mother, Bobby. I'm sure you miss her very much."

To her shock, Bobby flinched. She ached at the thought that the mention of his mother might have stirred up suppressed feelings.

JD's dark brown stare bore into her with an intensity that

made her stomach flutter and her lungs tighten. He swung a leg over the back end of the horse and landed on the ground with a thud, sending up a puff of gray dust. "You've got some nerve, lady."

At the steely note of warning in his voice, she almost lost her courage. "Nerve is my middle name."

"Then you can haul your nervy little back end into that car and get the hell off this ranch."

Josephine peeked at her nephew to gauge his reaction to his father's rudeness. Surprisingly, the boy ignored them, his attention centered on the horse as he stroked the animal's neck and wound his stubby fingers through the red-brown mane.

"I see we got company." The older man Josephine had noticed by the barn approached. He held out a hand. "Blake Sloan."

Obviously, the ranch hand had more manners than the ranch owner. Some of the tension inside her drained at the kind expression and lined smile creasing his weathered face. She grasped the leather-tough hand. "Josephine Delaney. Bobby's mother was my sister."

The cataract gaze darted between her and JD.

Grabbing her arm, JD flexed his fingers meaningfully against her flesh. "She was just leaving."

Because of her young audience, she refrained from yanking her arm back and plowing her fist into the arrogant cowboy's gut. "Actually, I'm in no hurry. I came all the way from Chicago to visit with my nephew."

The old man cleared his throat. "Supper'll be on the table soon. Got enough chicken for an army."

JD growled. Not out loud, but she felt the vibration of the sound rumble through his chest, which happened to be pressed against her arm. Like his horse, JD's hot breath puffed across the top of her head. She knew if she glanced up she'd see sparks shooting from his eyes.

She offered the old man a warm smile. "Thank you. I accept your invitation."

"While I go scare up the grub, JD can show you around the place." Blake Sloan moved to the horse and reached for the boy. "C'mon, rascal. I need your help in the kitchen." Hand in hand, the pair walked away, to disappear around the side of the house. A few seconds later, she heard the telltale squeak of a rusty hinge, then the sharp smack of a screen door closing.

Josephine opened her mouth to ask if she and JD could call a truce, at least until they'd finished supper, but his glowering expression stopped the words in the middle of her throat.

"I'll be damned if I'm going to be your welcome committee, lady."

BLASTED WOMAN! JD slammed his fist against the saddle hanging over the stall door. At first, he'd believed he'd imagined seeing the shiny silver rental on the ranch road leading to the house. He'd figured the sun's glare had played a trick on him. But when the car had moved, he'd realized trouble was on the horizon.

Cute, sexy trouble, but trouble, nonetheless.

Later tonight he'd have a long talk with Blake. What the hell had the old man been thinking...inviting this woman to supper? Men had to stick together, or before long, women like Josephine would run the whole world.

He shoved away from the stall and went into the tack room. Under the watchful green eyes of the mama cat, he quietly lifted a halter from a hook on the wall. Careful not to disturb the basket of sleeping kittens nearby, he removed a rag and a can of linseed from a metal storage cabinet in the corner, then sat down on an overturned pickle barrel and opened the paste. Maybe by the time he rubbed the hell out of the rawhide, he'd figure out a way to scare Josephine Delaney back to Chicago.

Scare her? He didn't think much scared the female. She didn't cower beneath his anger or rudeness. He admired that quality in a person, just not in *her.* He didn't understand why the lady brought out the worst in him. He'd always considered himself an even-tempered guy. But when Josephine tilted her defiant little chin, he felt ready to explode. He had to get a grip on his emotions or one of these times he'd really let loose and no telling what he'd say or do.

Actually, he knew what he'd do…kiss her. Minutes ago, she'd stood glaring up at him with her pink lips gleaming in the sunlight, making him feel things that would only complicate matters between them. How could one small woman make him angry enough to kick a fence post barefoot and at the same time yearn to sample that sassy mouth?

Aw, hell. He hadn't been attracted to a woman in a long time. He stared at the mama cat. "Why now? Why her?" Seconds ticked by, turned into minutes, and still the calico didn't answer. He tossed the strap aside, then removed his straw hat and punched the crown in. With a mumbled curse, he sent the Stetson sailing toward the doorway.

A sliver of guilt pricked his side when he considered how far Josephine had traveled today and the kind of reception she'd received. But Cassandra had left a bad taste in his mouth and he wanted nothing to do with her sibling.

A scuffling sound caught his attention. The woman, plaguing his thoughts like a bad case of the flu, stood in the doorway. As if taking a bead on a deer, he narrowed his gaze and studied her. Josephine bore little resemblance to her older sister…thankfully.

Cassandra had been porcelain-doll beautiful. The first time he'd laid eyes on her he'd noticed the absolute symmetry of her face. Remembered thinking her features had been too flawless, too proportioned. Unnatural.

The woman standing in the doorway was everything *but* unnatural. Josephine was warm, earthy…and very out of place dressed in that ridiculous skirt, silk blouse and leather pumps.

"I think we should talk before supper."

He couldn't put it off forever. Might as well let her have her say. Maybe then she'd go away and leave him alone. He rolled his shoulders as though he didn't have a care in the world, hoping the movement would loosen the knots that had formed the moment she intruded upon his sanctuary. "Okay, talk."

When she stepped into the room, her heel caught on his Stetson and she stumbled. Before he realized his intent, he sprang from the barrel and grasped her arm to steady her.

"Thank you." She scooped the hat off the floor, popped the dent out and handed it over. He had to force himself to let go of her arm to accept the hat.

The smell of rich perfume and a hint of her natural scent drenched the room. A nice change from the barn's usual manure-and-horse stink.

Her hesitant expression changed to delight when she spotted the kittens. Kneeling in front of the box, she peered over the edge. "Oh, how adorable," she whispered. Her hushed voice caused the skin along JD's shoulders to tingle.

With a silent curse he leaned against the far wall, crossed his arms over his chest and struggled to hold back a groan as he listened to Ms. Corporation cooing to the feline.

After a few moments, she stood and faced him. Hurt shadowed her eyes, deepening their blue. "Why didn't you notify my family when Bobby came to live with you?"

Anger from this woman he could handle, but the pain in her gaze made him yearn to tuck tail and run. "Because I didn't know you existed."

Her forehead creased. "You had to be aware of our family. You dated my sister."

"No, I didn't." Embarrassed and feeling like an idiot, he wished he didn't have to explain. "We didn't date. We had sex. One night." He had no intention of confessing another thing about his night with Cassandra.

Josephine's eyes rounded like an owl's. "But—"

"Sex. We did the down and dirty in a motel room." Remembering what he and Cassandra had done bothered him greatly, but speaking the words made him sick to his stomach.

Cheeks flushed, Josephine stared at the floor. "I see."

"No, I don't think you do. I knew nothing about your sister except her first name, and that was only because I'd heard some cowboys behind the chutes discussing her *talents*." He shrugged. "That's the way she wanted it."

Peeking at him from under her lashes, she insisted, "You must have talked about *something*."

"I guess you've never had a one-night stand."

Her chin rose a notch, and he noticed her cheeks had turned redder than one of Blake's garden-ripe tomatoes. "I guess you never heard of birth control."

Touché.

All this talk about sex and birth control shot the temperature up ten degrees in the small room. A trickle of sweat ran down his back, and he noticed little beads of moisture forming across Josephine's upper lip. He swallowed against the urge to move closer and run his tongue over the salty skin. "I always practice safe sex. The night with Bobby's mother was the first and only time condoms failed me."

She sighed, the feminine sound at odds with her defensive stance. "Okay, so you slept with my sister once, and she got pregnant. But I don't understand why she didn't tell you. My God, Bobby spent a whole month in foster care until social services located you."

JD cringed. How many nights had he lain awake after Bobby's arrival at the ranch, wrestling with guilt? The idea that his son had lived with strangers while the State of New York searched for JD tore him up inside. If Cassandra's roommate hadn't mentioned that he'd been a rodeo cowboy they'd probably still be looking for him. As it was, it had taken a bit of time to locate JD through the Professional Rodeo Cowboys Association.

Bitterness rose in his throat and he swallowed hard. "Take a good, long, hard look at me. What do you see?"

Her forehead creased and the tiny wrinkle across the bridge

of her nose distracted him almost as much as the rounded hips she perched her small fists on. "I see an ass."

Mocoso. His lip quirked, but he managed to hold back a grin. "Besides an ass, what do you see?"

She glared. "Fine. A too-handsome-for-his-own-good cowboy, with the personality of a rattlesnake and the sex appeal of a playgirl centerfold. Satisfied?"

The idea Josephine might be sexually interested in him inflated his ego like a hot-air balloon. Too bad nothing could ever come of the attraction between them. "I'm Hispanic, white and a little Indian thrown in for good measure."

Josephine did the owl thing again with her eyes. Damn, she was cute.

"What has your ethnicity got to do with Cassandra not telling you about Bobby?"

"Don't act so shocked, honey. Girls like your sister are a dime a dozen. They want to take a walk on the wild side, and that's exactly what I am, Josephine…a walk on the wild side."

Chapter Three

"What happens *after* they walk on the wild side with you, JD?" One of Josephine's perfectly arched eyebrows lifted.

He grinned. "They throw me away like last year's fashions."

A shrill bell clamored somewhere outside the barn.

End of round one.

"Supper," JD murmured. He made no move to leave.

Nor did Josephine.

The energy crackling between them sucked the air out of the room, leaving her gasping for breath. She couldn't remember the last time she'd been near a man so...*male.*

A horse's neigh shattered the sensual spell, making her head spin in relief. Another minute and she'd have begged JD for a taste of the wild side. With shaky resolve, she vowed he'd never learn it wasn't his words that shook her but his brown-eyed stare. "Thank you for allowing me to stay and visit with Bobby." She couldn't imagine having to leave after just meeting her nephew. There was so much she wanted to ask the boy. Questions about his mother, his life in New York. And she wanted to reassure him that he had family who cared about him back in Chicago.

JD shifted away from the wall. "I guess I wasn't clear." Motioning for her to precede him from the room, he added, "I don't want you here, and I didn't invite you for supper."

His muscular body blocked half the doorway and she

questioned whether he'd accidentally or intentionally brushed a broad shoulder against her back as she slipped by. In silence, they walked through the barn, JD keeping one step ahead. Through lowered lashes, she watched him move, awed by the strength emanating from his six-foot-plus frame.

When they reached the rental, she stopped. "I need to get something out of the car." She opened the passenger door and reached inside. "I bought this at the airport in Chicago." She held up a large stuffed brown bear with floppy ears. JD didn't even crack a smile at the silly-looking bear. Oh, well. Hopefully Bobby would appreciate her gesture.

She shut the door and followed JD around the corner of the house. Slowing her steps, she studied the backyard. Several oaks provided relief from the harsh Texas sun. A bike with training wheels leaned against a tree. A plastic play pool sat empty in the middle of the yard. Farther away, a football and soccer ball rested on the seat of a lawn chair. Upon first glance…all the ingredients for an afternoon of playtime fun.

But something nagged at Josephine. The bike's wheels were clean and new, and no worn path was visible in the grass to suggest the cycle had been ridden around the yard. The manufacturer's label remained glued to the inside of the pool, making her believe the pool had yet to be filled with water. And the balls appeared brand-new, as if their packaging had been removed minutes ago instead of months ago.

Oh, Bobby, why aren't you playing with these things? Maybe later after supper, she'd ask her nephew if he wanted to toss the ball with her. Or they could fill the pool and stomp through the water in their bare feet.

What she wouldn't have given to have had a bike or splashed in a play pool when she'd been her nephew's age. But the gardener would have had a heart attack if she'd ridden a bike across the perfectly manicured lawn or thrown a ball into the flower beds of her parents' *Home and Garden* estate.

"Are you through gawking?" JD asked, holding the screen door open for her.

As she hurried to catch up, she noticed the underground storm shelter on the far side of the porch steps. The shelter brought up concerns for Bobby's safety. Aside from the notorious Texas twisters that filled the evening-news programs each spring, she worried about other dangers rural living posed for her nephew.

Stepping past JD, she saw the back porch had been turned into a utility room. A washer, dryer and meat freezer occupied the far end. A yellow rope hung across the ceiling, cutting the room in half. Several pairs of colored B.V.D.s dangled from the makeshift clothesline. *Interesting.* She'd pegged JD as a simple, no-nonsense, whitie-tightie kind of guy. Her gaze slid past his waist and stalled on the fly of his jeans, as she wondered what color he wore today.

"Dryer broke," he mumbled, beating a hasty retreat into the kitchen.

While JD went to the sink to wash up, she hung back in the doorway. The sounds of frying chicken sizzling, silverware tinkling and water running filled the room. Linoleum, yellowed with age, covered the kitchen floor, the area in front of the sink worn black from years of standing there, washing dishes by hand. Faded red-and-white checked curtains hung above the sink window, billowing softly in the late-afternoon breeze.

A scarred oak table with matching chairs occupied the middle of the room. The Formica countertop had several dents, dings and scratches. At one end of the counter a stack of telephone books sat under a combination wall phone and answering machine. The extra-long cord dangled an inch above the floor. She envisioned JD pacing the room during yesterday's call, wishing the cord were her neck as he twisted the coils around his fingers.

All in all, the kitchen was...well...exactly what she'd expected after seeing the outside of the house. Shabby. But beneath the room's ragged appearance, Josephine sensed *warmth, love, security*—things she couldn't see or touch but that enveloped her in an invisible hug. She was sure Bobby felt those same things.

She could guarantee Bobby's grandparents would give him the best of everything if he lived in their elegant, impressive Chicago mansion—everything except the warmth and love. But *she'd* make sure her nephew received lots of hugs and kisses. And love.

Warmth and love aside, Josephine worried about JD's financial situation and the ranch's yearly profit margin. His intention to provide for Bobby might be honorable, but the run-down condition of the ranch suggested he didn't have enough money to provide the extras her nephew deserved.

Bobby entered the kitchen, cast a glance her way, but averted his gaze before she flashed him a smile. A pang pricked her side at her nephew's lack of interest in her. For a second, Josephine wondered if Cassandra had filled her son's head with not-so-nice tales of his grandparents and aunt. Although she and Cassandra had never been close, they'd never hated each other, either. She couldn't imagine her sister saying anything mean about her. Maybe Bobby just needed a little time to get used to the idea he had an aunt.

Bobby lifted a stack of heavy plates from the counter and she held her breath as he wobbled toward the table. Both JD and Blake kept their backs to the boy, as if the five-year-old handled antique china every day. She winced when he set the dishes on the table with a clank.

After he laid out the plates, he peeked at her, and Josephine had a smile ready. Even though his expression remained solemn, she felt ridiculously happy he didn't look away as quickly as he had earlier. "I can see you're a big help in the kitchen, Bobby." This time when he glanced her way, his eyes landed on the stuffed teddy bear and stayed there.

"I brought you a gift." She stepped farther into the kitchen and held out the bear.

Bobby stared at JD, then the old man, before hesitantly accepting the gift. "Thank you," he whispered, setting the bear in one of the kitchen chairs.

Before Josephine could ask her nephew if he had a favorite stuffed animal, the ranch hand turned off the gas burner and announced, "Supper's almost ready."

"Smells delicious." She studied the huge can of lard on the counter and shuddered when she considered how much artery-clogging grease would be pumping through her veins shortly.

The older man set the heavy cast-iron skillet on the counter, then removed a baking sheet of Texas-size rolls from the oven. "Ain't nothing better than fried chicken and biscuits to fill an empty stomach."

She cleared her throat. "I'd like to freshen up before dinner."

Hands and forearms covered with sudsy bubbles, JD stared over his shoulder, his face lighting with surprise. *What? Did he think that if he ignored her she'd simply disappear?* He motioned with his head. "Down the hall to the left."

"Thank you." She followed the narrow hallway off the kitchen and opened the first door on the left under the stairs. Slipping inside, she flipped the light switch, then turned to lock the door. The bolt was rusted and bent out of shape. *What a surprise.*

Careful not to bump her head against the angled ceiling over the toilet, she inventoried the veritable chamber of riches. No doubt, the pedestal sink would command a steep price in an antique store. And the commode had to be worth a fortune. The only place she'd seen an old-fashioned water closet with a chain pull had been in interior-decorating magazines. The upstairs bath probably had a claw-foot tub worth a few thousand dollars.

After washing her hands, she moistened some toilet paper and patted away the layer of dust on her face deposited by the never-ending Texas wind. Her lipstick had faded; only a hint of Strawberry Sorbet remained. Her mother would consider it a faux pas to come to the dinner table with a naked mouth; Josephine doubted the guys in the kitchen cared one way or the other.

Leaving the tiny hideaway under the stairs, she returned to the dinner table, surprised to discover all three males standing by their chairs, waiting for her. She found their old-fashioned chivalry charming. The ranch cook pulled out the chair next to him. "Thank you," she murmured, and slid onto the seat. JD sat across from her and Bobby to his right, the teddy bear in Bobby's lap.

The older man bowed his head and recited a blessing, an act occurring at her parents' table only on Thanksgiving, Christmas and Easter. Following the chorus of amens, he held out the breadbasket. "Biscuit?"

She selected a roll four times the size of the dinner pastries her mother's cook served with the evening meal. "Thank you, Mr. Sloan."

"We're not formal around here. Blake'll do just fine," he chastised with a wink.

"Thank you, Blake." Josephine added a meaty drumstick to her plate. Until she'd sat down, she hadn't noticed the stifling temperature in the room. Evidently, screen doors and windows were no defense against the Texas summers. How could anyone get a decent night's sleep in this sweltering heat without an air conditioner? Surely JD could afford a couple of window units for the house. She resisted the urge to adjust her bra's damp underwire.

Bobby sat quietly, eyes downcast as his father piled food on his plate. After setting the butter crock near the boy's elbow, JD lifted the lemonade pitcher and filled everyone's glass.

She wasn't used to silence during meals. The few times a week she dined with her parents, she discussed business accounts and clients with her father during dinner. "Blake?"

"Yes, ma'am."

Wrinkling her nose, she laughed. "I'm not old enough to be a ma'am yet." Bobby offered a tiny smile at her joke, and her chest swelled with pride, as if she'd just witnessed her own child take his first step. "How long have you worked on the ranch?" JD's shoulders tensed, making Josephine think she'd spoken out of turn.

"All my life. I'm a third-generation rancher. My grand-pappy bought most of the land. I added a couple hundred acres over the years." The piece of chicken in Blake's hand paused an inch from his mouth. "How many head we got running, JD?"

"About six hundred." JD set his drink down, then slathered butter on a biscuit. Half the bread disappeared with the first bite.

Hoping to hide the shock of learning Blake wasn't the hired hand but the owner of the Rocking R Ranch, she spent a good minute buttering her own roll. "JD works for you?"

Blake grinned. "He's the best darn foreman I've ever had. Been my sidekick for twenty years. Just bought into the ranch this past January. Now we're official partners."

If JD had become Blake's partner a few months ago, then she doubted JD had had time to recoup the money he'd had to use to buy into the property and all its assets. She had a hunch JD was flat broke right now.

What if something happened to Blake? JD would have to sell the ranch if he couldn't buy out Blake's half from the bank. Then where would JD and Bobby go? She shuddered at the idea of the two males roaming the back roads of America, searching for ranch work. Bobby deserved stability and security.

Maybe she should ask if JD had a savings plan or a financial portfolio. Did he have access to funds in case his son became injured or seriously ill? Which brought up another question. Did JD have health insurance?

Her forehead throbbed as a list of worries and concerns formed in her head. "Where did you say you're from, JD?"

She bit off a piece of crunchy chicken, her mouth watering at the spicy flavor.

JD reached for his drink, and she held her breath, waiting to see if the glass would shatter beneath his white-knuckled grip. "I didn't."

As Bobby's aunt, she had a right to ask questions. She had a right to answers. Why was he being so closemouthed? Didn't he realize his silence made her all the more suspicious of him? "Do you have family nearby?"

"Not that I'm aware of." He set his fork on the plate…none too gently.

Startled, she held her breath. Even Bobby had stopped eating and stared at his father.

"You're from Illinois?" Blake's question cut the thick tension in the air.

She almost laughed at the old man's blatant ploy to divert her attention from JD. Not wishing to ruin the first meal with her nephew, she played along. "I work in my father's investment firm."

Both men stared at her with blank faces.

Investment banking wasn't the most exciting career a woman could choose…if she'd had a choice in the matter. Which Josephine hadn't. Her father had expected her to join his firm after graduating from college. Of course she had. Defying him would have been out of the question. Lucky for her she happened to love numbers.

Her only regret was that she hadn't gone back to college to pursue a second degree, in fine arts. She couldn't care less that her father insisted *creative* was synonymous with *poor*. Now that Bobby was part of the family, she intended to lighten her workload in order to spend more time with her nephew. Maybe this fall she'd enroll in a drawing class. "I design and manage investment portfolios for our clients." She shrugged. "Bonds, securities, money market funds, trusts. Short- and long-term investments."

Blake's expression grew serious. "A numbers gal, huh?"

"You could say that." She glanced at her nephew. "Can you add and subtract, Bobby?" He shrugged, making Josephine wonder how much time Cassandra had spent teaching him his numbers and letters. At his age, he should at least know his colors, numbers to a hundred and the alphabet. She'd make sure she spent time each day working with Bobby on his arithmetic and reading.

Josephine had never been the type to flaunt her education, but if she was to convince Blake and JD to entrust her with Bobby's care, they deserved to know more about her. "I have an undergraduate degree in business from Brown University and a master's in finance from Yale."

JD pushed the food around his plate, as though he'd lost his appetite. She wished she knew whether her education credentials intimidated or impressed him. Then she scolded herself for even worrying about what he thought of her. Hoping to lighten the mood, she asked, "Bobby, how do you like living on a ranch?"

He squirmed in his chair, then lifted his head. "It's okay." The quiet answer was followed by a very audible sigh. JD sucked in a quick breath and Blake's forehead creased.

Ignoring the men, she focused on her nephew. "Texas is very different from New York. Do you miss the city?"

Bobby's lips curved upward. "You don't look like my mom," he stated, ignoring the question.

Feeling that she'd crossed some invisible line between them, Josephine cherished the warm flow of satisfaction the boy's smile sent through her.

"Finish your chicken, Bobby." JD sounded calm, but his eyes flashed Josephine a different message.

What? She'd done nothing to upset her nephew, so why did JD act as though he'd swallowed his fork sideways, blaming her in the process?

Bobby obeyed his father, popping a piece of chicken into

his mouth. While he chewed, Josephine questioned exactly how much he enjoyed his new life on the ranch. The boy must miss living in New York a little.

Unwilling to let JD bully her, she posed another question. "Have you made new friends here?"

"I don't got no friends," he mumbled around the food in his mouth.

None too gently, JD nudged the side of her shoe with the pointed toe of his boot. Josephine acknowledged the silent warning by grinding her high heel into the top of the offending boot. *Take that, you big lug.*

She ignored JD's hot glare and Blake's sudden coughing fit. "Bobby, are you saying you haven't made any friends since you came to the ranch?"

Her nephew nodded.

"I imagine you miss your pals back in New York."

"I don't got none there." His quiet declaration melted her heart.

The idea that Bobby didn't have any friends upset her, but she didn't understand why. When she'd been Bobby's age, she hadn't had time for friends. Her and her sister's days had been filled with private tutors, music lessons and etiquette courses. Anger filled Josephine. What kind of mother wouldn't notice her son was friendless?

JD patted Bobby's slumped shoulders. "I know two friends you've got."

Pushing a strand of blond hair away from his face, Bobby asked, "You do?"

"Yup. Me and Blake."

The tenderness in JD's expression reminded Josephine of how little emotion her father had invested in their relationship over the years.

A smile teased the corner of her nephew's mouth as he stared at JD. Josephine realized she'd yet to see a full-blown grin on the boy's face. She didn't have any experience with children, but Bobby seemed far too solemn for a child his age.

Deciding she'd grilled him with enough questions, she changed the topic. "This china is beautiful, Blake. Did these dishes belong to your mother?"

Rubbing his belly, the elderly rancher eased back in the chair. "I bought these fancy plates for my wife, Mary, on our honeymoon in Dallas. Had to sell my best dang cutting horse to pay for them." His face softened. "Never regretted it."

"I imagine your wife believed you'd handed her the moon that day."

"Mary was a fine woman. We had thirty-four years together before the cancer took her."

"No children?"

Sorrow flashed through Blake's eyes, before he blinked the melancholy thoughts away and grinned. "Lord, we tried more than most folks, I suspect."

Scooting his chair back, JD left the table and dumped the chicken bones on his plate in the trash can by the stove—a cue supper had officially ended.

"The least I can do after such a fine meal is clean up the kitchen." She carried her plate to the sink, then held out her hand for JD's dish.

He showed no surprise at her offer as he handed over the china. "I'll be in the barn. Bobby, you want to check on the kittens?"

Clutching the teddy bear in one arm, her nephew scurried down from his chair and dashed out the back door after his father.

For the next half hour, she and Blake worked side by side, clearing the table and putting away the leftovers. She washed. He dried.

"I'm just an old fart, and you'll think I'm being nosy."

Josephine tensed at the rancher's sober tone. "What's on your mind, Blake?"

"Did you come to take Bobby away from JD?"

A bang saved Josephine from answering. JD stood in the kitchen doorway, looking more determined than any man had a right to be. She couldn't recall hearing the squeak of the screen door, and wondered how he'd snuck up on them without making a sound. His face tightened. "We need to talk."

Blake threaded the damp towel through the oven-door handle, then clasped JD's shoulder. "I'll be in the barn with Bobby."

Alone, the overbearing cowboy leaned against the door frame and crossed his arms over his chest—a posture Josephine began to think he owned the patent for. She found his tough-as-nails pose too darned appealing, and realized she'd better keep her gaze on his face if she planned to hear a word of his *talk.*

"Finished?" he growled.

She straightened her shoulders, then set the rag on the counter and faced him. Feeling puny next to his large frame, she lifted her chin. "Yes."

"Let's take this outside."

Good Lord. He acted as though he wanted to brawl with her! She followed him out of the kitchen and down the narrow hallway to the front door. Taking care not to let one single inch of her person brush against him, she scooted past and stepped onto the porch.

At five-thirty in the afternoon, she expected some relief from the day's heat, but the temperature held steady at hot. On the bright side, the dry, gusty wind showed signs of dying down to a gentle breeze. She moved to the end of the porch and sat on the swing.

A safe distance away, JD leaned his hips against the porch rail. His relaxed stance didn't fool her, not when the muscles along his shoulders bunched with restrained anger.

With the tip of her shoe she set the swing in motion. Wanting to ease the strain between them, she asked, "Who uses the trailer under those trees?"

Her question had the desired effect—the bunching muscles relaxed. "José. He and his family live in Mexico. They help out during spring branding and fall roundup."

"What about the rest of the year? Aren't six hundred cows an awful lot for two men to take care of?"

His black eyebrows slashed downward. "Cattle. They're called cattle."

Waving her hand in the air by her head, she sighed. "Cows, cattle, whatever." Josephine pressed her lips together to keep from laughing at his slack-jawed stare. Evidently, he took offense to having his *cattle* slandered.

Studying his dark handsomeness, she attempted to convince herself that her shaky nerves and jittery stomach were the result of jet lag. But there was no sense denying the obvious—she was sexually attracted to the mulish, rude, arrogant, sexy, muscle-bound, silky-haired, tall, bedroom-eyed cowboy. *Lord help her.* Sex appeal aside, there was something compelling about JD that made Josephine wish Bobby didn't stand between them. In another time, on different ground, she would have enjoyed discovering the many fascinating layers making up the man.

He rubbed the back of his neck. "We've got two hands who help year-round. They live in a line shack on the south side of the ranch."

Josephine couldn't resist. "Wow, a line shack. Just like in the movies."

"Let's cut the crap and get down to business."

So much for her attempt to lighten the mood.

As though preparing to charge at the least provocation, he leaned forward. "What do you want?"

She couldn't recall ever dealing with a client this bull-headed. "First, I have to be sure Bobby is being properly taken care of—"

"What do you mean, *properly?*" His eyebrows dipped dangerously low, reminding her of an outlaw in a western movie. All he lacked was a gun belt slung around his slim hips.

"Hold on, Wyatt Earp."

Nostrils flaring, he glowered. "Are you accusing me of mistreating my son?"

Three strikes, I'm out. Clearly, her attempt at humor had failed. She cleared her throat. "I haven't seen anything yet to indicate you're mistreating my nephew." She hadn't meant to question JD's integrity and honor, but where her nephew was concerned, she couldn't be too careful.

"Does this have anything to do with the envelope you shoved up my nose outside the café earlier today?"

"Yes." She removed the folded paper from her skirt pocket and held it out to him. "This is from my father."

He made no move to take the envelope.

"I think you're going to want to see what's inside."

"Think again."

"It's a check from my father."

JD's entire body went rigid. "A pay-off." He clenched his hands against his thighs. "Swell guy, your old man. Sends his little girl to do his dirty work."

Darn her father for not taking her advice and contacting a lawyer to determine their exact legal rights in this situation. Her nephew's welfare was at stake and here she was, winging it! "He hopes you'll consider releasing Bobby into his care on a permanent basis."

JD's bronze face turned sickly white in a matter of seconds. His rigid posture crumbled before her. "He wants to *buy* his grandson?"

Josephine prayed her voice wouldn't betray her, and lied, "Of course not." Her father had insisted *every* man had his price. For Bobby's sake, and maybe even *her* sake, Josephine hoped JD wasn't *every* man.

"You can tell the bastard to shove the check right up his—"

"I get the picture." Time to backpedal before she lost complete control of the situation. "At least let me take Bobby back to Chicago for a visit."

"Not on your life, lady. You may be his aunt, but you're practically a stranger to my son." With reluctant amusement, JD watched anger brighten Josephine's blue eyes and her cheeks turn an appealing pink.

"From what I've seen this afternoon, Bobby doesn't treat me any differently from you. And you're his father."

Low blow, darlin'. Her words sliced through him like a castration knife. He wondered how many corporate executives Josephine turned into eunuchs on a weekly basis. "I won't lie to you. Bobby and I are still feeling our way around each other."

She leaned forward on the swing, and JD struggled to keep his gaze on her face and off the front of her blouse, which molded to her gently swaying breasts. "Even you admit your relationship with Bobby is strained. He's just a little boy, JD. A little boy who's too quiet, too somber for his age."

Another blow, this one knocking the air from his lungs. Bobby was only the second blessing JD had ever received in his life—the first, Blake's taking him in and giving him a real home. JD might not be the best dad in the world, but he was trying. Eventually, he and Bobby would find their way as father and son. But he needed time...something the sassy financier didn't intend to give him. "I'm not the bad guy. I'm not the one who ran off and had Bobby without telling anyone."

Josephine left the swing and edged toward him, stopping inches from his chest. To keep from shaking some sense into her, he wrapped his fingers around the porch rail and squeezed until a splinter of wood shot into his palm. He welcomed the pain. Anything to help keep his mind off the panic gnawing away at his body.

"What Cassandra did was wrong. But you have the chance to do what's best for your son." The last sparks of anger drained from her eyes, leaving them a soft, almost translucent blue. JD found the color fascinating and wished he could see for himself what shade of blue they turned when she made love. But he'd never find out, because he had no intention of traveling down that particular road with the lady.

Forcing his attention away from her face, he focused on the small tear at the bottom of the screen door. "Bobby won't be any better off in Chicago than he is here."

She flung her arms up in the air, her fingers coming dangerously close to whacking him in the face. "Get real, JD. Bobby is a Delaney. He has a right to all the advantages and privileges associated with the Delaney name."

JD shoved away from the rail, resisting the urge to reach out and steady Josephine when she stumbled back. He strode to the far end of the porch, turned and glared. "Back to money, are we? You had me fooled into thinking you might actually care about your nephew."

"I won't pretend money has nothing to do with Bobby living in Chicago." She swept her arm out in front of her, pointing toward the barn. "This life is fine for you, JD, but not for a small child."

More insults. The woman was ruthless. Anger made his blood boil and he prayed for her sake he could control his temper.

"Under normal circumstances, raising a boy on a ranch would be fine. A wonderful experience. But these aren't normal circumstances. I'm worried Bobby has no friends to play with, no nurturing female in his life, not even a housekeeper. At least in Chicago he'd have a grandmother and an aunt—"

"An aunt?" he shouted. "You mean a corporate junkie who gets high on sixteen-hour days and paychecks with no fewer than five zeros in them? Yeah, I'm sure you'll be a positive influence on the kid."

She sucked in a quiet gasp and turned her back to him.

Damn it, she'd insulted him first!

No matter how justified his harsh words were, JD wished he could take them back. *Oh, hell.* He stared down at his boots, feeling as if his feet were sinking in a mud bog. If only he hadn't hung up on her yesterday. Maybe all this insult slinging could have been avoided.

"The ranch may not seem like much to you, but it's my home. And this is where Bobby belongs. He gets plenty of attention from Blake and me. I doubt you or your father will give him the time of day in Chicago."

"How ridiculous!" The spitfire stomped her foot so hard JD was afraid her heel might go right through the weathered floorboards.

Enough already! In two strides he towered over her. "Ridiculous? Think again, honey. Ridiculous is *you* showing up uninvited, trying to take away *my* son when *you* have no legal grounds. Damn it, I'm his father!"

"I'm not trying to take him away."

"Then what do you call it? Borrowing Bobby?"

"You're his father, but Bobby has other family who can help him achieve his goals in life. Succeeding takes more than just love, warmth and shelter. I understand you want the best for Bobby…but can you afford to give it to him? You have to think about his future. His education."

"I've already registered him for kindergarten this fall."

"I'm talking about private schools, better teachers, advanced curricula, tutors if necessary. He'll receive a finer education than any rural school could hope to offer."

He had to move away before he did something stupid like toss her over his knee and swat her sassy fanny. He backed himself into the corner behind the swing.

She followed, but at least the swing stayed between them. "Not only education, but extracurricular activities and music lessons. Ranching doesn't allow you the flexibility or time for the extras Bobby deserves. My parents and I can ensure he receives those opportunities."

"A few questions at the dinner table and you're an authority on the life of a rancher."

She closed her eyes and rubbed her temple.

He hoped she had a hell of a banger, because his head felt ready to explode.

"He should have friends, JD. It isn't natural for Bobby to be with grown-ups all the time. He'll have trouble socializing with other children when he gets into school."

"The caseworker who brought Bobby out to the ranch claimed Cassandra had put him in full-time day care as soon as she left the hospital with him." He watched the color drain from Josephine's face, and felt a little better knowing the tidbit of news bothered her as much as it had bothered him when he'd first heard. "What Bobby needs is no clubs, no day cares, no activities. The friend thing can't be helped, at least until he starts school and meets other kids."

"What about his safety?"

He studied her across the narrow space. "What do you mean?"

"A ranch is a dangerous place to let a five-year-old run loose."

"He doesn't run loose. He's with me or Blake."

"Blake is an old man. What happens if he gets ill while you're out lassoing cows?"

She was like a dog with a bone. You didn't go near her unless you wanted your hand bit off. "Blake might be a little past seventy, but he's as healthy as a fifty-year-old."

Inching her way around the swing, she got right in his face. "I had hoped we could settle this without lawyers."

"Is that a threat?" Sexy or not, Ms. Corporation had gone one step too far.

"Contrary to what you probably believe, I don't use threats. In fact, I don't say anything I don't mean. You may be Bobby's birth father, but his grandparents and I have rights, too. If I need a lawyer to remind you of those rights, I'll get one."

Panic inched through him, tightening his muscles and joints into twisted iron. He didn't think for a minute the grandparents' rights outweighed the father's in a court of law. But he wasn't so blind that he didn't consider Josephine's father might have the power, money and connections to sway a court judge to rule in favor of the grandparents—especially if the Delaneys could prove he was an unfit father. JD could raise a ruckus, holler and balk, but in the end, the almighty dollar would win. Deep in his gut he believed he had to find a compromise, or he'd lose his son.

Her fingers tightened around his upper arm, the tips pressing into his skin with surprising strength. "There's more at stake than money or a better education. I'm worried about Bobby. He might not have recovered from Cassandra's death. How can I be sure if he remains here and I return to Chica—"

"Seems to me you ought to stay for the summer," a gravelly voice interrupted.

"What?" JD stared over the top of her head.

Josephine dropped her grip on his arm and spun away. "What?"

Blake stood at the bottom of the porch steps, eavesdropping. He rubbed his whiskered jaw. "You could get better acquainted with Bobby and see for yourself he's doing fine."

Had the old coot lost his mind? No way would JD allow the tempting blonde to spend the rest of the summer under his roof…make that half his roof. "You're kidding, right?"

Blake shoved his hands deep into the pockets of his overalls and rocked back on his heels. "Nope."

JD cussed under his breath. The last thing he needed was Josephine breathing down his neck, keeping score on how well he did with his son. He patted his shirt pocket for a cigarette. Christ, the woman had him so riled he'd forgotten he'd quit smoking right after Bobby arrived last Christmas.

Josephine walked over to the porch steps. "There has to be another way to handle this." Staying the summer was out of the question. She couldn't afford the time off from work.

Rubbing the ache pulsing against her right temple, she considered what JD would do if she forced his hand and brought Bobby back to Chicago with her. Would he make good on his threat and call the police? Lord, what would her father say if she was brought up on kidnapping charges? "Now isn't a good time for a leave of absence from my job."

Blake grinned. "I figured all you financial wizards used them fancy portable computers and cellular phones."

Drat, the *toot.* He was smarter than he led on. "I don't think I'd survive a whole summer in some dingy off-the-beaten-path motel."

"We've got an extra bedroom upstairs and an office to work in downstairs."

Josephine caught the way JD's face tightened when Blake mentioned the extra bedroom. Well, she wasn't too happy about that arrangement, either. She held up her hand and counted off on her fingers. "Today's already July 15. Employee appraisals are due the middle of August. Not to mention all the business meetings I'd have to reschedule. And my clients. If word gets around I'm no longer accessible I could lose some of our most valued accounts."

JD grinned. "Sounds like staying's too much trouble."

Yeah, you're hoping, cowboy. Without taking her gaze off JD, she asked Blake, "Do you have an Internet connection in the house?"

"Had one put in last year."

Josephine felt the first flicker of victory. "Fine, I'll stay."

JD's grin flipped upside down. "Two weeks. Take it or leave it."

She was out of her ever-loving mind. "I'll take it."

Chapter Four

"Did you tell this JD character I'll hire the best custody lawyer in Chicago?"

Josephine sighed into the cell phone. She'd thought her father would be tied up in Monday-morning meetings, but he'd managed to catch her as she'd pulled into a parking spot outside Milner's Feed and Tack in Brandt's Corner. After spending her entire Sunday hidden away in a run-down motel room, answering e-mails and writing employee appraisals, she wasn't in the mood to go head to head with the mulish man.

"Yes, Father. I mentioned lawyers." *Sort of.*

From experience, Josephine knew his lectures could go on forever, so she'd left the car running and turned up the air conditioner. At ten in the morning, the temperature hovered near ninety. How did people in West Texas stand this heat? "I brought up visitation rights with JD."

"Visitation rights? Josephine, you're getting soft on me. Next time, go for the jugular and threaten a custody suit if he doesn't hand over my grandson immediately."

Oh, good grief! Her father's obsession with gaining custody of his grandson wasn't healthy. After learning of Cassandra's death, he'd confessed that he should have kept a closer eye on his elder daughter instead of allowing her to run loose all over the country. Josephine suspected guilt played a large part in her father's resolve to raise Bobby.

William Delaney's outbursts weren't unusual, but some sixth sense told Josephine to proceed cautiously and not offer too much information about JD, the ranch or Bobby. At least until she figured out what her father had up his sleeve.

"For now, Bobby's fine where he is." Cringing at herself in the rearview mirror, she added, "He's well and he seems happy." She wasn't completely sure about her nephew's happiness, but after hearing his mother had dumped him off at day care every day of his young life, his trailing around after JD and Blake all day had to be an improvement.

"What about the check I sent with you? He's holding out for more money, isn't he?"

"I don't think you'd like to hear where JD suggested you put your check." She smiled as her father's sputtering outrage echoed through the connection loud and clear.

"Every man has his price. Tell him no sum is too much for my grandson."

Bitterness filled Josephine. She'd never heard her father talk about her with such possessiveness in his voice. From as far back as she could remember, her parents had always showered her sister with more attention. Cassandra had been their shining star. Prettier than their younger daughter. More outgoing. More popular. Although Josephine had never resented her sister for being the favorite, she had hoped she and her parents would grow closer after Cassandra's death. But Bobby had taken Cassandra's place in their hearts, shutting her out once again. Surprisingly, she felt no animosity toward her nephew, only a strong instinct to protect him.

"Tell me about his ranch. What kind of assets does he have? Cash reserves? What am I up against, Josephine?"

Nothing put a fire under William Delaney more than a competitive game of financial warfare. And he never played by the rules. Several times she'd witnessed his quick mind search out the enemy's weak spot, then go in for the kill before the opponent even realized he'd been a target. He might be her father, but she wouldn't offer information that would aid him in defeating JD when the playing field wasn't even level to begin with.

"Slow down, Father. We're strangers to Bobby. He won't return to Chicago with me until he trusts I have his best interests at heart."

"A child his age doesn't have a clue about what's best for him. However, there may be some truth to what you're saying."

Some? Typical. He never gave her full credit for any of her ideas or advice no matter how well received they were with the other members of his firm—including him.

"I'll have to rely on your judgment, Josephine."

Gee, thanks for the vote of confidence.

"You've got two weeks to bring my grandson back to Chicago, or I'll come to Texas and get him myself."

"I can't promise anything more than a visit."

"Once Robert sees his new home, he won't wish to live anywhere else."

"I'll do what I can." She'd only just met JD, but her instincts insisted he wouldn't give up custody of his son to anyone. Not willingly.

"I expect to see you and Robert before the end of the month."

Before the end of the month? Josephine flipped through her personal planner. JD had offered two weeks and she'd need every one of those days. Today was Monday, the seventeenth. "I'll try to speed things up, but let's plan on July 30." Before he could object, she changed the subject. "About my business meeting in New York this Thursday."

"Concentrate on winning over my grandson. I'll delegate your work and your business trips."

"I'll have Internet access later today if anyone needs to reach me."

"I expect an update in a few days."

Stubborn cuss. "Yes, sir."

"And Josephine?"

"Yes?"

"We owe this to Cassandra. Don't let her down."

Thanks for the guilt trip. She snapped the cell phone shut and stared at the display window of Milner's Feed and Tack. Yuck. She hated shopping. She preferred to order her clothes out of a catalog. But that wasn't an option.

Once she'd removed the key from the ignition, she left the car and entered the store. The cowbell above the door clanged, announcing her arrival. The sharp smells of polished wood, new leather and cleaning disinfectant assaulted her nostrils.

"Well, howdy," a cheerful feminine voice called out.

Josephine blinked. Shook her head. Frowned. Then blinked again.

"You must be new around these parts." The young woman smiled. "Everyone else is used to me."

Josephine returned her smile. "You look exactly like the country singer—"

"Dolly Parton." She patted the white-blond explosion of curls cascading halfway down her back. "The dimples are real, too." She pointed to the little dents in her cheeks. "The only thing I'm missing is a mole next to my lower lip." She touched the tip of a nail to the left side of her mouth.

"Amazing." Josephine couldn't get over how much the younger woman resembled the famous singer. "I guess you wear your Halloween costume all year-round."

Enthusiastic laughter reverberated throughout the store. "Aren't you a stitch. I've won tons of look-alike contests for sure." She sighed dramatically and leaned closer. "I get high scores on everything except these." She cupped her massive breasts and lifted them in the air.

Josephine stepped back, to avoid being bumped in the face by the voluptuous mounds. "What's wrong with your chest?"

"I'm two cup sizes smaller than Dolly. But Ma won't let me get implants." Her mouth turned down in a sexy pout.

"I can't tell the difference," Josephine offered.

"Well, ain't that a nice thing to say. You sound like a city girl. Dallas? Houston? San Antone?" Josephine didn't have a chance to answer before the young woman continued, "You can't be a native Texan. You ain't got the twang."

"Chicago."

"Ah, the Windy City. Always dreamed about shopping on State Street and seeing the big building…what's the thing called?"

"Sears Tower."

"Yeah, that's the one."

"Josephine Delaney." She held out a hand. "Pleasure to meet you."

"Bonnie Milner. Pop owns the store."

Josephine couldn't help but stare at the glittering lime-green talons with tiny ladybugs painted across them.

Bonnie wiggled her fingers in the air. "Like 'em?"

"I've never seen nails so elaborate."

"Gloria, over at the Nail 'n More, does mine. Tuesday's discount day. You get an extra ten percent off."

Josephine never had her nails done on a regular basis. She simply couldn't spare the time away from work.

"You passing through or visiting?"

"Visiting. I'm afraid I didn't pack anything appropriate to wear."

Bonnie's gaze roamed over Josephine's cream linen pants, low-heeled pumps and coffee-colored silk blouse. "Yep, them duds are mighty fancy and we country folk ain't too formal. You'll need blue jeans. And a pair of boots."

"Boots won't be necessary. I brought along a pair of Cole Haan mules."

"Mules? The only mules I know walk by themselves. Will they protect you from snakes? We got plenty o' snakes during the summer."

Josephine shuddered. The only snake she'd ever seen up

close was on the Discovery Channel. "I guess I should buy a pair of boots to go along with the jeans." Staring at the selection of Wranglers reminded Josephine she had little patience for trying on clothes. Probably because finding flattering outfits for an out-of-date Marilyn Monroe figure was next to impossible. "I'm not sure what size I wear."

"Jeans are made to fit a woman's body differently than those fancy pants you're wearing. C'mon. I'll help you out." Bonnie flitted around the clothing tables, stacking various brands and sizes of jeans in Josephine's arms. By the time the woman escorted her to a dressing room, Josephine was convinced she'd be trying on clothes all day.

"When you get the first pair on, I'll take a peek and make sure they fit right."

After a few minutes, Josephine walked stiff-legged out of the dressing room. "Bonnie? These seem a little snug." The pants were so tight she feared the seams would leave permanent creases in her skin.

"Oh, my. Those don't work at all." Bonnie ran her hand down Josephine's backside.

Startled by the intimate gesture, Josephine jumped.

"Better try the eight."

Eight? The ten felt snug. "I don't think I'd be able to move or sit—"

"Honey, jeans stretch. Gotta start smaller than you think, or you'll end up with a big pouch hanging under your butt by the end of the day. Don't want folks wondering if you've gone and messed your pants."

Oh, Lord. "Okay. I'll try the smaller size. I wouldn't want people to think I'm not potty trained." She smiled as the sound of Bonnie's tinkling laughter followed her back into the dressing room.

A moment later Josephine's smile turned into a frown. Following several unsuccessful attempts to stand and slip into the jeans, she sat on the bench and tugged. Pulled.

Struggled. Cursed. When she managed to coax the denim over her hips, she punched the air with her fist and whispered, "Yes!"

Panting, she glared down at the zipper. Bonnie wouldn't be any help, not with her ladybug nails. Clutching the handrail in the room, Josephine hauled herself into an upright—and locked—position. She sucked in her breath and yanked the zipper. Success! Then she exhaled loudly and the zipper reversed direction. "Fine. I just won't breathe."

"What was that, Josephine?"

"Nothing!" She sucked in one more deep breath. "Just." She clenched her teeth. "Zipping." She tugged the tab. "Up." Her overzealous effort produced the desired result…and then some. She lost her balance and went careening backward, slamming her shoulder into the mirror and causing the walls to shake as if an earthquake had struck the store.

"Everything all right in there?" Bonnie asked.

"Fine. I'm fine," Josephine panted as she secured the button at the waist.

"Come out and let me see."

"I don't think I can."

"Why?"

"I can't move my legs."

Bonnie giggled as she flung open the dressing-room door. Her gaze roamed up and down Josephine. "Perfect."

Horrified, Josephine gaped at her backside in the mirror. She'd known her fanny wasn't petite, but when had her rear gotten so…so curvy? Apparently, her work wardrobe concealed more than she realized.

"They'll loosen up after you move around some."

As if her knee joints were fused, Josephine walked awkwardly through the store, searching for T-shirts.

"The weather's so dang hot you'll be wanting one of those." Bonnie pointed to a rack of tank tops several feet away. "Blue would make your eyes stand out."

Josephine never considered herself the tank-top type, but the pretty cotton material with lace trim appealed to her feminine side. She chose one in blue and another top in soft butter yellow.

"Come on over and sit down. I've got a snazzy pair of boots you're gonna love."

Josephine hobbled to the small shoe section, then stopped and stared at the chair, wondering how to fold herself in half so she could sit.

Setting the boots aside, Bonnie instructed, "You gotta kind of slide onto the seat." She dipped at the waist and swayed her hips in a move that would have put an exotic dancer to shame.

With a few adjustments, Josephine followed Bonnie's example. The result wasn't as smooth. She collapsed on the chair, her legs popping straight out in front of her.

"Takes a little practice." Bonnie wiggled a black boot with yellow and red flames shooting up the sides over Josephine's foot.

"They're very…flashy, but I'm not sure I need anything this lavish."

"Why? You planning to work during your visit?"

Work? She remembered the employee appraisals she wanted to finish herself. "Not the kind you're thinking of." Honestly, she wouldn't mind helping around the ranch, but she doubted JD would let her. However, she would like to learn to ride a horse during her stay. She'd ask JD if he'd allow Bobby to give her riding lessons. Josephine would enjoy using the time to become better acquainted with her nephew and hopefully gain his trust. "I might try horseback riding."

"Well, golly, girl, why didn't you say so. You'll have to wear Ropers." Bonnie removed a pair of black, low-heeled boots from a box. The shaft was shorter and laced up the front.

After putting both boots on, Josephine rolled to one hip,

planted her palms on the seat of the chair and pushed herself upright. A couple of steps later, she smiled. "These feel great." Stiff-legged, she followed Bonnie to the front of the store to pay for her purchases. "Has business been slow lately?" Josephine had been the only customer for the past hour.

"Slow?" Bonnie glanced at her watch. "We might get a straggler, like yourself every now and then today, but rush was several hours ago."

"Rush? I don't understand."

"See that door?" Bonnie pointed to the back of the store. "That's the warehouse. You'll find all kinds of ranch and farm supplies back there. Feed, fence wire, tools. Some tractor parts. We open at 5:00 a.m. and most cowboys are here and gone by eight in the morning."

Feeling stupid, Josephine mumbled, "I see." Of course ranchers didn't shop during the middle of the morning unless there was an emergency of some kind. She wondered if JD or Blake had already come and gone.

The bell above the door clanged.

"Speaking of stragglers…our second of the day. Howdy, Gerard."

"Whoo-wee, what a pretty sight for these tired eyes."

Josephine imagined Bonnie got that reaction from men all the time. Smiling to herself, she buried her head in her purse and searched for her credit card. She considered herself the queen of organization and expediency in her work life, but she sure had problems keeping her personal things in order. One of these days she planned to clean out her purse. "Found it!" she exclaimed, handing the card to… *Where had Bonnie gone?* She glanced over her shoulder, but the only other person in the room was a blond-haired cowboy who happened to be gazing at her butt. *My butt?*

"Yer 'bout the sweetest-looking thing I've seen this morning."

"Keep a leash on your wicked tongue, Gerard, or you'll scare our visitor away," Bonnie warned as she approached.

She stepped behind the counter and set a can of leather spray next to Josephine's empty boot box. "Gerard's harmless. He's big and dumb, but kinda cute like a stuffed teddy bear."

Gerard sidled up to Josephine at the counter. "Bonnie's right. I'm a big ol' teddy bear. You just wanna hug and squeeze me to death."

Since the cowboy had a belly the size of a beach ball, she assumed he played Santa Claus each year for the local children. "Pleasure to meet you, Gerard. I'm Josephine Delaney."

He tipped his hat. "Pleasure's all mine, sweet thing."

Oh, brother. Did all cowboys use such hokey lines? She knew of at least one who didn't—JD.

He studied her purchases. "You fixin' to stay awhile?" He edged closer. And closer.

Josephine inched away. And away.

"Darn credit machine's actin' up again. I'll try the one in the office." Bonnie paused in the doorway. "Mind your manners, cowboy."

Gerard grinned. "Who're you visitin'?"

Josephine didn't hear the question; her attention remained focused on the large belly drifting toward her as the cowboy leaned against the counter. Since her stiff jeans prevented a quick escape, she swayed sideways, avoiding a belly bump in the nick of time. "Pardon?"

"I gotta know where to pick you up for a little honky-tonkin' on the town."

Josephine imagined a night on the town in Brandt's Corner didn't include fine dining and a Broadway show. More like chili-cheese fries and tap beer. She shuddered.

Bonnie returned with the credit slip. "Sorry about the wait."

After scrawling her signature on the receipt, Josephine answered the man. "I'm staying at the Rocking R."

Gerard stiffened. "You a relative of Blake's?"

"No. Actually, I'm visiting JD and his son, Bobby."

Gerard shoved his bulk away from the counter, tipped his

hat at Bonnie. "Be back later for the harness I ordered last week." He spun on his boot heels and stomped out of the store.

Dumbstruck, Josephine stared at the closing door. "Was it something I said?"

Bonnie laughed. "Nah. He just keeps his distance from JD, is all."

"I'm not sure what you mean."

Bonnie slid the clothes into a large plastic bag. "JD whipped his hide in eleventh grade and Gerard hasn't forgotten."

Given JD's size and dark handsomeness, Josephine admitted he cut an intimidating figure. But she didn't believe for one minute he was a man who brawled without a good reason—not after witnessing the love and fierce light of protectiveness in his gaze when he looked at Bobby.

"There ain't much to the story," Bonnie went on. "Gerard forced his *unwanted* attentions on the daughter of a local migrant worker. JD warned Gerard to stop. Gerard didn't listen. The girl didn't speak English and couldn't tell the teachers what was going on." Bonnie shrugged. "JD stepped in and fixed the problem. After knocking Gerard around, he made him apologize to the girl in front of all the other students, then fess up to the principal that he'd been harassing her."

"All those years ago and they still don't get along?"

Bonnie shook her head. "After high school they both hit the rodeo circuit. JD did better than Gerard and they tangled a time or two the first couple years. Finally, Gerard up and quit the circuit. Went back to ranching with his daddy. JD won a couple of buckles. Made a name for himself."

"Sounds silly to me."

"They mostly just ignore each other nowadays."

"I see." Josephine wasn't sure she saw anything. She questioned what kind of relationship JD had with the people of this community and how growing up in a small town would affect Bobby. She opened her mouth to ask how the locals treated JD, but changed her mind. Talking about him behind his back didn't seem right. If she wanted information, she'd ask him face-to-face.

"Pleasure meeting you, Bonnie. Thank you for your help this morning."

"Don't be a stranger while you're visiting. And if you stop in at the Nail 'n More, tell 'em Bonnie sent you. I get a free pedicure for referrals."

"I sure will. Take care." Josephine left the store and clumsily wobbled down the steps toward the car. Bonnie was right. The more Josephine moved in the jeans, the more the material gave. Maybe if she wore them twenty-four hours a day until next Friday, they'd fit just perfect.

Josephine pulled away from the parking spot and headed out of town toward the Rocking R, doubting her reception at the ranch would be as warm as the one Bonnie had given her. She glanced down at her jeans and boots. The new duds gave her confidence a boost.

Now she was ready to tangle with the nasty cowboy on his turf.

SHE'S LATE.

Dark, ominous clouds gathered along the horizon. The sky crackled with electricity and the smell of rain saturated the air. JD stood at the bottom of the porch steps, his gaze glued to the ranch road.

After Josephine Delaney had left last night, he hadn't stopped beating himself up over his hasty decision to allow her to invade his home and privacy for two weeks. He'd never been a man to lose his temper or make rash decisions. Until Ms. Sassy Pants dropped into his life and shot his control all to hell and back. And that worried him almost as much as the idea of Bobby living in Chicago.

In the darkest hour of the night, he'd admitted he was scared. Scared of losing his son. He'd recalled the cold, gray afternoon Bobby had arrived at the ranch. They'd stared into each other's eyes and something had passed between them, something tangible, something unbreakable, long-lasting… forever. At that moment, JD understood he and Bobby were kindred souls.

Josephine would find out soon enough he'd fight until his dying breath to keep Bobby with him.

JD might not be the smartest man in the world, but he didn't have to be a genius to figure out that honorable intentions and love wouldn't stand a chance against money and power if Bobby's grandparents decided to sue for custody. He had to prove beyond a doubt he was a good father and Bobby was better off with him at the ranch than in some gated mansion in Chicago with a geriatric Don.

Proving anything would be next to impossible if he couldn't keep his mind off his son's aunt. But he wasn't a monk. And he hadn't been attracted to a woman in a long, long while. If Josephine crooked her finger, he wouldn't have the strength to turn her down. Nor would he care to. He had a hunch that sliding under the sheets with the lady would be like sleeping with a bundle of TNT.

He could handle only *sex* between him and Josephine. What he couldn't handle was the yearning to know her on a deeper level. He hated admitting he admired her for hopping a flight to Texas to make sure Bobby was in good hands—only a day after learning of his existence. For a woman who thrived on corporate power, giving up the office for two weeks to get acquainted with her nephew impressed the hell out of him. He'd wager she had a bit of maternal instinct buried between the papers in her briefcase and the messages on her cell phone.

Kicking a clump of dirt near his boot, he reminded himself Josephine's stay was about Bobby. Not about him or his lusty ideas. He had to keep things in perspective and not let the little financier push his buttons—something she had an uncanny ability to do without much effort on her part. A squall of dust rose on the horizon and his insides churned at the sight of the car cresting the hill a half mile from the house.

Two weeks. Fourteen days. Three hundred thirty-six hours. *No problem.*

She parked the silver-colored rental near the porch and got out, flashing her perfect white teeth. "Good afternoon, JD."

"What's so good about it?"

Her smile slid sideways. "Sorry I'm late. I had some last-minute shopping to do."

"I don't remember setting a specific time for you to report in today."

She shut the door and rounded the hood of the car.

Holy cow. Automatically, his hand reached for the porch rail. As if her curves had been poured into the fabric, Josephine gave a whole new meaning to women's Wranglers. He glanced at her feet. At least she'd had the sense to choose decent shoes. The Ropers would be safer to wear around the ranch than those pile drivers she'd shown up in yesterday. His gaze roamed back up her body, stalling at chest level. As he'd noticed on too many occasions already, Josephine was by no means skimpy in the breast department. With every breath she took, the horse logo looked as though it was galloping across her chest.

She glared at him. "You've made it clear I'm not welcome. I hope I've made it just as clear I intend to stay." Stopping near the bottom of the porch, she shrugged her slim shoulders. "We can be miserable together, or we can try to get along. Your call."

He didn't answer right away; instead, he took a moment to finish studying her. Today she wore her hair in a simple ponytail high on her head. Dressed in jeans and a T-shirt, she could pass for a bona fide country girl. Taking a gulp of humid air, he rubbed the knot bunching at the back of his neck. "Let's get a couple of things straight from the get-go."

"Straight?"

He stepped closer. "First, you're not a guest. You stay—you work."

She planted her fists on her rounded hips and lifted her chin. "I don't expect to sit around and be waited on. You might believe I'm a prima donna, but I can cook and clean—"

"Can you do laundry?" He didn't have time to baby-sit her all day. If he could keep her in the house, then he wouldn't have to worry about her getting kicked in the head by a horse or trampled by cattle.

Her face reddened. "Yes, I can do laundry."

JD swallowed a chuckle at the heightened color leaking across her cheeks. The gusty wind loosened some of her hair from the ponytail, and he clenched his hands to keep from brushing the strands away from her face.

He shouldn't tease, but her expressive face and the uninhibited way she allowed her feelings to show intrigued him. He wished they'd met under different circumstances. Josephine Delaney was definitely a woman worth a man's time.

"Other than the fact I'm not welcome and I have to earn my keep, what else is bothering you?"

Hell if he didn't admire her spunk, too. He'd get around to the sex thing in a minute. First, he wanted to make sure they covered everything else. "You don't leave the ranch with Bobby. Understand?" He steeled himself against the flash of hurt in her eyes. He didn't believe she'd try to take Bobby back to Chicago without telling him, but he wasn't taking any chances. Not with his son's welfare.

"I'm not going to snatch my nephew out from under your nose."

"I may not be as well educated as you, lady, but my instincts are right on. You came here for one reason and one reason only—to persuade me to let Bobby go back to Chicago with you."

She crossed her arms under her breasts, and he forced himself to keep his gaze off the horse logo and on her face. "Ease up a little. I just want to get better acquainted with my nephew. My family's been through a lot since Cassandra's death."

Moving closer, he got right in her face. Big mistake. The sexy one-hundred-dollar-an-ounce scent she wore whirled around him, knocking him off balance. "I won't allow you or your family to use Bobby as a substitute for his mother."

Her shocked gasp gave him pause. He stared into her baby blues, glinting with hurt and anger, and thought maybe he'd gone one step too far. Part of him wanted to apologize and the other part wanted to keep slinging insults until he ran her off for good. God, he was a mess around this woman.

"Have we covered everything? Or do you have something else you wish to get straight with me?"

He slipped a hand under her ponytail and curved his fingers around her neck. Her eyes widened, but she didn't pull away. Slowly, he coaxed her head forward. "We haven't covered this." He pressed his lips to hers. When she gasped in surprise, he slid his tongue into her mouth.

His chest tightened with some indefinable emotion as he explored the cool, sweet, peppermint-tasting interior. He couldn't tell if she was evading his tongue or playing with it—whatever, the movement drove him nuts. When her hands pressed against his chest, he softened the kiss, taking a moment to caress, suckle and nibble her lower lip before running his tongue over the edge of her front teeth. He coaxed and cajoled until her jaw slackened and her moist sigh drifted into his own heated mouth.

He knew it! Deep in his gut he'd sensed kissing Josephine would be all fire…urgency…sizzle. Hidden inside the uptight corporate financier was a woman full of passion. She had a body made to please a man, and he craved to smell and caress and kiss every gorgeous feminine inch of her.

The distant rumble startled her and she tore her mouth from his. Keeping his hand on her neck, he rubbed the callused pad of his thumb across the tender patch of skin below her hairline.

Her soft breath puffed against his neck as she stared at the top button of his shirt. "So, um, I guess we've got everything straight now?"

He fought the grin tugging the corners of his mouth as he reluctantly released her and stepped back. Her flushed skin and shimmering gaze made him wish he could toss her over his shoulder, haul her into the house and dump her in the middle of his king-size bed.

Shoving a hand through his hair, he squelched the erotic musings. "If you're looking for someone to scratch your itch while you're here, I'm willing to accommodate." He snapped his fingers in front of her face. "Just say the word and I'm yours."

She sucked in a sharp breath and the rosy flush across her cheekbones darkened to red. "Jerk."

"Go ahead, honey. Call me anything you like. But I won't let you use me to get to Bobby."

"Use you?" She laughed, the sound too shrill to be genuine. "Thanks for the offer, stud, but I don't do affairs."

His chest tightened with satisfaction at her confession. He didn't understand why, but he was glad Josephine wasn't *easy,* as her sister had been. "Who said anything about an affair?"

She stamped her foot and sputtered something unintelligible. He wiped a hand down his face to hide a smile. She reminded him of a schoolgirl who'd just had her pigtail yanked. "We understand each other, then?"

"Perfectly."

Chapter Five

Josephine stared in a daze at JD's retreating back as he headed for the barn. She licked her lips and shivered at the tangy taste of him lingering in her mouth. He'd kissed her as if she were…were…easy! And she'd let him.

Her emotions had been under control until she'd touched his chest, felt the raw power quivering beneath the crisp cotton. Even now, her belly burned with the urge to feel all that hard, sleek muscle rubbing against her. What in the world was wrong with her? Sure, he kissed like a fantasy lover. But sex with JD would only complicate matters.

Remember Bobby. Josephine didn't dare return to Chicago without the boy. Unless she wished to subject herself to her father's wrath—not! The fact that JD made her knees wobble and her heart race like a greyhound had had absolutely nothing to do with the decision to take a two-week leave of absence from the office.

Nice try, Josephine.

Oh, shut up! She hated when that whiny voice in her head played devil's advocate with her.

Returning to the car, she removed her suitcase, cosmetics bag and her recent purchases from the store in Brandt's Corner. Then she lugged them through the empty house and up the short flight of stairs. The doors on the second floor were closed, except the one at the far end of the hall. She stood outside the room—rather, cubbyhole—and stared. A far cry from the luxurious guest suite in her parents' home.

The ceiling sloped downward, connecting with the top of a small square window two feet above the floor. None of the whitewashed walls were the same size or length. She had a hunch the room had once been part of the attic.

A double bed rested against the wall opposite the doorway. A set of clean sheets sat at the bottom of the mattress. Another sign JD wasn't bending over backward to make her feel welcome. A beige oval rug covered a good portion of the floor. And a narrow, three-drawer dresser sat to the left of the door. All in all, the room would have made a lovely sitting area off a nursery. Josephine imagined a white rocker by the window, where a mother could nurse her baby while gazing at the stars.

Stop daydreaming, Josephine.

After arranging her toiletries on the dresser top and making up the bed, she peeked into the room next to hers. Bobby's room. The walls were painted blue, with a race-car border around the top. Bright red plastic bins filled with toys and building sets were stacked under a window. A race car lamp sat on the bedside table and the bed linens had colorful cars and trucks printed on them. The teddy bear she'd given him yesterday lay in the middle of the bed next to a stuffed monkey. A case with books and games occupied the wall near the door. JD had spared no expense in making his son feel welcome in his new home.

Speaking of the taciturn cowboy...his habit of hiding out with the horses when things got testy between them intrigued her. The men she worked with thrived on confrontation. She sensed JD avoided conflict whenever possible, which made her question why he always got the last word in with her.

As she stepped out the front door, she spotted movement by the dilapidated trailer. Bobby dashed out from behind the rusted mobile home, a huge grin on his face.

The expression snatched Josephine's breath away as an image of Cassandra's face flashed through her mind. Bobby had inherited his mother's smile. Recognizing her sister's features in her nephew made Josephine feel that a small part of Cassandra would forever be with her. She'd always assumed that one day she and her sister would grow close. Now that there was no future for them, Josephine felt a sense of urgency about building a strong, lasting relationship with Bobby.

Blake followed the boy into the barn. A minute later, the old man came out, got into JD's pickup and drove off.

Never one to waste an opportunity, she hobbled down the porch steps in her new boots. Instead of a brisk walk, she settled for a graceless mosey to the barn.

Once inside the structure, she paused a moment, allowing her eyes to adjust to the dim interior. She inhaled deeply, her nose twitching at the smell of fresh hay and animal. Voices drifted toward her from somewhere in the back. A warm flush suffused her body as she recalled yesterday's conversation with JD in that same room. She moved past the stalls quietly, hoping not to disturb the horses.

"How come you don't like her?" Bobby's hushed question floated through the doorway.

She pressed a hand to her heart as she hovered in the shadows. Were they talking about her?

"I didn't say I don't like her." JD, his voice not so hushed, protested.

"Sometimes you look mean at her."

Silence loud enough to shatter her eardrums filled the barn. She felt rotten her nephew had picked up on the animosity between her and JD. From this point forward, she'd do everything in her power to get along with the reticent cowboy, even if she had to eat crow every day of her visit.

"I like her well enough, Bobby."

Well enough? Next he'd tell the boy she was disease free

and had good teeth. Josephine inched closer and peered around the edge of the door. His back to her, JD sat astride a wooden stool, oiling a saddle in his lap, while her nephew lounged on a hay bale.

Her nephew's mouth formed an adorable pout. "How come my mom didn't tell me about Aunt Josephine?"

The soft rag slid to a halt on the leather. "I don't know, son."

JD resumed oiling the leather, his strokes rough and fast, as if he was taking out his anger and frustration on the rawhide. "I wish I could tell you what your mama had been thinking, but I can't."

Josephine wanted to stomp her foot at her sister's selfishness. Obviously, Cassandra hadn't given a thought to the possibility she might not always be around to raise her son.

"Can I like Aunt Josephine?"

At her nephew's question, Josephine's eyes blurred and she blinked back the moisture threatening to escape.

"You bet." That JD wasn't allowing his true feelings for her to show in front of Bobby made Josephine want to hug the grumpy man.

The boy hopped off the hay bale and inched closer to his father, but stopped just far enough away that he couldn't be pulled close for a hug.

JD set the saddle on the floor by the stool and waited patiently for his son to speak. Although the obstinate man was surly with her, he had an abundance of patience with Bobby.

"If I like my aunt, is she gonna take me away?" The quiver in the high-pitched voice ripped through Josephine, and she bit her lip to keep from protesting out loud.

"Remember the talk we had when you first showed up at the ranch?"

Bobby sniffed, his gaze glued to the tips of his miniature cowboy boots.

"I'm your father and this is your home. No one is going to change that."

Her nephew wiped his nose on the back of his sleeve. "Even when I get old like Blake you won't never send me away?"

JD reached out to wipe the tears dripping off the small trembling chin, but Bobby turned his head at the last second. JD's shoulders slumped in defeat. Josephine's chest ached for the big lug, who yearned to comfort his son but wasn't allowed. "Even when you're walking with a cane you can live with me."

Bobby stared long and hard, as though weighing his father's words. "I don't miss Mom anymore. But I'd miss Blake 'n you if I had to go away."

Josephine held her breath, waiting to see if JD would reach for Bobby again, but he didn't. "You're not going away, son. You're staying right here with me."

"Are you gonna like Aunt Josephine?"

JD's mouth turned down in a grimace at the mention of her name.

Well, fine. He didn't want to like her. News flash—she didn't *want* to like him, either. Tired of eavesdropping, she backed up several steps, then made a scuffling noise and called out, "Hey, any cowboys around here?"

A moment later, Bobby stood in the doorway, dried tear tracks staining his cheeks, but his eyes shone with welcome.

"Howdy, cowboy. What do you think of my new duds?" Josephine twirled, then lost her balance and staggered into the stall door next to her. "Hmmph!"

Bobby giggled.

"Oops." She smiled at her nephew. "Guess I could use a little practice spinning in these Wranglers." This time Bobby returned her smile.

And that was how JD found her and his son when he stepped out of the tack room: grinning like fools at each other. JD's shoulders tensed and his mouth thinned into a straight line.

"I was hoping I could play cowgirl with you two cowboys this afternoon."

Her nephew giggled again, but JD remained stone-faced. "Bobby and I are heading out to check a watering hole."

"Sounds like fun. I'm game," she added, not the least bit remorseful she'd invited herself along.

JD's gaze slid down her body slower than spilled honey. "Have you ever ridden a horse before?"

"No. But I'm a fast study." She increased the wattage of her smile. How hard could sitting on top of a horse be? They weren't going on a cattle drive; they were searching for holes in the ground filled with water.

He stared at her jeans. "Sugar, those tight-as-sin Wranglers look mighty fine on you, but you'll never be able to spread those thighs over the back of a horse."

Heat seeped into her face. If he counted on scaring her away with sexual innuendos, he was in for a big surprise. Being a woman in a predominantly male occupation, she'd heard everything and then some. "Let me worry about my thighs. You get the horse." She spun, took one step, then gasped when she felt her hips being tugged backward.

A loud ripping sound rent the air. She whirled. "How dare—"

"Forgot to remove this, Ms.—" JD waved a leather tag in the air "—Size Eight." He winked. The exasperating cowboy had *winked* at her!

Annoying man. Josephine snatched the tag from his fingers and marched out of the barn with quick tiny steps instead of long strides.

"Hold up, Aunt Josephine!" Bobby called after her.

Stopping midstride, she waited for her nephew. "He's gonna saddle Turnip for you."

"He?" Josephine couldn't recall if she'd ever heard Bobby call JD *Dad* or *Daddy.*

Head bent, her nephew traced circles in the dirt with the toe of his boot.

Kneeling in tight jeans was out of the question, so she settled for placing a hand on the boy's shoulder. "Bobby, why don't you call your father Dad or Daddy?"

Silence.

A moment later JD approached, holding the reins of two horses. By the pained expression on his face, he'd heard her question and the nonanswer his son had given.

"Let's ride. Don't have all day to waste standing around jawing."

Deciding to drop the subject for the time being, she motioned to the smaller of the two horses. "Is this Turnip?" The mare's beautiful light brown color blended with large white patches above her rump and across her shoulders.

"Turnip is a paint. She's got the best disposition of any horse on the ranch. I don't think you'll have any trouble with her."

"When I get bigger, I get to ride Turnip all by myself," Bobby added.

"What do I do first?" she asked, amazed at the excitement zipping along her spine at the prospect of doing something so…so…nonwork related. She couldn't remember the last time she'd taken a day off and played.

"First, you put this hat on." JD placed a straw hat on her head. "Did you buy any long-sleeved shirts to go with those jeans?"

"No. I didn't want to overheat."

"Better hot than sunburned. Here." He removed sunscreen from his saddlebag and tossed the bottle in her direction.

Surprised, Josephine stared at the label. JD was trying so hard to be a good parent. For his sake she wished a woman other than Cassandra had been Bobby's mother, then JD wouldn't have to worry about his son's grandfather making threats.

After slathering the lotion on her arms, neck and face, she handed the sunscreen to Bobby. He rubbed a small amount on his face and the back of his neck. He handed the bottle to JD, who to her surprise put lotion on his own neck and face.

She admired him for trying to set a good example in front of his son.

"Up you go, Bobby." Her nephew set his boot in his father's cupped hands, and JD easily lifted the boy onto the stallion.

Josephine eyed the larger horse suspiciously. "What's his name?"

Moving around the animal, JD answered, "Warrior."

Aptly named. The beast stood at least two feet taller than Turnip.

JD cupped his hands near the paint's stirrup. "Ready?"

He had to be kidding. No way could she lift her leg high enough to set her boot in his palms. Grabbing the edge of the saddle for support, she leaned back and stuck her foot in the air. JD hunched over until his hands were under her boot, then hoisted her up.

The jarring movement caused her to lose her grip on the pommel. Arms flailing, she fell backward. JD lunged, jamming his shoulder under her rump, then straightened his legs as if he were doing squats with a two-hundred-pound barbell. She shot through the air like a cannonball and landed on her belly in the middle of the saddle with her butt sticking straight up. "Oomph!" If she hadn't had the air knocked from her lungs she'd have shouted a very unladylike word.

Lifting her head, she gasped, "This is certainly an unusual way to ride a horse." Her nephew burst into a fit of giggles and Josephine decided her embarrassment was worth the sound of her nephew's laughter.

"Grab the pommel and swing your right leg over," JD instructed.

Easier said than done. After listening to her grunt and moan for a good minute, JD set his hands on her backside and pushed.

Lord, the man is obnoxious! She shifted her hip, and with one final grumble managed to force her leg over the saddle and sit upright. Wincing as the tight denim pressed into her thighs, she estimated twenty minutes before her legs turned blue and fell off from restricted blood flow. She glanced down, ready to give JD a tongue-lashing, but his poker face caught her off guard and the words shriveled in her throat.

JD guided Warrior next to Josephine's horse, then swung up in the saddle behind Bobby. "Hold the reins this way."

She really had no business riding a horse without taking lessons first. But she yearned to be with Bobby. JD, too. After witnessing the tender moment between father and son in the tack room, she craved to learn more about the sexy, cantankerous man.

Thankfully, she didn't have to steer Turnip. The mare followed the stallion without any prompting. After ten minutes, Josephine's back ached and her jeans rubbed against her thighs like sandpaper. She forced the uncomfortable feeling aside and studied her surroundings. Miles of flat grassland spread out before her, marred only by an occasional outcrop of rock or sloping hill. She counted a few lone trees, but mostly clusters of scrub oak dotted the land. If she had to describe the area with one word she'd use *bleak.*

Upon closer examination, she changed her mind. Yellow, daisylike weeds along the fence line flourished despite the lack of rain. And even though the limbs of the oak tree in the distance reminded her of an old arthritic hand, the gentle curve of the umbrella-shaped canopy invited one to rest in the comfort of its shade.

After another ten minutes, they came upon a large pond. They stopped the horses near the edge, then JD dismounted and lifted Bobby from the saddle. JD stared at her. "Be best if you stayed up there. This won't take but a minute or two."

Her cramped leg muscles cried for release, but an image of her struggling to climb back on the horse changed her mind. "Fine."

He glanced at Bobby, "You go right—I'll go left." Both

males walked in opposite directions around the water's edge, stomping their boots against the ground, occasionally bending over to pick up something. After five minutes they returned to the horses.

JD put the few pieces of garbage he and Bobby had collected into a plastic bag tied to the saddle horn. "Thanks for the help, buddy."

Respect for the way JD strived to make his son feel important filled Josephine. She compared her own father with JD and cringed inside. How would Bobby deal with a grandfather who was quicker to criticize than compliment? "What were you guys doing?"

Bobby spoke up. "Checking the mud."

"What for?"

"Over time, the cattle can turn the ground around the hole into a mud bog." JD set Bobby up on Warrior, then mounted behind him. "Mud isn't good for the animal's hooves. If the bank gets too soft we bring a load of gravel in and build the sides back up."

Crinkling her nose at the green scum covering parts of the surface of the pond, she stated, "The water doesn't look very healthy."

"The hole is spring-fed. We've got two on the ranch. In the other pastures we use metal watering tanks and those have to be cleaned out periodically or the water can become contaminated." Clicking his tongue, JD turned Warrior east and Turnip followed.

"So ponds and tanks are the only source of water on the property?" Josephine didn't understand squat about raising cattle, but she assumed the ranch would be worth more money if the land contained a constant water supply of some sort.

"There's a stream in the south pasture that runs most of the year. During dry spells we haul barreled water to those animals."

After another fifteen minutes of riding, JD stopped. "It'll take a half hour to tighten this section of fence. Be a good time to climb down and stretch your muscles."

Josephine studied the ground, wondering if her numb legs would support her once they touched the dirt.

"Let me help you." JD appeared at her side, stretching out his arms. She set her hands on his shoulders and attempted to lift her bottom off the saddle, but nothing happened. "I think I'm paralyzed from the waist down."

Grumbling something unintelligible, he hoisted her dead weight from the back of the horse and set her down, none to gently. Her knees buckled, and she clutched his shirtsleeves to keep from folding at his feet.

"First time's the worst." He clasped her upper arm and guided her to the tree a few yards away. "You and Bobby rest." He waited to let go of her arm until she was seated on the ground. Never had anything felt more comfortable than the lumpy tree roots poking at her bottom. She stared at her bowed thighs, worried that they'd never go back together again.

"Bobby, make sure you and your aunt drink something." He handed her nephew two water bottles and a bag of cookies. "Blake packed you a snack, too."

Plopping down next to her, Bobby stuffed a cookie into his mouth and mumbled, "Want one, Aunt Josephine?"

"No, thanks. But I'll take one of those waters."

JD gathered an assortment of tools from the saddlebags and walked away. Josephine's gaze followed his lean stride. She loved watching him, his movements sure and efficient. Although he wore long sleeves, the muscle hidden under the cotton fabric rippled and bunched as he tugged the barbed wire. Her attention drifted down his backside. JD sure filled out his Wranglers nicely. The center of her palms tingled as she imagined what the firm muscle would feel like bunching under her hands.

"Aunt Josephine, your face is red. You better drink some more water."

"Good idea." She uncapped the bottle and guzzled. What had gotten into her? She had no business lusting after her nephew's father. "Do you like hanging out with your dad?"

Bobby shrugged. "He lets me help a lot and I like riding Warrior." Although Bobby seemed eager to help his father, he acted nervous and unsure around JD.

"Are you afraid of your father, Bobby?" She hated having to ask the question, but she had to be sure her nephew felt safe at the ranch.

"No. He doesn't never yell at me." Bobby put a half-eaten cookie back in the plastic bag. "My mom yelled at me."

"Tell me about your mother. Even though we were sisters, we didn't see each other very often."

"Mom didn't tell me about you. Did she tell you about me?"

"No, honey, she didn't."

"If you know'd about me would you come'd see me sometimes?"

At his earnest expression, Josephine drew him close for a hug. At first, he stiffened, then relaxed and leaned into her, snuggling his head against her bosom. "Of course I would have come to see you. Goodness, I have five birthdays and five Christmases to make up for."

He smiled up at her. "I like presents."

Laughing, she cuddled him tighter. Right then she happened to catch JD standing by the fence, staring in their direction. Even from a distance, the longing in his gaze made Josephine's eyes sting. She had to figure out a way to help father and son become closer. She couldn't stand seeing the suffering on JD's face every time he looked at the boy. After a few moments, JD turned his back to them and continued working.

Bobby had done nothing to earn his father's love, yet JD offered it freely. She'd labored all her life, and continued to do so in the hope of meeting or exceeding her father's expectations...praying each of her accomplishments would strengthen their father-daughter relationship. The minuscule progress she and her father had achieved over the years made her question whether taking Bobby back to Chicago was really in the boy's best interest. Yet part of her wondered if her nephew's presence might help her father, mother and her become a tight-knit family.

Lord, you're pathetic. The fact that she considered putting her own interests ahead of her nephew's made her chest tighten with shame.

"Aunt Josephine?"

She shook her head, scattering her worries, and nuzzled her nose in his sweaty hair. "What, honey?"

"Mom said my dad was poor, and we wasn't never gonna see him."

Cassandra, how could you! Obviously, JD hadn't made the kind of money her sister had needed to maintain her spoiled, rich-girl lifestyle. In truth, Josephine was surprised Cassandra hadn't had an abortion or given Bobby up for adoption once he'd been born.

Before she could think of something appropriate to say, Bobby blurted, "Mom said he was never gonna want me."

Dear God, did JD have any idea what he was up against? "Sometimes mommies can be wrong. I believe your father loves you. I think he gets sad sometimes because he wishes he could have been with you all those years you lived with your mom."

"Really?" Bobby watched JD, who had his back to them at the moment. "He says he loves me after my bedtime story."

"That's because he does love you." She brushed a lock of hair off his forehead. "Do you love your father, Bobby?"

Ignoring her question, he yawned, then closed his eyes and burrowed against her. "Aunt Josephine?"

"What, honey?"

"I like you."

Hand shaking, she gently rubbed his back. After a few minutes, the steady rise and fall of his little chest told her he'd drifted off to sleep. The poor child was afraid of getting hurt. What a mess she'd unknowingly gotten involved in. How would any of them come out of this with their hearts intact?

"You two are a couple of lazy, good-for-nothing cowpokes," JD murmured as he approached the tree.

"I don't know anything about kids, but Bobby's probably young enough to still require a nap during the day." She patted the ground next to her. "Do you have time for a break, or should we move on?"

He hunkered down next to her. They sat in silence for a while, content to share the peace and quiet. Then JD reached across her chest and stroked Bobby's head. Her heart almost broke at the sight of the big man's trembling hand.

"Would you like to hold him?"

"No, don't wake him." JD plucked a blade of dry grass from the ground and twirled it between his fingers. Josephine had no idea of the pain he felt watching her hug *his* son—something he'd yet to do since Bobby had arrived last December.

The realization that she had wormed her way into his son's affections in a few short hours, when he'd attempted to break the barrier between him and his son for over six months, burned like battery acid in JD's gut.

He set his hat aside and rubbed the back of his neck. He wished he could blame Josephine for his failure as a father, but he couldn't. She'd done nothing wrong. *He* was the problem. For the life of him, though, he couldn't figure out how to fix things with Bobby. The temptation to ask Josephine for advice made him squirm against the ground. "Bobby seems to have taken to you real quick." *Damn.* Why couldn't he keep his mouth shut?

"I suspect he misses having a maternal figure in his life. Little boys need their mothers more than they think."

JD clenched his jaw to keep from spouting his opinion about the kind of maternal figure Cassandra had been. He had to let go of the past and focus on the future. He couldn't change what his son had gone through the first five years of his life. But he could make sure Bobby had a happy future and a loving home from this day forward.

"Give it time, JD." Her fingers gripped his arm, and his heart flipped over in his chest.

Not realizing how close their heads were, he turned his face toward her and sucked in a quiet breath at the sight of tears shimmering in her blue eyes. *Tears...for him?* He tamped down the urge to kiss her, to show her how much her concern meant to him. Instead, he leaned sideways, putting an extra foot of space between them. "Time is something I don't have much of anymore, or had you forgotten?"

Her face drained of color, and he cursed himself for being a jerk. He didn't make a habit of lashing out at people, but he'd never felt this sense of helplessness before. "Sorry, didn't mean to take out my bad mood on you."

Josephine's alluring scent and sexy perfume drove him crazy. Needing to clear his head, he went to Turnip and stroked her neck. "I figured Blake and I would be enough for Bobby." He motioned to his son, still snuggled against Josephine's side. "I can see I was wrong."

"Is there a Mrs. JD in your future?"

Her smile seemed innocent enough, but her piercing gaze told him his answer meant *something* to her.

He had his pride and he wasn't about to admit he didn't have a steady girlfriend. His whole adult life had been a series of miserable hit-and-miss affairs. But damned if he'd tell Josephine. "Maybe." Curiosity got the best of him. "What about you? Any Mr. Corporation in your future?"

"Father's hoping I'll hook up with a man back in Chicago who's in the railroad business. They both love money. Love making money. Love investing money."

Well, there you go. Always comes back to the same old thing—money. JD couldn't compete with the almighty dollar. Disappointment hit him square in the chest, knocking his emotions sideways. Why should he care if she had a significant other in her life?

Because just the mention of another man snuffed out any

hope of hauling her up into the hayloft these next two weeks. "Sounds like a perfect match."

"I have no intention of marrying a man whose first love is money." Her face took on a dreamy glow as she stared off into the distance. "What good is money without love?"

So Josephine had money…but no one to love.

And he had someone to love…Bobby…but no money.

Well, hell. Sometimes life just plain *sucked.*

Chapter Six

Two hours later, Josephine's thighs screamed and her butt burned as though it were being roasted over the flames of hell.

If only Turnip hadn't decided to chase after a rabbit. She hadn't had time to think about her backside banging against the hard leather saddle, as she'd hung on for dear life and contemplated death by broken neck or crushed skull. After a mile, JD had caught up with Turnip and yanked on the reins, which slowed the horse to a bone-jarring trot for another quarter of a mile.

When they'd returned to the barn, she'd bravely attempted to hide the pain as she'd half stumbled, half hobbled toward the house. But as soon as JD had put the horses in the corral, he'd swept her up in his arms, then hauled her through the house to the upstairs bathroom, where he'd insisted she soak in a hot bath while he searched for a tube of ointment for her aches and pains.

A timid knock startled her. The lock on the upstairs bath shared the same malady as the lock on the downstairs bath—busted. She sank lower in the water, making sure only her head showed above the mountains of bubbles in the tub. "Who's there?"

"Me, Aunt Josephine." Bobby's soprano voice filtered through the crack under the door.

"What do you need, honey?"

"I got some rub for you."

JD had been right about one thing. The hot water had gone a long way in easing some of the aches from her lower back and thighs. Hopefully, the cream would relieve the rest of her pain—if she could convince her hard-as-concrete muscles to relax long enough to haul her sorry self out of the tub and massage some on. "Come in."

Bobby poked his head around the edge of the door, his face lighting up when he spotted the mounds of foam threatening to overflow the tub.

"Wow. You got lots of bubbles." He stepped farther into the room and held out a long, thick tube. She noticed a picture of a horse on the label and had a sneaking suspicion the ointment was meant for livestock use.

"Are you sure JD gave you that?" Maybe Bobby had grabbed the wrong cream.

"Yep. He says you gotta put this on your butt cheeks." Her nephew set the cream on top of the toilet tank, then stood next to the tub, staring down at his feet. "Sorry Turnip scared you."

Oh, bless his little-boy heart. "I'm okay, honey. I didn't get hurt."

His eyes implored her. "So you isn't ascared to go riding again?"

Ah, now she understood. He was afraid her incident with Turnip this afternoon would keep her from riding with him again. "Well, I am a little nervous about getting back up on a horse."

"I can ride with you so you isn't ascared."

Her heart melted. "I'd like that, Bobby." They'd been together one full day and already her nephew was reaching out to her. She didn't understand all the reasons why…maybe he craved her hugs or gentle touches. Whatever need she filled in her nephew she planned to continue doing so.

His thin shoulders relaxed. "Where'd you get all them bubbles?"

"I brought bath foam with me. You can use some the next time you take a bath."

He wrinkled his nose. "Smells kinda stinky."

"Yes. But if you don't mind the scent of roses, the bubbles are fun to play with." She lifted her hand, palm up and blew a mound of white suds in his face.

He squealed and jumped back.

Laughing, she nailed him again with another blast of bubbles.

"That's not fair," he protested, flinging a handful of foam at her. A mound of bubbles landed on top of her head.

Narrowing her eyes, she declared, "This is war, young man."

His face gleamed with mischief. Within thirty seconds, he stood in a puddle of water covered from head to toe with melting bubbles, both of them screaming battle cries.

"What the hell's going on?" JD's booming voice jolted Josephine, and she sloshed a gallon of water over the edge of the tub. She swallowed a laugh as he took in the mess, including the suds trailing down the mirror.

Bobby clamped a small pudgy hand over his mouth. She had a sneaking suspicion she wasn't the only one who heard the muffled giggle.

When JD's stunned gaze landed on her, his eyes darkened. Josephine peeked down at herself, shocked to see only a thin layer of sudsy soap floated over the surface of the bathwater, concealing her from view. She slid lower in the tub until her chin bobbed in the water.

"Everything okay?" Blake poked his head around the door. "Looks like we got ourselves a first-rate bubble fight."

Despite the rapidly cooling water, Josephine's face heated.

JD glared at Blake. Blake grinned back.

Josephine didn't know whether to laugh or cry. Not many women could boast they'd bathed in the company of three males between the ages of five and seventy-five. "I'll clean up the mess," she offered, then gagged when an inhaled soap bubble hit the back of her throat.

"Take your time. Supper ain't ready yet." Blake left the room, mumbling something about a litter of puppies being less trouble than her and Bobby.

One down, two to go.

"As soon as your aunt is out of the tub and dressed, you get back in here and clean up this mess. Now, go change out of those wet clothes." If not for the twitch near the corner of JD's mouth, Josephine might have assumed he was angry.

"Okay." Bobby squeezed past his father but hesitated in the doorway. His sweet little face broke into a wide smile directed right at her. "I won."

The stinker! "Rematch!" she yelled after him, enjoying the sound of his laughter echoing down the hallway.

As soon as Bobby disappeared, the bathroom walls closed in around her. JD shut the door, leaned back and crossed his arms over his chest. Seconds ticked by. Then a full minute.

"Is there something else you wanted?" Oh, Lord. Did that husky voice really come out of her mouth?

His gaze boldly raked over her as he pushed away from the door. Each step toward the tub spiked the temperature of the cooling water up several degrees.

She held her breath as he studied the milky-white surface. A tingling sensation shot through her thighs, and she crossed her legs to keep from squirming. He dropped down on one knee, and her breath escaped her lungs in a loud whoosh.

When he grabbed a towel and began mopping up the water on the floor, she felt foolish at her reaction. "I'll clean up," she protested.

Ignoring her, he sopped up the puddles. He finished, then tossed the soaked towel into the sink and turned to her. His steady gaze began at the top of her head and slowly moved down her face, her neck.

Although he couldn't *see* her, the heat of his stare skimming over her shoulders, chest, thighs, legs, even her feet, made breathing next to impossible.

He inched closer until his chest bumped the rounded edge of the tub. He trailed his fingers through the water, coming dangerously close to her skin.

Intending to protest, she opened her mouth, but to her horror nothing but a squeak came out.

He grinned, then lowered his head. No escaping his kiss unless she intended to vault from the tub naked. *Not likely!* When his mouth hovered directly over hers, she admitted that running from JD's kiss was the last thing she wished to do.

Their breath collided. His rich masculine scent overpowered the rose-smelling bathwater, making her dizzy. Satiny brown eyes stared, hot with desire…for her.

They watched each other as he sampled her mouth, testing, seducing, coaxing. She fought to subdue the moan crawling up her throat, but when he laved a tender spot in the middle of her lower lip, her control snapped. The moan escaped on a quivering sigh.

Then his mouth opened wide over hers. She gave herself up to the moment and succumbed to the shivery sensations JD's kiss caused along her nerve endings. His masculine lips nibbled and caressed a path along her jaw, his tongue flicking away the droplets of moisture from her skin. When he suckled her earlobe, she arched her neck, gasping in delight, unaware of the view she offered from above.

"Supper's ready!" Blake hollered from the bottom of the stairs.

JD shoved away from the tub, slipped on the wet floor and landed on his rump. "Crap." He stared at her, chest heaving, eyes a little wild. "Coming!"

Startled by his shout, Josephine let out a squawk and sent a wave of water over the edge of the tub right into JD's lap.

He scrambled off the bath mat and dived for the door.

"JD?"

His hand froze over the knob.

"This didn't happen, right?" She held her breath, waiting for his reassurance. Silence. "JD?"

Some of the tension eased from his shoulders before he flashed a cocky grin over his shoulder. "It was just a kiss, Josephine." Then the blasted cowboy strode from the room as if accosting a woman in her bath was an everyday occurrence on the ranch.

Just a kiss, my aching butt!

JD WOKE TO THE CLATTER of pots and pans. He rubbed a hand over his face and cursed the racket interrupting his dream.

A dream of him and Josephine mattress-dancing.

Sliding his legs off the bed, he sat up and glared down at his lap. His misbehaving member nudged the trapdoor of his B.V.D.s. *Sorry, buddy. You can't come out and play today.* Groaning, he fell back on the mattress. He couldn't remember the last time he'd woken in such a state of arousal. And knowing that the source of his discomfort slept peacefully down the hall didn't help matters.

He stared at the alarm clock on the nightstand. *Four-thirty?* What was Blake doing up so early?

No sense trying to catch another hour of sleep, not with all the noise in the kitchen. At least he'd be able to eat and sneak out of the house before Josephine crawled out of bed.

First things first—a cold shower. After grabbing his jeans and a fresh pair of drawers, he padded down the hall to the bathroom. Standing under the cool spray, he called himself every kind of fool. Yesterday, he'd read Josephine the riot act about trying to seduce him to get custody of Bobby, then he'd gone and practically molested her in the bathtub.

Oh, hell. He'd figured out right away that Josephine wasn't the kind of woman to use her body to get what she wanted. But thinking the worst of *her* was easier than believing *he* was capable of selling out.

Lifting his face to the water, he winced as the stinging spray pelted his skin. He accepted the blame for the fiasco in the bathroom. He'd gotten caught up in the moment. Walking in on her and his son, seeing Bobby smile, hearing his laughter, had warmed his insides. For one split second he'd pictured them as a family.

Now, how crazy was that? The odds of a successful career woman living happily ever after with the owner of half a ranch were next to nil. On the surface, Josephine had everything a man could desire. Intelligence, beauty, wealth. But JD had seen a glimpse of what lay beneath her no-nonsense demeanor…a fragile heart. Several times he'd noticed how her face softened when she stared at Bobby. As if she needed his love more than he needed hers. Which made him suspect the men in her past had only wanted her for her money or the prestige associated with her father's investment firm and not for herself. If that was true, then they were all idiots.

Stepping back from the spray, he squeezed a dollop of shampoo in his hand, then rubbed it through his hair, the bubbles a cruel reminder of yesterday's tub incident.

He recalled the expression on Josephine's face when he'd burst in on her bath. She'd been startled at first, then her blue eyes had grown bold and hot. He'd about gone crazy from wanting right there in the doorway. He could no more have walked away at that moment than given up his son. And the hell of it was, she hadn't resisted him. *At all.*

Her image swam through his mind. Damp strands of hair had curled against her neck and had drawn his attention to her gently sloping shoulders. A droplet of water had clung to her lower lip, quivering with each indrawn breath. Then, when he'd kissed her, she'd raised up until the rosy nubs of her breasts bobbed against the water surface. *Oh, man.* One thought had entered his mind…he'd yearned to stake his claim on her.

He stared down at himself. *Hell.* The cold shower hadn't

helped. He shoved his head under the spray, hoping to rinse the memories of their kiss down the drain with the shampoo.

Having *just sex* with Josephine was out of the question. Each time he saw her, heard her voice, caught her smile, his chest ached with feeling. A feeling to protect her, to keep her by his side. To please her.

You are one, certifiably crazy yahoo. You only met the woman two days ago.

True, but already Josephine's presence at the ranch had eased some of the strain between Bobby and him. His son looked him in the eye now when he spoke, and yesterday in the tack room, Bobby had initiated a conversation for the first time. They still had a ways to go, but JD had felt closer to Bobby the past two days than he had the past several months. And he had Josephine to thank for that.

Yeah, *just sex* with Josephine would be messy. No way would he be able to bar his feelings from the intimate experience.

For a man who went through life trying to block out feelings, the sensations his son's aunt evoked in him were pretty incredible. But he had nothing to offer a woman like Josephine. She deserved what those fancy-pants businessmen back in Chicago could give her—a pampered life. Beginning today, he'd keep his hands to himself. He finished his shower, dressed and headed downstairs to retrieve his boots from the back porch.

"Good morning."

He froze in the kitchen doorway. Josephine stood at the stove, flipping pancakes, wearing a frilly apron tied crooked at her waist. Her hair in a ponytail, she had on her skintight jeans and a tank top that threatened to make him swallow his tongue.

Damned if she didn't remind him of a down-home country girl. How the heck did she go from Ms. Corporation to Miss Daisy-Maisy overnight? He inhaled deeply, then choked back a groan as he got a whiff of yesterday's rose-scented bathwater still lingering on Josephine's skin.

He studied her warily, but didn't detect any signs of anger over his Neanderthal stunt twelve hours ago. "Up kind of early, aren't you?"

"I'm not a guest, remember?" She smiled, and his heart zigzagged in his chest.

He felt stupid standing there with his shirt unsnapped and his socks balled in his fist. But he couldn't stop staring at her. Without makeup, she looked more like a teenager than a corporate financier. He wanted to tug her ponytail until their bodies touched, until he had her in his arms. On the verge of losing control, he growled, "Don't you have anything else to wear?"

She carried the mixing bowl with the remaining batter to the sink. "What's wrong with my outfit? Bonnie at Milner's Feed and Tack helped me pick this out."

"Your outfit is fine if you plan to work in a cathouse."

"A cathouse!"

JD forced himself to calm down. Josephine didn't realize that sweet little Bonnie turned into the local feline-on-the-prowl when the sun went down, flaunting her Dolly Parton boobs at every available male within a hundred-mile radius.

"After breakfast I'll take you into town to get another pair of jeans and a couple of long-sleeved shirts." So much for his *plan* to steer clear of her.

"I don't need another pair of jeans."

He clenched his jaw. "Yes, you do need another pair of jeans...the kind that won't split open when you bend over."

Her face flushed bright red and he expected her to tell him where he could go...then her mouth curved into a thoughtful smile and his shoulders started itching. *No way.* She couldn't know he fussed over her sexy outfit because he didn't like the idea of other men making a pass at her.

"I'm a big girl. I can handle a man's unwelcome attentions."

Shoot. He couldn't get anything past her. He admitted, albeit grudgingly, that her sassy little mouth could probably take down any man intent on harassing her.

He should back off and send her into town by her lonesome. But he never claimed to be smart. Determined to show Josephine he could behave like a civilized man, he insisted, "I have to pick up some supplies, and I promised Bobby the next time I went into town he could go along. You'd be doing me a favor watching over him while I load the truck."

The pinched expression on her face smoothed out. "When should I have Bobby ready to leave?"

He squished the socks tighter in his fist. The woman had a hell of a knack for making him forget what was at stake. No way would he allow Josephine to step in and take responsibility for *his* son while she stayed at the ranch. "I'll make sure Bobby's ready to go."

JOSEPHINE HELD FAST to Bobby's small hand as she watched JD drive the truck around to the back of Milner's Feed and Tack. She had no intention of entering the store and asking Bonnie to help her find a larger size pair of jeans.

As the lone female on her father's team of corporate executives, she went to great lengths to hide her feminine curves beneath loose-fitting suits. She wanted men to see her as an intelligent, confident co-worker, not as a pair of breasts and hips. But the ranch was a different world from the high-rise office building she worked in. Here, she could let her guard down and be herself. Surprisingly, she discovered *herself* liked wearing jeans and slinky tank tops. The fact that JD found her sexy in the clothes gave her feminine ego a big boost.

She glanced at her nephew. "I'm hungry for ice cream. How about you?"

"Do they have chocolate?"

"I think so." Hand in hand they walked three doors down to Lacey's Drug Emporium. A sign in the front window advertised homemade desserts and ice cream.

The wind chime, hanging from the ceiling near the door, tinkled when they entered. Ceiling fans whirred above their heads, carrying the scent of lemon cleaner through the air. At the back of the store, Josephine spotted an old-fashioned soda fountain. The floor creaked and moaned as she and Bobby strolled down the main aisle.

"Well, hello!"

Turning at the sound of the high-pitched greeting, Josephine spotted a woman in her early fifties, with a toothy smile and sun-wrinkled skin, heading toward her. The lady lifted a pair of eyeglasses attached to a jewel-studded chain and perched them on the end of her hawkish nose. She spared Bobby a fleeting glance as she raised a pencil-thin eyebrow. "I don't believe I've seen you in town before."

Josephine didn't like the woman. She'd bet her 401K this lady headed the local gossip ring. Gossiping aside, anyone who saw a boy as cute as Bobby and didn't smile was missing a heart. A lifetime of good manners and what her mother referred to as breeding forced her to offer a hand. "Josephine Delaney from Chicago."

"Oh, my, such a long way from home. Laura Brannigan. I own the place. My mother's name was Lacey."

Bobby shuffled his feet and sighed with boredom, but the store proprietor didn't notice. Josephine squeezed his shoulder. "I see some toys." She pointed toward an end cap one aisle over. "Why don't you go check them out."

Her nephew smiled. "Okay."

"Are you the mother of that boy?" the store owner asked after Bobby walked away.

"Who, Bobby? No, I'm—"

Gasping, the older woman placed a hand over her heart. "I can't believe what a sorry mess the whole situation is out at Blake's. The man's done nothing to deserve all the gossip the boy's scandalous father has caused."

"Scandalous?" If Josephine wasn't so confused she might find the woman's dramatics entertaining.

"I figured that Mexican boy would grow up and amount to

no good. I can't understand why Blake took him in all those years ago." The woman touched Josephine's elbow and whispered, "We think his parents were drug dealers from Mexico."

We? Josephine didn't want to know exactly whom *we* included. She'd heard enough. If JD wished to share his past, he'd tell her. She didn't care to hear some twisted version of his childhood from a bitter, past-her-prime busybody. "Mrs. Brannigan?"

"Call me Laura, dear. I've never been married."

Figures. Josephine pictured herself thirty years down the road and grimaced. Would she ever fall in love and marry? Or would she end up a spinster like Laura Brannigan? "Bobby and I came in for some ice cream."

The storekeeper ignored Josephine's attempt to change the subject and motioned toward Bobby. "Social services dumped him on Blake's doorstep last Christmas." She shook her head, her mouth turning down at the corners. "What kind of mother would give up her child?"

"A dead mother, Ms. Brannigan."

"Oh, Lord!" The woman's outburst drew Bobby's attention, and he stared. Josephine grasped the woman's arm and guided her away from the toy aisle.

"How terrible. I can certainly understand the mother not having anything to do with that JD character while she lived. The man looks like an outlaw. The least he could do is cut his long hair."

Pressing her lips together, Josephine counted to ten, afraid that if she didn't, she'd lose her temper and let loose one of her famous corporate tongue-lashings.

"I ask you, what kind of an example is he for a young boy?"

"Ms.—"

"I'm sorry, dear. I get carried away sometimes. Are you a relative of Blake's?" She pursed her lips. "I don't recall him having any kinfolk left."

A twinge of admiration for the woman's tenacity pricked

Josephine. She'd be hell-on-wheels in her father's firm. "Actually, I'm visiting my nephew." She nodded toward Bobby.

The older woman's eyes widened. "The youngun' is your nephew?"

"My deceased sister is…was Bobby's mother."

Two bony shoulders hunched forward and she whispered, "Have you come to take the boy away from his heathen father? He'll be better off with you than that…that good-for-nothing Mexican."

Josephine's hand fisted at her side. If the woman called JD *Mexican* one more time she'd haul off and punch her in the nose. "Ms. Brannigan—"

"The boy belongs with your family. Actually, I'm surprised his father has stuck around this long."

Ignoring the twinge of conscience, Josephine murmured, "Stuck around?"

"He was one of those rodeo cowboys." Her nose curled. "After graduating high school, he never stayed at Blake's place more than a few weeks at a time. Until the boy showed up. Won't be long before he gets the itch and takes off again. Then what will Blake do with the boy, and the man in his seventies?"

Josephine motioned to her watch. "I'm afraid we're running late. If you wouldn't mind getting us our ice cream."

"Goodness, plumb forgot." She hurried toward the soda fountain. "We've got chocolate, vanilla, strawberry, maple—"

"Two chocolates, please."

The bell above the door clanged and Josephine glanced over her shoulder. *Oh, dear.* JD, his face set in stern lines, started down the aisle toward her.

Josephine flashed a smile, hoping to wipe the scowl off his face.

"We came in to order ice cream. Would you care for some?"

"Bobby, let's go," JD growled.

Guess not.

She touched his wrist. When he would have pulled away,

she tightened her hold. "Let him have his ice cream," she whispered.

Her nephew approached his father with slow, hesitant steps.

JD's gaze zeroed in on the back of the store. His body stiffened, and his face settled into a blank mask. Even his voice held no emotion when he spoke. "C'mon, Bobby. Your aunt will bring the ice cream out to the truck." He grasped his son's hand, turned and exited the store without another word.

"He's such a rude man."

Josephine jumped inside her skin. The Brannigan woman stood behind her, holding two cups of ice cream.

"How much do I owe you?"

"Yours is on the house." The woman's mouth curved into a cold smile. "It'll be a dollar for the boy's."

Josephine's hands shook so badly she had trouble removing her wallet from her purse. She handed over a five-dollar bill. "Keep the change." Afraid that if she didn't leave immediately she'd tip the cups of ice cream over the woman's head, she grabbed the treats and stormed toward the front door. As her hand reached for the handle, Laura Brannigan got one last word in.

"Don't be a fool and fall for that no-good cowboy."

Without answering, Josephine left. She stood for a second on the sidewalk, gulping air. JD and Bobby sat waiting in the idling truck. JD's mirrored shades concealed his eyes, but she noticed a suspicious tightening around his mouth.

Until her run-in with the Brannigan woman, Josephine had never given JD's ethnicity much thought. Now she wondered if others in town were prejudiced toward him. JD was a grown man and could handle the snide remarks. But what about Bobby? How would Bobby cope if people judged him unfairly simply because of who his father was?

She hopped into the front seat and handed Bobby his treat.

"Thanks, Aunt Josephine."

Each time her nephew called her *Aunt Josephine,* she rejoiced at the fragile bonds of trust forming between them. She'd only known her nephew for a couple of days, but already her heart wished she were more than just his aunt. She yearned to be his mother.

Startled by the realization, she swallowed her ice cream wrong and collapsed into a coughing fit.

"You okay, Aunt Josephine?"

"Fine, honey," she wheezed. The only way she could become Bobby's mother was to marry his father. *Marry JD?*

Shifting in her seat, she stared at JD, not caring that he squirmed uncomfortably under her watchful eye. Josephine's stomach tingled at the idea of being this man's wife…at night…in his bed. But what about during the light of day?

No. JD had too strong a personality for her to coexist peacefully with him. She didn't think she could survive a week, let alone twenty years of "his way or no way" philosophy. She fought a smile. Oh, but the fun she'd have challenging JD at every turn.

Not a day would pass without arguing. Not a night without…making up.

Chapter Seven

"Bobby's sound asleep," Josephine announced as she joined Blake on the front porch.

He patted the seat next to him on the swing. "You'll spoil the rascal reading all those stories before bed."

Swallowing a sigh, she sat down. "I hope JD wasn't too upset Bobby asked me to read to him tonight. He enjoys spending that time with Bobby."

The rancher's chest shook with silent laughter. "He'll live."

Josephine nodded, wondering if she should confess she and Bobby had talked more than they read. Her nephew had asked several questions about her life in Chicago and his grandparents. She'd answered his inquiries truthfully until he'd asked if his grandfather would read to him.

She hadn't been sure what to say. Neither her father nor her mother had ever read her a bedtime story. At an early age, Josephine had learned her parents were too busy with their own lives to spend much time with her. She'd figured out the only way she'd get a story was if she'd read herself one. So she'd taught herself to read by age four. The years following, she'd stayed up past her bedtime reading books under the covers with a flashlight.

Tonight when she'd kissed Bobby's sweet-smelling forehead and whispered *I love you* into his ear, she'd realized that she'd been cheated out of hundreds of good-night kisses and hugs because her parents hadn't been around to tuck her into bed. Bobby's sleepy smile and the way he clutched the teddy bear she'd given him had reminded her just how lonely her childhood had been.

Blake pointed toward the west. "Beautiful sky tonight."

She admitted Chicago couldn't compete with a Brandt's Corner sunset. Not that she'd noticed many sunsets back home. Normally, she ended her evenings behind her desk or parked in rush-hour traffic.

"Mary and I made a habit of sitting on the swing at the end of each day. Even when she'd been real sick, she insisted on coming out. Had to carry her the last few times."

Josephine's heart hurt at the love she heard in Blake's voice when he spoke of his deceased wife. "You must miss her very much."

He dropped his gaze to his lap. "I don't know how I would have survived if JD hadn't stayed with me that first summer."

Sensing the old man had more to say, she remained silent.

"I spent every minute of every day taking care of Mary those last few months until the end. After she was gone, I went a little stir-crazy without anyone to look after." The lines on his weathered face deepened. "JD needs Bobby the same way I needed JD."

She yearned to tell Blake everything would work out between JD, Bobby and her parents. Rather than making promises she wasn't sure she could keep, she held her tongue.

"Bobby said the store lady acted angry today." His gentle smile failed to hide the shadow of concern in his eyes.

Unsure of the rancher's relationship with Laura Brannigan, Josephine settled for a noncommittal shrug.

Blake rubbed his jaw. "I should have warned you about the busybody."

The note of disgust in his voice made Josephine believe he didn't care for the woman any more than she did. "Why?"

"Laura's always been hostile to JD. Even when JD was a youngun'."

"What has she got against him?"

"Mary once heard gossip about Laura's having fallen in love with a young man who'd worked on her family's pecan farm."

"Let me guess—the man was Hispanic?"

"Yep. Seems the young man broke her heart when he returned to Mexico and married the daughter of a family friend."

"Can I ask you something, Blake?"

"Sure."

"What have you found out about JD's past? His family history?"

Old, arthritic fingers plucked at the buckles on the straps of his overalls. "Not much."

Shocked, she waited a moment to digest the implications of his answer before asking, "You brought him into your home without bothering to check into his background?"

Blake patted her hand, as if she were simple in the head. "I'm a darn good judge of character, Josephine. JD's one of the finest human beings I know. Loyal, honest, dedicated and considerate."

Josephine frowned.

Squint lines crinkling around his eyes, Blake added, "He's a mite slow in the consideration department, but it's there." When she didn't respond, the laughter drained from his expression, and he cleared his throat. "I've never been more proud of JD than the afternoon Bobby showed up at the ranch. Should have seen the surprise on his face when the social services woman claimed Bobby was his son." Blake's face softened. "He accepted the boy as his, no questions asked. That day I wished JD had been my own blood son more than ever."

Would her father have behaved as nobly if Josephine had been dumped on his front porch? No, he'd have wanted some sort of proof first.

Blake's loyalty to JD prevented him from confiding in her.

"I guess I'll talk to JD myself." She crossed her arms over her chest and grumbled, "He's not a garrulous man."

The night breeze carried off the sound of Blake's rumbling chuckle. "He's down in—"

"The barn. He hides with the horses when he doesn't want to deal with me."

"Like horses, you got to be patient and gentle with him, then he'll break easier." Blake left the swing and gimped across the porch, old age and arthritis making his steps jerky. He entered the house with a muttered "See you in the morning."

Glaring across the ranch yard, Josephine decided the only way to get answers was to ask questions.

Several lights gleamed above the horse stalls when she stepped inside the barn. A clanking off to the left drew her attention, and she spotted JD hammering a shoe on Turnip. The horse was tethered to a post outside a stall.

She froze, mesmerized by the sight before her. Not the horse…JD. His tanned naked back, glistening with sweat, made her knees tremble. Broad shoulders bunched as he shifted Turnip's leg to his other hand.

"Easy, girl." He smoothed his fingers down the animal's foreleg, and Josephine yearned to experience the feel of those callused fingers stroking her own bare calf. The horse nuzzled JD's neck, knocking the hat right off his head. "Bossy girl, aren't you?" He grinned and the normal stern set of his lips gave way to sexy creases alongside his mouth.

Her breath hitched at the beauty of his smile. The man was gorgeous when he flashed those pearly whites. If she waited any longer to announce her presence he'd catch her with drool dripping off her chin. "Did Turnip injure herself chasing after the rabbit yesterday?"

JD's head swiveled in her direction. His smile slowly faded. "No, her shoe came loose, is all." He narrowed his gaze. "Figured you'd turned in for the night."

She wandered closer, her stomach tingling as she breathed

in JD's aftershave mixed with the scent of hardworking male. "Too much on my mind."

He nodded, then resumed pounding nails in Turnip's shoe. The bright lights bounced off his jet black hair and emphasized the harsh lines of his face. Maybe Laura Brannigan had been right about his appearance. With his inky hair tied back in a strip of rawhide, his naked chest gleaming and a fierce light flashing in his eyes, he could pass for an outlaw or a renegade warrior.

After hammering in the final nail, he led the horse back into her stall. He latched the gate, then snagged the towel from his back pocket and wiped his hands. "I'm busy. If you've got something to say, spit it out."

Inching closer, she lifted his hat from the floor and tapped the brim against her thigh. Dust particles danced through the air. She held out the Stetson, forcing her gaze away from the dark brown nipples on his hairless chest. "After our trip to town today, I realized I don't know much about you."

He took the hat from her, set it on a hook protruding from the stall door and moved away. "Not much worth telling."

"I'm Bobby's aunt. I believe I have a right to know more about his father."

JD stopped midstride. She held her breath, watching his shoulder muscles bunch one by one until his back resembled a slab of granite. Hands clenched at his sides, he faced her. "What did she say?"

"She mentioned you used to rodeo before Bobby came to live with you." She had no intention of hurting him by repeating the insults the shop proprietor had spouted.

Some of the stiffness eased from his body, but the wary look in his eyes remained. "Yeah, well, that's all history."

"Are you sure?"

The corners of his mouth turned down. "What are you getting at, Josephine?"

"Rodeoing is an exhilarating sport." She gestured around the barn. "This is hardly as exciting."

Moving forward, he didn't stop until his breath fanned across her forehead. Until she had an in-your-face view of his well-defined pectoral muscles. She could even see the short black hairs peeking out from under his arms. "If you think for one minute I'd take off and leave my son alone for weeks on end with Blake, you're crazy."

She forced her gaze to his face and her heart winced at the hurt darkening his brown eyes to black. Clearly, he took offense at her assumption that he'd put rodeo before the welfare of his own son. Something inside Josephine insisted JD was telling the truth. "I believe you."

Inch by inch, his body relaxed, which lent her the courage to forge ahead with her questions. "The other night at the dinner table you mentioned you didn't have any family." He tensed.

Ah. Obviously, *family* was a touchy subject with JD. "What if Bobby asks about your family? What will you tell him?"

"Did he ask about my relatives when you put him to bed?"

"No, but I'm sure he wonders if he has other aunts or uncles. Cousins. Grandparents."

His jaw tightened. "Bobby has no family other than you and your parents."

She couldn't recall ever dealing with a more stubborn man, save her father. She suppressed a smile as she envisioned William Delaney and JD going head-to-head. If there was one man who could take her father down in the stubborn department, it was JD. "Will a private investigator come up with the same conclusion?" As soon as she voiced the words, she regretted them. Darn, the cowboy had a knack for pushing her buttons.

"I'll be damned if I'll stand here and help you make a case against me keeping custody of my own son."

Judging by the vehemence in his voice, she doubted she was the first person to show an interest in his background. Unwilling to cave in under his angry glare, she lifted her chin.

"I could have simply believed all the garbage Laura Brannigan spouted about you. But I wanted to hear the truth from you. If you can't even give me that, then what am I supposed to believe, JD?" She spun, angry she couldn't have a normal, calm conversation with the man.

"Wait."

She wasn't sure if it was the whispered word or the deep, gut-wrenching agony in his voice that made Josephine freeze in place.

"I'm sorry."

Bracing herself, she turned around. The stark pain in his eyes stole the breath from her lungs.

He unlatched the stall door to his left. "Let's talk."

A secluded spot, privacy, a half-naked man…all the ingredients for a classic seduction. But the utter defeat in JD's expression convinced her she would be a fool to believe the man had hanky-panky on his mind right now.

"I won't bite."

She entered the stall, careful not to rub up against his naked skin. The seating selection consisted of hay bales and…more hay bales. She chose the one closest to her. JD sat next to her, leaving only inches between them. He balanced the heel of his boot on the edge of the straw and leaned against the wall.

He boldly met her gaze. "I told the truth about not having any family." His eyes flashed with defiance; bitterness edged his tone. She refrained from commenting, allowing him the courtesy of explaining without interruption.

"I grew up in an orphanage on the American side of the Rio Grande across from El Porvenir, Mexico."

She swallowed hard as the image of JD as a little boy, lost and alone among strangers, flashed through her mind.

"When I was old enough to understand, the *padre* told me my father had been Mexican and my mother an American. He claimed he had no other information about my family."

"So how did you end up with Blake?"

"Every year, men from El Porvenir crossed the Rio Grande to work the cattle ranches or pecan farms in West Texas. They'd stop at the orphanage and take along the younger boys to cook and wash for them. But the *padre* never allowed me to go. When I turned ten, he died. The next time José came to the orphanage, the new *padre* let me tag along with him. We ended up at the Rocking R." JD rubbed a spot of grease on his jeans and continued.

"Blake's wife had just died. He asked José and me to help through the summer. At the end of August, José returned to his family in Mexico." JD swallowed hard. "Blake let me stay."

Judging from the hoarseness in his voice, Josephine realized the rancher's offer had meant the world to a ten-year-old boy.

"Didn't the *padre* send someone for you when you didn't return to the orphanage?"

"José insisted he'd take care of it." JD shrugged. "One less mouth to feed."

Sadness filled Josephine at the thought of a small boy believing he didn't matter to anyone. No child should ever have to experience that feeling. Now she understood why JD felt such a strong connection to Bobby. In a sense, they'd both been abandoned.

"Have you made an attempt to locate your parents?"

He tapped his fingers against his knee. "No."

"Why?"

"*Why?* Would you want to track down two people who threw you away like a bag of stinking rubbish?"

"Yes, I believe I would."

He snorted. "You're crazy."

"JD, what about extenuating circumstances? Maybe your parents *couldn't* keep you."

"No. They just didn't want me."

"You're not being fair. What about Bobby's situation? You weren't aware of his existence because Cassandra didn't tell you. But that didn't mean you didn't want him or didn't love him."

He stared at her, his chest barely moving with each indrawn breath. After a long moment, he glanced away. "Don't waste your time trying to make me feel better. There's no fairy-tale ending to my story."

The urge to hug him was so strong; she wrapped her arms around herself to keep from reaching for him. She ached to insist his parents hadn't intentionally abandoned him. But what good would it do without proof? "What does JD stand for?"

"Juan Diego."

Surprised he'd told her right away, she asked, "Is Diego your last name?"

His fingers gripped his knee until the knuckles turned white. "The summer I turned twelve José insisted I take his last name—Gonzalez. Blake helped me get a social security card, and the rest as they say is history."

Josephine smiled. "JD fits you. I can't quite picture you as a Dave or a Mike."

"Dave, huh?" His lips quirked and his expression lightened.

"I understand what JD stands for on Bobby's birth certificate. But why didn't Cassandra fill in your last name?"

"I guess because she didn't care to find out what it was. Most people knew me only by JD. I even insisted they print my name in the rodeo standings as JD." He shrugged. "Once Bobby's caseworker in New York called the PRCA, Professional Rodeo Cowboy Association, it wasn't hard to track me down."

"What about Bobby?"

He frowned. "What do you mean?"

"His last name. Will he use Gonzalez?"

JD's jaw tightened. "I used Gonzalez to register him at school."

Josephine assumed by his defensive posture that he expected her to object. She had no problem with Gonzalez as Bobby's last name. But she knew her father would object. He'd insist his grandson use Delaney in order to take advantage of the prestige and clout the name carried in the financial world. Not for a minute did she believe her father would get his way. She sensed JD didn't care much about prestige or clout. He'd teach Bobby to wear his name with pride. But she couldn't help worrying about the kinds of challenges her nephew might face. "I have a request I hope you'll consider."

When he remained silent, she continued, "I'd like to take Bobby back to Chicago for a short visit." JD opened his mouth, but she held up a hand, stalling his protest. "He deserves a chance to meet his grandparents and get acquainted with them."

Tell JD the whole truth, Josephine. Tell him if he doesn't allow you to take Bobby back to Chicago your father will make trouble for him. The kind of trouble that good intentions and honor are no defense against.

Since she'd informed her father of her intent to stay at the ranch for two weeks, he'd called daily on her cell phone, demanding she up the date she'd planned to return to Chicago with Bobby. One message had been particularly threatening: he'd sworn he would arrive at the ranch with an entourage of lawyers if she didn't bring his grandson back pronto. Josephine believed him. Her father didn't issue useless threats. "Please, JD. Three or four days. No longer, I promise."

He shook his head.

"Don't answer now. Just say you'll think about it." She wished she could read his mind, but his face remained blank. "Seeing Bobby in person will help my parents come to terms with Cassandra's death and the fact that she kept Bobby a secret from our family." Not for a minute did Josephine believe Bobby's presence would instantly change her parents into loving, affectionate people, but she hoped that after meeting their grandson, the older couple would acknowledge the need to do what was in Bobby's best interest.

He rubbed his forehead, a definite sign he was weakening, so she went in for the kill. "Bobby asked me tonight if he could go visit his grandparents."

Stark fear glittered in JD's brown eyes. His chest rose and fell heavily, his anxiety palpable.

"You can't hide Bobby away forever on the ranch, JD. He'll grow up resenting you for keeping him from his family."

His gaze shifted frantically around the stall, as if desperately trying to locate an avenue of escape.

She reached for his hand, but he pulled away. "Please. Trust me enough to take your son to visit his grandparents and return him safely to the ranch."

He bounced off the hay bale. "I'll consider the idea." Then he was gone.

Well, it was what she asked, and better than a flat-out *no*. She just hoped time didn't run out before he reached a decision.

"WHAT SHOULD I DO, Blake?" JD stood at the kitchen window, watching Bobby and Josephine ride double on Turnip inside the corral. Every night this week the two had spent time together with the horse. His son looked forward to being with his aunt each evening and that made JD jealous as hell. But his hide was nailed to the wall. He didn't dare try to keep Bobby away from Josephine, for fear the boy would resent him and ask to go back to Chicago with his aunt—for good.

Blake wandered over to the window and stopped next to JD. "You don't have much choice, son."

JD swallowed hard at the casual way *son* slipped out of the old man's mouth. As a young boy, he hadn't understood the significance attached to the word. Now that JD was a father, he realized the importance, the sentiment, the word carried. "What if she doesn't bring him back? What if she calls and says Bobby wants to stay with his grandparents? What if—"

The touch of Blake's knobby fingers on his shoulder stopped JD midsentence. "Those are a lot of what-ifs. If she doesn't keep her promise, then you fly to Chicago and bring Bobby home yourself."

Nerves tied JD's stomach in knots. If the Delaneys refused

to let Josephine bring Bobby back to Texas, they'd make sure he couldn't get within a mile of their grandson.

Blake returned to the sink and continued washing dishes. "Be good for Bobby to meet his grandparents."

The knot in JD's gut tightened as he watched the pair practice backing up the mare. He flexed his fingers, feeling as though his son was slipping away and he could do nothing to alter the course of the future. *Damn* it! He hadn't even had a decent grip on Bobby to begin with.

His son might deserve to meet his grandparents, but his gut insisted the Delaneys were not an ordinary storybook grandma and grandpa. Even so, JD remembered sleeping countless nights on a dirty cot in the orphanage, dreaming one day of being rescued from that hellhole by family who hadn't known he'd existed.

He admitted the Delaneys had a right to see for themselves Cassandra's child was well, healthy and happy. But deep down, JD feared this was the older couple's first step in their fight to gain custody of Bobby. If he proved he had no intention of keeping their grandson from them, maybe the pair would back off and settle for an occasional visit from Bobby.

"When does she plan to take him back?" Blake's voice shattered JD's thoughts.

"Yesterday."

The rancher wiped his hands on a towel. "What about plane tickets?"

"She said the company plane will meet her and Bobby at the Blackhawk Municipal Airport."

"Sounds simple enough."

Simple? Hardly. To JD's way of thinking, everything was a mess. "Do me a favor and help Bobby with his bath tonight, while I talk to Josephine."

"Sure thing."

By the time Bobby and Josephine put Turnip in the barn,

brushed her down and fed her some oats an hour had gone by and JD was a nervous wreck.

"Don't forget to say good night, Aunt Josephine," Bobby hollered as he ran up the porch steps, Blake gimping after him.

Every word, look and laugh Bobby and his aunt shared made JD worry he was that much closer to losing the boy. Not for the first time did he agonize over Josephine replacing him in his son's affections. Chest tight, he stared at the ground, afraid his feelings might show on his face.

"You wanted to discuss something with me?"

He glanced sideways. She smiled, her beautiful face glowing. How someone so tiny, so beautiful, so soft could land in his life with the force of an atomic explosion baffled him.

He nudged the lower corral rung with his boot and hung his arms over the top rail. She sidled closer. He hadn't been this close to her since their talk in the barn four days ago and her scent threatened to make him forget why he was out there with her in the first place. "If I let you take Bobby back to Chicago, when would you leave?"

"Tomorrow."

The one-word answer cut him to the bone. "And when would you return?"

"Let's see. Today's Thursday. How about next Tuesday, the twenty-sixth?"

Wishing the dusty soil beneath his boots would crack open and suck him under, he shoved away from the fence and headed for the barn. "Tuesday. Not a day later."

JD'S FINGERS CLENCHED the steering wheel of the truck until his knuckles turned white. He glanced at Bobby, who sat between him and Josephine in the front seat. No use cursing again. He'd already called himself every kind of fool for caving in and allowing his son to visit his grandparents in Chicago.

Next Tuesday was a lifetime away. During the dark hours of the night, when he wasn't out of bed standing in Bobby's doorway watching him sleep, he'd almost convinced himself he'd be so busy preparing for fall roundup he'd hardly miss the boy. And the herd had to be moved to a different grazing area. Then, if he had any time left, he'd clean out the trailer for José's family. As he turned the truck into the municipal airport's minuscule parking lot, he gave up trying to justify a decision he'd begun to regret the moment he'd made it.

For a second, he considered going along with them, then he studied himself in the rearview mirror. When the Delaneys caught sight of him they'd run to the police, insisting a Mexican illegal had kidnapped their grandson. Better for everyone if he stayed behind.

He parked the truck near the back of the lot and stared out the windshield at the runway. "Those planes are mighty small."

"Commuter jets. They fly at a lower altitude, so Bobby will have a great view." Josephine's smile didn't do a damn thing to reassure him. She unbuckled her seat belt, then helped Bobby with his. JD stepped from the truck and lifted two soft-sided duffels out of the back seat before following Josephine and Bobby into the terminal building.

Once inside, Josephine checked in at the counter, while he and Bobby stood by the floor-to-ceiling windows, staring at single-engine props taking off and landing on the lone runway.

JD rubbed his aching chest. The moment he'd agreed to this bound-to-lead-to-no-good gamble, the simple act of breathing had become an arduous chore. He tousled Bobby's blond hair, thinking he should have given the boy a haircut before he left the ranch. "I'm going to miss our bedtime stories at night, pardner."

Instead of a smile, a somber face stared up at JD, sending a jolt through his body. His son lifted his hand, and he grasped the small fingers tightly. "Your grandparents will be excited to meet you."

Bobby dropped his gaze to the floor. JD went down on one

knee and clutched the child's narrow shoulders. "You don't have to go if you don't want to."

He peeked out from under his ragged bangs. "Will you come, too?"

Even if Blake could manage the ranch on his own, JD refused to get within two states' distance of the man who'd offered to *buy* his grandson. The temptation to use his fist and not his mouth to tell Delaney off would only create more trouble…something he had enough of already. "No, Bobby." He nodded to the small brown sack with handles. "What's in the bag?"

His son pulled out the brown, floppy-eared teddy bear Josephine had given him. Bobby fingered the big red-and-green plaid bow around the fuzzy neck.

"What's your pal's name?"

"Rascal."

Blake's nickname for Bobby. The tightness in JD's chest crawled into his throat. "Rascal will be good company during the trip."

Bobby touched JD's knee. "Are you gonna be sad when I leave?"

JD wrapped his arms around his son and pulled Bobby close for a hug, hoping the feel of the small, warm body would squelch the panic escalating in him. "You bet I am." He sucked in a deep breath. "I'll miss you every day." *Every hour. Every minute. Every second.*

Bobby squirmed, and JD reluctantly loosened his hold. "You take Rascal." His son thrust the bear at him. "He sleeps under the covers."

With a shaking hand, JD accepted the stuffed animal, cursing the tightness in his throat.

Shoving papers into her carry-on bag, Josephine approached. "All set. We can board the plane."

After giving Bobby one last squeeze, JD stood, Rascal dangling from his hand.

Josephine's gaze shifted between him and Bobby. Her eyes narrowed thoughtfully as she held out a business card. "Home, office, cell phone, e-mail and assistant's number. I won't be hard to find. We'll call when we land."

The numbers on the white card blurred, and getting air into his lungs took more effort than staying on top of a rank bronc for eight seconds. He tried to recall if he'd ever done anything this hard in his life—didn't think so.

He must have done a poor job of hiding his feelings, because Josephine draped her arms around his neck and whispered near his ear, "Trust me, JD. I'll bring your son home. You have my word."

JD did believe she was a woman of her word. Josephine, he trusted; her parents, he didn't.

Burying his face in her neck, he breathed in her scent, wishing she'd change her mind about going. He didn't keep track of the time they stood locked in each other's arms; long enough to draw stares from several people. He realized what an odd couple they made. Josephine, small and businesslike in her suit and heels. Him, tall and scruffy in his jeans, ratty boots and threadbare shirt.

"We have to go, JD. The pilot is waiting for us."

Panic surged through him, making him reckless. He kissed her. Branded her. Burned her into his memory.

He met no resistance when he forced his tongue between her lips and savored her sweet taste. He couldn't get enough. Wanted more. Needed more. Clutching her head, he devoured her mouth, Rascal bumping against their faces. He yearned to tell her without words he would miss her…that she'd become more to him than just his son's aunt.

Bobby tugged on his jeans. "Are you gonna miss Aunt Josephine?"

JD smiled against her soft, swollen lips, then nuzzled his nose along her cheek, inhaling her fresh, feminine scent before stepping back. Unable to resist one last touch, he brushed a strand of honey-blond hair from her cheek. “Yeah.” He cleared his throat. “I’m going to miss you both.” Josephine might not have spoken the words, but the dreamy sparkle in her eyes insisted she’d miss him, too.

Then they were gone.

From his spot at the window his gaze followed the pair as they walked out to the plane. The pilot lifted Bobby inside, then offered Josephine a hand up. He figured his last glimpse of her would be her sassy fanny swish-swaying as she climbed the stairs. Instead, she turned at the door and waved. The gesture eased the tight band around his chest a fraction.

He watched the sky swallow up the small plane. He wasn’t sure how long he remained at the window, his insides filling with emptiness, when the announcement of another flight startled him.

With purposeful strides he left the building, Rascal swinging in his hand.

Chapter Eight

The silence was killing him.

JD paced the kitchen floor, shoving his fingers in the back pockets of his jeans. His gaze locked on the phone. *Ring, damn it.*

He missed his son. He just never expected to miss him *this* much. The first day without Bobby had been hell. He'd constantly checked over his shoulder, expecting to see a pair of little legs pumping to keep up.

"Pacing won't do nothin' but wear a hole in your boots," Blake commented, his tired eyes filled with understanding, as he walked into the room.

Until tonight, JD hadn't realized how much the sound of Josephine's reassuring voice on the phone soothed the sting of her and Bobby's absence. Not to mention that he'd enjoyed his conversations with Bobby, even if the discussions had centered on the Delaneys' mansion and all the new toys they'd bought for their grandson and a dog named Fi Fi who wore pink bows in *his* fur. Obviously, the kid had been dazzled by his first introduction to lifestyles of the rich and famous.

"I haven't heard from Josephine today." JD clamped his mouth shut, wishing he hadn't spoken. He didn't want Blake thinking the little corporate barracuda had burrowed under his skin. Even though she had.

The old man patted his back. "She'll phone."

He wished he felt as confident as Blake sounded, but the knot in his gut refused to unravel. Josephine had kept her promise and had contacted him as soon as the plane had landed in Chicago on Friday. Saturday and Sunday evening she'd called at exactly six o'clock. Now, the night before their return flight home, he couldn't shake the feeling something was wrong. Very wrong.

Fear twisted his insides. "What if they had an accident?" God, he despised this feeling of helplessness.

Compassion warmed Blake's age-weary face. "Don't borrow trouble. I'm going to work on the truck." He hunkered down on the stool by the porch door, wormed his feet into a pair of work boots, then left without another word.

"I'll holler at you when they phone," JD shouted as the screen door slammed shut. Guilt pricked him. He'd been selfish in assuming only he missed Bobby. Blake missed the boy, too. JD hadn't meant to neglect the old man, but he hadn't been good company since he'd dropped Bobby and Josephine off at the airport. He'd thrown himself into ranch work from sunup to sundown. The only way he knew how to keep from going crazy wondering what the Delaneys were doing with Bobby and if they were poisoning his young mind with untruths about his father.

Jeez. He was a wreck—feeling sorry for himself because he missed the company of a five-year-old.

He blinked the dryness from his eyes. He'd slept like crap the last three nights. Without Josephine around to tick him off and send him running to the barn, he'd gone to bed early, hoping to catch some extra Zs. Not a chance.

Memories of the sexy blonde had danced through his mind into the wee morning hours. The first night, he'd convinced himself his insomnia had been due to worrying about Bobby. But after the second night, when he'd lain wide awake at 3:00 a.m., he'd admitted his sleeplessness had nothing to do with his son and everything to do with lush breasts, curvy hips and long, blond hair. And a pair of the most striking blue eyes he'd ever seen.

He missed the sway of Josephine's full hips in the too-tight jeans she insisted on wearing. Missed the way her cute little nose curled when she stepped into the barn and got her first whiff of horse and hay. Missed her stubborn chin jutting in the air when he bossed her around. Missed the covert glances she tossed at his backside when she thought he wasn't paying attention.

Fighting the slow-building throb between his thighs, he wished more than ever he and Josephine had more in common than Bobby. If he thought they had a chance in hell of meeting in the middle he'd do his damnedest to coax her into bed with him. He had no doubt that sliding between the sheets with the woman would be one unforgettable experience.

A doctor should examine his head for even *considering* getting close to the lady. But Josephine captivated him. She made no excuses for her intelligence, her family's wealth. He appreciated her for not pretending to be anyone other than herself. In that regard, they were a lot alike.

In the past, he'd never given a care what other people thought about him. Why, all of a sudden, did he have the urge to make Josephine proud of him? Because of Bobby? *No. Because of you.* Her opinion of him as a man and a father mattered more than he cared to admit.

She might not approve of raising Bobby on a ranch, but he sensed she approved of the way he worked his tail off, assuming most of the responsibility for the day-to-day cattle operation. Which meant a lot to a man who'd spent half his life being called one of those lazy-good-for-nothing Mexicans.

Until Bobby had shown up at the door, JD had been content with minding his own business and living life one day at a time. But fatherhood changed a man. Made him think about the future. A future for his son.

Deep inside, he hoped Josephine would always be part of

Bobby's life. Mainly for Bobby's sake, but also for his. He couldn't imagine never seeing her again.

He looked at the kitchen clock: 7:20 p.m.

He slapped his open palm against the counter and cursed. He'd give Josephine ten more minutes. If she didn't call by then, he'd dial every frickin' number on her business card until he tracked her down. He shoved his stinging palm into the front pocket of his pants and wrapped his fingers around the delicate hair ribbon nestled inside.

After pulling the ribbon from the pocket, he rubbed the satin material between his fingers. The first evening after they'd left, he'd stood in the empty guest bedroom, breathing in the lingering scent of expensive perfume, and missing Josephine like crazy. Then he'd spotted the pink ribbon on the nightstand, and before he'd realized what he'd done, he'd stuffed the string into his jean pocket. In a weird way—a way he refused to analyze—the piece of fluff comforted him.

The minute hand circled the clock face again. Had Josephine gone out on a date with that railroad guy her father liked so much? A picture of her decked out in a sequined gown, twirling around a dance floor in the arms of a rich playboy, formed in his mind, causing his blood to boil.

What right did he have to be jealous? The only thing he had to offer Josephine was a do-si-do around a smelly barn. She belonged with her own kind. Still, he rebelled at the idea that Josephine would never fit into his world.

Seven-thirty. Time was up. As he reached for the receiver, the phone rang, rattling his nerves. "Josephine?"

"Hello, JD."

"Is Bobby all right? Are you okay?"

A deafening silence filled his ear before she answered, "We're both fine."

Was that a hitch he'd heard in her voice? "I've been waiting for your call." *Aw, heck.* Why did he have to sound as though he was pining away for her?

A soft sigh echoed through the connection. "Sorry. Things are hectic here."

Something's wrong. He felt it in his bones. Beads of sweat popped out across his forehead. "What's going on?"

"Nothing."

"Is Bobby with you?"

More silence.

"Josephine?"

"No. I'm still at the office. He's home with my parents."

JD rolled his shoulders, his skin prickling with apprehension. "You're sure everything's okay?"

"I'm sorry, but I don't have time to chat."

"Josephine, what's going on?" He winced. He hadn't meant to shout, but her evasiveness scared the crap out of him.

"Nothing's going on."

Fear clawed his insides until his stomach felt as if it had been flayed open. "You're still coming back tomorrow, right?"

Silence again. "Yes."

Her voice sure as hell didn't ring with conviction. "When should I be at the airport?"

"I'm not positive what time the plane will take off. I'll call to update you on Bobby's flight time."

"Okay. I'll wait to hear from you."

The buzzing dial tone sent chills down his spine. She hadn't even murmured a goodbye. He hung up the receiver, frustrated, angry, worried.

Trust her. She won't let you down. And if she did, he'd be on the next flight to Chicago. No matter what, his son would come home tomorrow.

He headed outside to find Blake. Halfway to the barn, he stopped in his tracks. *I'll call to update you on Bobby's flight time.* Just Bobby? Wasn't Josephine flying back with his son? He stared at the dust-covered rental car twenty yards away.

She had to turn in the car. Didn't she?

"ARE WE GONNA CRASH, Aunt Josephine?"

Josephine snuggled Bobby closer to her side as rain and blustery winds buffeted the six-seater company plane in the skies over central Texas. "We're not going to crash, honey." She smoothed a hand over the clump of hair sticking up at the back of his head. "Any minute the plane will break through the clouds, and we'll see the sun." *I hope.*

She stared out the window, her stomach clenching and unclenching with each dip and roll of the plane. A second later, the Cessna lost altitude, plummeting through a mass of swirling black clouds. She tugged Bobby's belt tighter, until he protested.

"I can't breathe."

"Sorry, honey. Just making sure your bottom doesn't leave the seat." When the plane leveled off, she let out a quiet sigh of relief.

He yawned, his mouth opening wide. "I'm tired." No doubt. He'd been up since 4:00 a.m. and it was now one in the afternoon.

"Rest your head in my lap." Bobby squirmed until he found a comfortable position. In minutes his eyes closed, and his mouth sagged open. She stared at the sweet face, thinking the turbulent flight was a fitting end to their trip to Chicago.

In the four days she'd spent away from the ranch, she felt as though she'd aged fifty years. She had expected her father to appreciate her effort in gaining JD's approval to bring Bobby home for a visit—he hadn't. Maybe in her subconscious she'd already acknowledged her efforts wouldn't be appreciated.

She rubbed her forehead, sure the pounding in her head had more to do with her father's words echoing through her memory than did the rocking plane.

Josephine, you dropped the ball on this.

Her father had continued to berate her for not taking a tougher stand with JD and convincing him to relinquish his parental rights. Then her mother had joined in the bashing and accused Josephine of being immature and jealous of her nephew.

Feathering her fingers through Bobby's blond locks, she turned her thoughts to JD. Her parents could learn a thing or two from the stubborn cowboy. JD wasn't a perfect father. He had his share of faults. But he loved his son unconditionally and would always put Bobby first in his life.

After Bobby had gone to bed last night, her parents had insisted Josephine phone JD and inform him she was extending Bobby's visit. Evidently, her parents' lawyer needed more time to investigate the possibility of filing for temporary custody of Bobby on their behalf.

She shivered as she recalled the stern grimaces of displeasure on her parents' faces when she'd refused. For over an hour, Josephine had argued in JD's defense, but her parents had stood firm, insisting they'd do everything in their power to see that Bobby was raised right.

JD had entrusted his son to her, and she'd been determined not to fail him. Which brought her back to the reason they'd arrived at the airport at 4:00 a.m. Afraid her parents would make a scene when she and Bobby left today, she'd decided to sneak out before her parents awoke.

Without allowing Bobby the opportunity to say goodbye to his grandparents, she'd whisked him from the house and caught a cab to the municipal airport, where she'd made arrangements for the company pilot to meet them. Due to the change in plans, she hadn't had time to call JD and inform him of their arrival time today.

The aircraft dipped to the right for several seconds, then burst through the clouds into clear blue skies. She sent up a silent prayer of thanks the small plane had weathered the storm. Peering out the window, she spotted the airport below. As soon as they landed, she'd phone the ranch.

Then what?

The idea of returning to Chicago and facing her parents' wrath held about as much appeal as shoveling horse manure in JD's barn. After her actions today, she doubted she'd have a job with her father's firm, or a place to live. Mentally, she went over a list of the financial companies in the Chicago area, but the idea of starting over with a different firm depressed her. She'd always considered herself a career woman. So why did the thought of working in corporate America suddenly feel like putting the right shoe on the left foot?

Because you met a man who showed you that inside your high-powered corporate body is a woman with needs and wants and desires that have nothing to do with making money or pleasing other people.

She'd missed JD. After two days at work dealing with overbearing men, men who demanded her attention, her time, who shoved their accomplishments in her face—me-me-me men—she'd missed JD's uncomplicated ways. His quiet demeanor. His humbleness. His earthy sex appeal. He was nothing like some of the executives she worked alongside, whose suits reeked of dry-cleaning fluid and whose hair stayed in place with gels, sprays and weekly trims.

JD was pure m-a-l-e. His kisses were more than physical displays of affection. With his mouth and eyes he'd allowed her to see and feel his vulnerability, his need for her. She admitted the feelings she harbored for her nephew's father were deep and rich and more serious than she'd first thought when she'd left four days ago. She yearned to find out where they stood as a man and a woman…together.

She didn't care if being with JD was proper, right or wrong. She'd waited all her life to feel this way about a man. For once she sought to choose what *she* wanted and not what others thought was best for her.

The pilot's voice announced their arrival at the airport. The plane bumped twice against the runway, then slowed to a smooth stop. She woke Bobby and managed to get him to walk off the plane, but the tired little boy refused to march to the terminal, so she carried him. Once inside, she searched the seating area for a spot to set him down. Her gaze landed on JD.

JD?

Chin resting on the center of his palm, he slouched in a seat by the windows, dozing with Bobby's teddy bear in his lap.

Joy and anticipation made her heart clamor like the dinner bell at the ranch. He was even more handsome than she remembered, maybe because his face appeared relaxed and at peace in sleep.

Stopping a few feet from the chair, she quietly observed him. His long hair and beard stubble reminded her of an outlaw in a Hollywood movie. Her heart turned over when she spotted the dark rings beneath his eyes. They were identical to the half circles shadowing her own. He'd missed Bobby and no doubt fretted over his absence. Half of her wished his sleepless nights had also been caused from missing her.

Hoping not to wake Bobby, she whispered. "JD."

His lashes flew up, and he went from asleep to instantly awake and on his feet in a matter of seconds. He stared at her and Bobby, his face filled with such relief her throat tightened. Shifting Bobby's dead weight to her other hip, she offered him a watery smile.

He clasped her face between his work-roughened hands, his tender gaze zeroing in on her mouth. She rose on tiptoe, meeting him in the middle. She anticipated a gentle, welcome-home kiss. She got so much more.

His mouth covered hers hungrily, his tongue tracing the seam of her lips. When he bit her lower lip, her knees buckled, and she sank against his chest. JD's strong arms pressed her and Bobby close as he devoured her mouth.

He kissed her as if he craved to inhale her, absorb her into his body, become one with her. How could a simple kiss make her feel so much?

Because it's not a simple kiss. The man is making love to your mouth.

"I missed you," he murmured.

She sighed, welcoming his tongue, shivering when his arm wrapped around her and stroked her back before settling low on her hip.

He dragged his lips across her cheek, her temple, then back to her mouth for one more long-slow-wet-thorough welcome home.

Bobby squirmed. JD stepped back and lifted him from her arms. His eyes, near black with desire, flashed with questions Josephine wasn't ready to answer. Still asleep, Bobby snuggled his head in the crook of his father's neck.

JD's hand cupped her cheek, and she turned her head, brushing a kiss over the center of his palm. His gaze smoldered. She doubted either of them had the strength to move.

Ask me to stay, JD. They'd never talked about extending her stay after bringing Bobby home. When he didn't say anything, her racing heart stumbled, then resumed beating at a much slower pace. She motioned toward the parking lot, visible through the windows at the far end of the terminal. "Did Blake follow you in the rental car?"

His face tightened. "No, why?"

"I had planned to turn in the car, then fly back to Chicago after the pilot refuels the plane."

His mouth thinned in determination. "Sorry. You'll have to send the pilot home without you." He didn't look sorry. In fact, he acted darned pleased with himself.

Her heart rate sped up again and a breathy excitement filled her. The smart thing to do would be to leave today. Before they reached the no-turning-back point. Before she laid her heart on the line.

Just because she was smart didn't mean she was a fool.

"I guess I could stay awhile longer."

Chapter Nine

JD hadn't realized he'd been barely breathing until Josephine returned from sending the company pilot on his way. He exhaled loudly, relief making his head woozy. He gestured to the small duffel next to Bobby's larger one. "Is that all you brought back with you?"

"Yes."

Refusing to give her a chance to change her mind he settled Bobby on his hip and grabbed the boy's bag with his free hand, then headed for the exit. "Good thing you left your boots and jeans at the ranch."

Josephine flung her carry-on over her shoulder and hurried after him, taking two steps to every one of his. "I think my jeans are in the laundry basket on the back porch. I'll throw a load of clothes in the machine tonight."

He grinned over his shoulder. "I already did the wash."

Her eyebrows shot up. "*You* did the laundry?"

"I see you're in a sassy mood today." Hell, not only did he do the laundry, he'd mopped the kitchen floor. Scrubbed the toilets and the bathtub. Swept the porch. Wiped down the stove and cleaned out the refrigerator. Amazing what a person could accomplish when afflicted with insomnia.

"Did you press my jeans?"

He stopped, allowing her to catch up. "You iron your jeans?"

"I had to. The dryer's broke, remember?"

He shook his head. "Sorry, darlin'. I draw the line at ironing."

Bobby stirred and lifted his head from JD's shoulder. "Hi, Dad."

JD's throat thickened at finally hearing his son call him *Dad.* "Hey, big guy. 'Bout time you woke up. I missed you."

"Me, too." Bobby laid his head back down on JD's shoulder. With his son in his arms, the world seemed right and good again.

Stepping aside, JD motioned for Josephine to precede him through the automatic doors. As they crossed the parking lot, his gaze zeroed in on the twitch of her hips and sexy little tush. He couldn't blame the hot, muggy air for the beads of sweat popping out across his forehead.

Bobby squinted against the bright sunlight. "I'm tired."

"But I want to hear about your trip." Heck, he'd welcome listening to his son brag about his grandparents, their big house and the stupid dog, Fi Fi. As long as Bobby remained awake, JD wouldn't be tempted to touch Josephine. Or kiss her.

Oh, man, was he dying to kiss her again.

They stopped next to the truck and he set the bag on the ground, then fished his keys from his pocket.

"Bobby needs to catch up on his sleep. We left rather early this morning." She set down her carry-on next to Bobby's bag.

"Yeah, Dad. The sky was dark, and I saw the moon."

"The moon?" He stared at Josephine, but her gaze skirted his face and landed on the hood of the truck.

Why leave so early if they flew the company plane? The stilted telephone conversation last night came to mind. Later, when he and Josephine had some alone time, he'd question her. He had a hunch he wasn't going to like what she had to say. He set Bobby on the pavement and opened the passenger door. "Tell me about this dog, Fi Fi."

"He bit me."

"Bit you—where?"

Bobby held up a finger.

JD examined the nonexistent wound. "Already healed." He ruffled the blond head. "Why did Fi Fi bite you?"

"I tried to take his bows out."

He got caught up in Josephine's smile and for a second lost himself in her eyes. When Bobby shuffled toward the front seat, JD grabbed the back of his shirt collar.

"Hold on, pardner. Let's run the air conditioner a minute before getting in." He went around to the driver's side and cranked the engine. Then he stowed the luggage in the truck bed and removed a blanket from the toolbox.

"Can I get in?" JD clamped a hand on the tiny shoulder and held him in place. "Let your aunt sit in the middle." Josephine's mouth opened, but he cut her off before she could protest. "I'll bunch up the blanket, and Bobby can sleep against the door."

Her gaze moved from the pavement, to the bench seat, back to the pavement. *This ought to be interesting.* The truck didn't have running boards.

JD shoved his hands in the pockets of his jeans and rocked back on his boot heels. He waited for her to ask for help. She didn't. No surprise there. After little sleep the past four days he was just ornery enough not to offer assistance.

She wore her trademark power skirt, silk blouse, hose and heels. After setting her purse on the seat, she stepped back, then raised her left leg as far as the tight material would permit.

He swallowed a chuckle. Her foot was four inches above the pavement. She had a long way to go.

Manicured pink fingernails inched the material a little higher on her thigh.

Nope. He grinned.

Her mouth thinned in determination. One thing for sure, the lady wasn't a quitter.

JD couldn't remember ever getting such a kick out of teasing a woman. *Because you've never felt this comfortable around a woman.* What was it about Josephine that made him let his guard down?

One more tug on the skirt revealed a good six inches of silk-covered thigh.

The smirk slid off his face.

Her toe bumped the truck frame, and she grumbled something about men and their toys. She yanked the skirt the rest of the way up her thigh.

Holy cow! She might as well have smacked him upside the head with her purse, he was so stunned. *Garters?* What else did she have on under her prim-and-proper business skirt?

With an unladylike grunt, she hoisted herself into the cab. He set Bobby next to her. "Aunt Josephine, I'm squished."

She let out an exasperated sigh and scooted over a few inches.

Fighting a grin, JD shut the door, walked around the hood and hopped in the driver's side.

Josephine Delaney was wearing a garter belt!

"Unless you're both starving," he said, "we'll wait until Rineland to gas up and grab snacks."

"Fine with me." Josephine caught him staring at her legs and slammed her knees together. He doubted even a crowbar could pry them apart.

"How about you, Bobby?" His son shook his head, yawned, then buried his face in the blanket. JD noticed Bobby hadn't put on his seat belt.

Automatically, he reached across Josephine to grasp the strap. His forearm grazed her breasts and she sucked in a deep breath, the movement pushing two, hard little nubs against his forearm. This time it was his turn to suck in a deep breath. Arousal played havoc with his coordination as he struggled to secure the belt. Finally, he managed to click the buckle and move the shoulder strap behind Bobby's body.

Purposefully, he angled his arm so his knuckles skimmed her blouse again when he sat back in his seat. *Amazing.* The light touch made her eyes glow and her face flush as though she'd run a marathon. Man, he bet she was something to stare at after a long night of loving.

His gaze slid to his sleeping son. He shouldn't. This wasn't the time or place. But he'd been an emotional wreck since last Friday. His nerves were shot to hell, and he admitted he wasn't thinking too clearly at the moment. He had to touch her. To taste her one more time before they hit the road.

Gripping the tight bun at the back of her head, he tugged until her chin came up and her lips bumped his. "God, I missed you." Her breath puffed across his cheek as he waited for a signal telling him she wanted his kiss.

She tilted her chin a fraction, bringing their mouths in line.

Thank goodness.

Gentle was out of the question. He crushed her lips beneath his at the same moment he cupped her breast. He thumbed her nipple, then tested the weight, the lushness, groaning at the way her flesh overflowed his hand. He'd been with his share of women over the years, but none of them drove him this wild. Made him feel reckless, needy.

Bobby sneezed, and the sound jarred JD back to reality. He moved his hand to her shoulder. Lips still clinging, he opened his eyes and felt the pull of those beautiful blue orbs watching him. She blinked, her lashes fluttering against his cheekbone like butterfly wings.

He frowned at the marks his beard stubble had left behind on her face. With the pad of his thumb, he caressed the angry red patch near the corner of her mouth.

"What are you waiting for, cowboy? Let's go home."

Home. Pleasure shot through him. He didn't know what road he and Josephine were headed down or how long she wanted to travel it with him. But damn, he was eager to see where it would take them.

He backed out of the parking spot and left the airport. The first few miles passed in silence, leaving time to think. Josephine was special—the kind of woman who deserved to be courted, not manhandled in the front seat of a truck with a sleeping kid next to her.

In truth, he had no experience wooing a woman of Josephine's upbringing. The only ladies he'd been around were the burger-and-beer types he encountered in roadside taverns and sleazy dance halls.

The silence stretched into fifteen minutes. He wasn't much of a talker and he sensed Josephine had a lot on her own mind. But he'd take a stab at conversation if only to keep from pulling over to the shoulder and kissing the daylights out of her again. "How was the flight?"

"Bumpy. We flew through a storm."

He thought she might elaborate and explain why she and Bobby had left so early in the morning, but she dropped her gaze to her lap and picked at a piece of lint on her skirt.

After a minute she lifted her head. "I didn't expect you to be waiting for us at the airport."

Should he lie and tell her he'd arrived minutes before their plane landed? He doubted she'd believe him. Not when she found him sawing logs in the chair. "I was a worried after the phone call last night. I came straight to the airport as soon as I woke up this morning."

Her fingers fluttered over his thigh, a barely there caress. If he hadn't glanced down, he'd have never known she'd touched him. "I'm glad you were waiting."

His body tensed at the whispered confession. This whole *whatever* he and Josephine had going on between them was nerve-racking as hell. Half the time he felt as though he was dangling from a stirrup, headfirst, over a fresh cow turd.

She sighed and the forlorn sound went straight to his heart. "Everything is such a mess, JD. I'm not sure where to begin."

"Don't begin anywhere. We'll talk later."

The relief on her face startled him. Exactly what had gone on in Chicago?

Josephine tucked the blanket around Bobby's shoulders and angled the air vent away from his face. Then she wiggled her fanny against the seat and turned toward him. Well, heck. He couldn't ignore an invitation like that. Setting his hand on her leg, he stroked her knee, enjoying the hot friction moving his thumb over the nylon created.

"Did you get the chance to compete in a rodeo while we were away?"

The breathy way she asked caused chaos in his jeans. "I considered riding in the Las Cruces rodeo." The money had been tempting, especially after he'd used up his savings to buy into the ranch, but the bloodthirst to compete wasn't in him anymore. Without the adrenaline rush, he wouldn't have lasted eight seconds in the saddle.

"Why didn't you?"

He shrugged. "Too much work around the ranch. Didn't want to leave Blake alone."

"I guess you'll catch the next one."

Hadn't she believed him when he'd insisted he'd never leave Bobby alone with Blake while he took off for a rodeo? He clenched the wheel tighter. "My days of rodeoing and breaking my ass, among other bones, are over."

"For good?" Her big blue eyes stared at him. He hoped she had a personal stake in his answer.

"I'm getting old." An impolite snort escaped her pretty mouth and he smiled. "Old by rodeo standards." He cast a peek at Bobby and sobered. "Bustin' broncs is dangerous. I've got a son to provide for."

Josephine's soft smile made him believe she understood exactly what he'd given up for his son—the money, the excitement and, yeah, the women. "I've been discussing with Blake the idea of breeding bulls on the side."

"Is there good money in raising bulls?"

Typical financier's question. "Yes, if you understand the business." He didn't share his thoughts much with anyone, but he sensed Josephine wouldn't ridicule him or his ideas. "I've done some research on the subject, compiled a list of breeders in the state, made a few calls and gathered some information."

"You did your homework."

His chest puffed up. "I've got a meeting with a breeder up in the Panhandle next month. He's going to show me his operation, give me a few pointers." He didn't tell her the ranch owner was the father of an up-and-coming bull rider he'd met two years ago.

"Will you sell off your cattle, then?"

Finding her interest flattering, he relaxed a little more each time she asked a question. "We'll stay in the cattle business because beef pays the bills. Breeding bulls will see us through the tough times. Drought, bad hay crop, disease." Hopefully, pay for Bobby's college education.

"I didn't realize how dicey ranching could get. Must be awfully stressful. Kind of like the stock market in my line of work. You start out the day with nine hundred thousand in your portfolio and end up with a hundred thousand after a disastrous turn on Wall Street."

Yeah, right. Keeping his attention on the road, he offered an unintelligible grunt. His and Blake's combined savings wouldn't pay the phone bill, let alone buy Wall Street stock. And speaking of nine hundred thousand, was that how much Josephine had in her portfolio? And what the hell was a portfolio, for Christ's sake? Some kind of glorified bank account?

He'd better keep his mouth shut before Josephine realized she was sitting next to a real live hayseed. Flipping on the blinker, he exited the highway. At the first light he turned right and pulled into the gas station. He parked the truck next to a pump and lowered the windows. "Need to use the rest room?"

"No, thanks."

"I'll pick up a couple of snacks to tide us over until we get to the ranch."

"Something chocolate." She smiled. "Please."

If she fluttered those eyelashes at him, she could ask for

anything and he'd do his damnedest to accommodate. "Chocolate. Got it."

He selected the gas, shoved the nozzle in the tank, then leaned against the truck bed and waited. Even with gas fumes filling the air, Josephine's sexy perfume scent clung to his clothes. The numbers on the pump blurred as his thoughts turned to the garter belt she was wearing under that straitlaced business skirt. All this *thinking* made his jeans feel as if they'd shrunk a size. He adjusted his pants with a discreet nudge and told himself to settle down.

By the time he paid for the gas and purchased drinks and a sack of junk food, he had his body under control. Back at the truck, he noticed Bobby still slept soundly. Josephine set the drinks in the cup holders, then rummaged through the bag and selected a chocolate candy bar.

She sank her teeth into a big bite. "Mmm."

"Taste good?"

"Heaven. Pure heaven," she groaned, licking her lips.

He couldn't help it—couldn't stop his body from reacting to every move, sigh, sound Josephine made. He was a drowning man who had no wish to be saved. Her ocean-blue gaze reeled him in until his chest crowded her against the seat and tiny puffs of chocolate-scented breath hit his chin.

A smudge of the treat clung to her lower lip. "You missed a spot." Slowly and thoroughly, he licked the sweet confection from her lip. When her mouth opened in surprise, he thrust his tongue inside. Chocolate velvet. Like the candy bar, Josephine was addicting.

"Aunt Josephine, why are you kissing Dad?"

She pulled back so fast their mouths made a loud popping sound. JD enjoyed the pink tint spreading across her face. With swollen lips, rumpled clothes and mussed hair, she resembled a sexy siren, not his son's aunt.

Straightening her shoulders, she smoothed her clothes and insisted, "I didn't kiss your father. He kissed me."

Bobby glanced from one adult to the other, visibly confused. "Oh."

"She's right, son. I'm afraid I started it."

Bobby shrugged, the kiss forgotten when his gaze landed on his aunt's candy bar. "I'm hungry."

Josephine offered him the bag. "Take your pick."

"Wow." Fully awake, Bobby rummaged through the bag.

Shifting into Drive, JD pulled back onto the access road and headed for the interstate. No chance now of sneaking another kiss from Josephine before they returned to the ranch. The next time he and she went at it, he'd find a place with no interruptions.

And there would be a next time.

"IF YOU'D LET ME EXPLAIN..." Josephine held the receiver away from her ear as her father bellowed in anger. After a few seconds, she added, "I gave JD my word I'd bring Bobby back to Texas today." The idea that her parents had gone behind her back and arranged for their grandson to stay indefinitely in Chicago made her blood run cold.

"Extending our grandson's visit was wrong?"

Guilt flooded her. Stealing her nephew away in the predawn hours had hurt her parents deeply. But she'd had no other choice. Every attempt to reason with them had failed, and in the end, they'd attacked her loyalty to the family. "You're Bobby's grandparents, not his guardian. You can't decide what's best for him."

More bellowing.

Drat! She could kick herself for waiting until nine o'clock in the evening to phone her father. She should have talked with him as soon as they'd arrived back at the ranch late in the afternoon. But Bobby had asked to ride Turnip with her and then demanded a bedtime story following dinner. After tucking him in, she'd spent an hour soaking in the tub, going over in her mind what she planned to say to her father.

"When are you coming home, Josephine?"

"I'm taking several vacation days."

"You'd better have my grandson with you when you do return."

"No, Father. I won't be bringing Bobby along." She watched the doorway, afraid Blake or JD would walk into the kitchen and overhear the conversation.

"I don't understand you, Josephine. This defiant attitude and uncooperativeness are shocking."

Josephine studied her outfit. Her father would probably suffer heart palpitations if he saw her in the tight jeans and slinky yellow halter top she wore now. Time to end the conversation before one of them said something they *really* couldn't take back. "I have to go."

"You leave me no choice. If you don't return my grandson to me, I'll fire you from the firm."

Swallowing back a heavy sigh, she mumbled, "Do what you have to." She'd figured her father would stoop this low to attempt to force her to do his bidding. Even though she'd been prepared for something like this, it still hurt. "I'll clear my desk the moment I return to Chicago."

"I'm serious, Josephine."

"So am I, Father. Goodbye." Gently, she hung up the receiver. In a trance, she went outside and sat on the porch swing, set her sandals on the edge of the seat, her arms wrapped around her legs and her chin resting on her knees. Ignoring the lump in her throat, she stared at the last streaks of orange and red across the horizon as day gave way to night. Sadly, even nature's beauty failed to console her.

Decisions needed to be made. She couldn't stay at the Rocking R forever and live the rest of her life off her investment portfolio. But concern for Bobby's future took precedence over her own worries. Her parents didn't have their grandson's best interests at heart, and once her father set his mind to something…

And what about her and JD? Her attraction to him jumbled her emotions. She was a grown woman—certainly old enough to have sex with a man if she chose to. But this *something* between them didn't *feel* like just sex.

No matter how hard she tried, she couldn't convince herself that all she felt for the man was lust. Not after spotting JD asleep in the chair at the airport with Bobby's teddy bear in his lap. Right then she'd realized her feelings for JD were deep and tangled.

She recalled the first time she'd met him in front of Lovie's café. Tall and proud, he'd walked toward her with purposeful strides, his jaw tight with determination. She'd pretended his arrogance had had no effect on her, but her insides had trembled at all the masculinity he'd shoved in her face. His sheer physical presence had taken her breath away.

Broad shoulders had blocked the sun from her eyes, allowing her a close look at his strong jaw, long hair and grim mouth. His utter maleness had called out to her feminine side. Smiling to herself, she thought it had been too bad he'd opened his mouth and ruined the effect.

His rudeness had bothered her until she'd caught a glimpse of his trembling fingers when he'd reached for the café door. She'd suspected his anger had come from his fear of losing Bobby. She'd received no satisfaction in recognizing the power she'd held over him. As a matter of fact, JD had stolen a little piece of her heart when she'd witnessed his vulnerability.

Later, when they'd talked in the barn and he'd confessed that his parents hadn't wanted him, Josephine had been drawn even closer to JD. She'd felt his pain as though it were her own. How she'd wanted to take him in her arms and reassure him...convince him of his goodness, his worthiness as a human being. But how could she have, when she struggled with the same issue herself? She may have grown up with parents, but she'd known only conditional love. Neither of their early childhoods had been filled with warmth and security.

There were other instances when she'd been near JD that

something in her heart had shifted and expanded. Even though her feelings for him were deep, she didn't dare put a label on them.

She and JD were worlds apart in some ways and similar in others. She was city; he was country. She considered herself intense and demanding; JD was laid-back and accepting. Yet she sensed in him the same yearning to be loved she hadn't admitted existed in her until lately.

And then there was Bobby. They both loved him. She'd be a liar if she didn't admit she'd pictured the three of them as a family when she'd caught herself daydreaming in her office while back in Chicago.

Desperately, she yearned to lose herself in JD, his touch, his warmth. Although she considered herself bright, intelligent, driven and successful, where matters of the heart were concerned, she had the experience of an intern in the Wall Street Exchange program. Even if she were willing to risk her heart for this man, the odds of everything working out in the end were stacked against them.

The creak of the screen door caught her attention and JD stepped onto the porch, fresh from the shower, wearing nothing but a faded pair of Levi's and his favorite boots.

Her heart stuttered, then struck up a brisk tempo. JD without a shirt was a sight every woman deserved to see once in her lifetime. He moved toward her, a solid, hairless, tanned wall of muscle, bunching and rippling.

A leather thong held his gleaming damp hair away from his face, accentuating the strong angles and hollows. She longed to set the silky mass free, to let the strands slide through her fingers, sweep across her heated flesh.

He stopped inches from the swing. His deep brown eyes flashed with desire. Desire for her. Desire to finish what he'd started in the truck hours ago. His nostrils flared as he caught her scent. A delicious tingle raced down her thighs. Hardly breathing…she waited.

He held out a hand.

No pretty words. No promises.

She stared at his hand, imagining the long, callused fingers trailing over her breasts, her stomach. Her heart and mind waged a fierce battle. Taking this next step with JD was risky.

But so was life.

Sliding her fingers across his rough-skinned palm, she clasped his hand. His strong, reassuring grip convinced her this was meant to be. At least for tonight.

On shaky legs, she rose from the swing. He grabbed her upper arm, steadying her swaying body. His intimate gaze clung to her face as he set his hand above her breast, then pressed her hand to his heart. The tender moment brought tears to her eyes.

Inching closer, she wrapped her arms around his waist and snuggled against him. His soap-scented skin made her lightheaded. With her mouth and nose she nuzzled his smooth, hot flesh. She felt his lips against her hair, the lightest of caresses, before he took her hand and led her off the porch and down to the barn.

When she'd dreamed of making love with JD, she'd imagined a big, comfy bed, not a smelly barn. But they couldn't take the chance Bobby or Blake might wake in the middle of the night and discover them in bed together. And truthfully, she yearned for JD so badly that he could take her standing up against a stall door, and she'd be helpless to stop him.

Once inside the barn he lowered his head and softly moved his mouth over hers. Her eyes burned at the gentleness of the caress. He left her standing in a daze while he grabbed a saddle and a huge camping pack. Side by side, they left the barn and walked to the corral, where Warrior waited.

After saddling the stallion, he strapped the camping pack to the back of the horse, then turned to her. He didn't say a word. Just stood there, strong, powerful and proud. Understanding dawned. If she planned to change her mind, this was her chance. The heat in JD's stare warned there would be no turning back for either of them once they rode away together. His noble gesture made Josephine ache to offer him her heart for safekeeping.

She held out her arms, and he visibly shuddered before lifting her onto the horse. He murmured to the skittish stallion, and immediately the animal calmed. A hot tremor shook Josephine as she imagined what words JD would whisper in her ear this night.

He hoisted himself up behind her. "Scoot back."

Scoot back? There wasn't an inch of space left between them. When she hesitated, he lifted her bottom until she sat in his lap. In this position, there was no mistaking his desire for her.

Clicking his tongue, he guided the horse out of the corral, then leaned forward and ordered against her cheek, "Latch the gate."

As she reached down to flip the lock, her hips flexed against his arousal. His hand tightened over her stomach as he pressed an openmouthed kiss to the back of her neck and groaned. The sound of his moan, the feel of his touch, made sitting still nearly impossible.

At a slow walk, JD maneuvered Warrior through the wooded land behind the barn. The gentle sway of the stallion's rhythm lulled her, and she sank against JD's chest, letting him take all her weight. "Where are we going?" She searched the darkness ahead.

"Be patient." The arm around her middle moved upward, settling under her breasts. She squirmed, trying to bring her flesh in contact with his masculine fingers.

A chuckle rumbled in his chest. Then his mouth was on her neck, nibbling the tender patch of skin behind her ear. When he suckled her earlobe and bit tenderly, she arched away from his chest, her head falling back on his shoulder as she absorbed the passionate vibrations tingling through her body.

His hand lifted her breast, squeezed and molded the soft

flesh until her bones threatened to melt. She raised her arms and wrapped them around JD's neck. His lips nuzzled her cheek, the edge of her jaw, then suddenly, he gripped her ponytail and tugged her toward him.

His mouth…hungry…searching…demanding…

The horse's gait created a delicious friction, and moisture pooled between her thighs. Never before had she felt this intense need.

JD moved his hand between her thighs. Slow and steady, the rocking rhythm of the horse and his palm pressed against her heated core brought her body dangerously close to exploding.

She yanked the rawhide strap from his hair and grabbed fistfuls of the silky dark mass, bringing the strands forward to fall across her face and shoulders. Her hips twisted as she *begged* for more, *needed* more.

Then his hand was gone, leaving her trembling and shaky. Softly spoken Spanish words floated past her ear, soothing her ragged nerves.

"Hang on, darlin'." He freed her ponytail, tightened his hold around her middle, then spurred the horse to a gallop.

The smell of muggy-night air blasted their faces as they raced through the darkness. Gusts of wind lifted their hair high into the air, entangling blond strands with inky black. The fierce wildness of the moment stole her breath.

As they approached an outcrop of craggy rock, he slowed the horse to a walk. The sound of gurgling water came from somewhere behind the rocks. JD dismounted, then dragged her off the horse after him. He pulled her close, kissing her as if he was afraid she'd change her mind.

The throb between her thighs flared to life again. He crowded her, flexing his hips against her stomach, showing her how much he desired her. Then his tongue slid into her mouth, matching the rhythm of his hips.

Her hands caressed his heated skin, slick with perspiration. When her nail caught on a nipple, he groaned. She repeated the caress, then trailed her fingers lower to the snap on his jeans. She fumbled with the fastener, gave up and wiggled her fingertips beneath the waistband. He sucked in his stomach, and her hand inched lower until she managed to sneak her fingertips under the waistband of his B.V.D.s.

He pressed his mouth to her temple. "Oh, darlin'. I am so hot for you."

"Me, too." She removed her hand from his pants and pressed her palm to the front of his jeans, running a fingernail down the hard length of him. His erection jumped under the denim, and he lurched out of reach.

"Damn. If I don't get a hold of myself, I'll take you right under the horse."

He walked the animal several yards away, where he tied the reins to a tree limb. He returned with the backpack, then led her toward an opening in the rock. "Stay here." Taking a flashlight from the pack, he disappeared through the opening. He returned in less than a minute. "Coast is clear."

She hesitated. "What's in there?"

He flashed his gleaming white teeth. "Our secret hideaway."

She followed him inside, pleasantly surprised at the clean, cool cave. The smell of damp earth filled the small chamber. He knelt on the stone floor and rummaged through the backpack. After removing a battery-operated lamp, he set the light in the far corner. The intimate glow cast their shadows against the rock walls. JD's form appeared larger than life huddled over the pack. Next, he removed a thick quilt and spread the material across the hard ground.

Their labored breathing echoed inside the intimate enclosure, interrupted only by an occasional wind gust whistling through the opening in the rock. Seconds ticked by and still he made no move to touch her.

She licked her suddenly dry lips. "Have you changed your mind?"

Chapter Ten

"Not on your life, babe." JD's pulse jumped at the challenging gleam in Josephine's eyes. Like wavy heat lines off hot blacktop, her body shimmered with desire.

"Then why are you way over there when I'm way over here?" She inched forward across the blanket.

"Don't move."

She froze.

"I want to look before I touch." The dim lamp cast an ethereal glow inside their cozy quarters. Hair flowing loose around her shoulders, Josephine resembled an angel more than a corporate career woman. Her small stature, fine porcelain skin and delicate shape of her face reminded JD to treat her with great care and reverence.

She deserved better than a tumble in a cave with a rough-around-the-edges man, but he didn't have the strength to deny her or him what he figured would be one hell of a ride. Better than the ride that had earned him a national rodeo title six years ago.

Rising up on her knees, Josephine gathered the hem of her tank top, exposing her midriff. "Maybe you'd like a peek at the goods?" Switching from angel to siren, she whisked the T-shirt over her head.

She wore only a barely there melon-colored lace bra and a pair of Wranglers, and JD swore he'd never seen anything so sexy in his life. What a shame she hid those feminine curves beneath loose blouses and suit jackets. Man, oh, man, he couldn't wait to bury his face in all her softness.

Her hands went to the snap on her jeans.

"Slow down, honey." He cleared the hoarseness from his throat and edged nearer. The heady combination of perfume and damp clay wrapped them in an earthy, sultry cloud. Lightly, he ran his hands over her hair, skimming the silky strands. Then he dipped his head and nuzzled the warm skin behind her ear.

He could spend hours smelling her, touching her. But his lips grew restless. With his mouth, he kissed a trail down her neck. When he laved the hollow at the base of her throat, she purred like a feline and rubbed herself against him.

Wrapping his arms around her, he fitted her close until her heart pulsed against his bare chest. Her nails raked his back and he groaned, battling the urge to lay her down and put an end to this torture.

"Kiss me, JD."

Eager to please, he clasped her head between his hands and began an all-out assault on her mouth. Forget slow and easy. He wanted wet, open and lots of tongue. He could have kissed her this way for hours, if not for the need to breathe. He lifted his lips a fraction and their moist breath caressed each other's faces as they gulped oxygen.

When he smoothed his hands up her rib cage, her blue eyes turned smoky and drowsy. He rubbed his thumb over a lace-covered nipple. Her gaze clung to his, allowing him to witness how his touch excited her. Humbled by her openness, he wished he could be all she sought in a man.

With a flick of his fingers he opened the bra's clasp and slid the silky straps off her shoulders and down her arms. He urged her to stand, then nuzzled her belly button. After removing her sandals, he worked the tight denims over her hips and down her thighs. Each inch of exposed flesh demanded attention from both his hands and mouth. When she stood before him in nothing but her panties, he rocked back on his heels and stared at her. *Magnificent.* "You're so damn lovely."

She reached for the snap on his jeans. "Let's see how lovely you are."

Chuckling, he swatted her hands away and stood. If he let her touch him in his current state of arousal their lovemaking would last about as long as a TV commercial. He removed his boots and set them to the side, then shucked his jeans and underwear, dropping them on top of Josephine's clothes at the bottom of the blanket.

He hoped his body pleased her. He hadn't been with as many women as Josephine probably assumed. Those he had slept with had assured him he had a nice body. But Josephine's opinion was the only one he cared about.

Inching nearer, she trailed her fingertips across his shoulders, down his arms and over his chest. Everywhere her fingers touched his skin burst into flames. Her gaze dropped below his waist and he sucked in a breath when she wrapped her fingers around him and firmly stroked.

"C'mere, honey." He tugged her down to the blanket. Clasping both her wrists in one hand, he raised her arms above her head. "I get to go first."

Heaven. Sweet heaven. Placing tiny kisses in a circle pattern over her skin, he drank his fill of her. She moaned her appreciation and squirmed, thrusting her hips, her body begging him not to stop.

With a shaking hand, he nudged her panties down her hips and over her knees. Josephine wiggled the skimpy material the rest of the way off with her pink-painted toes. He stared at the triangle of honey-colored hair between her thighs, awed and amazed he and this woman had come this far. His fingers feathered across the curls, testing the softness, the thickness. He lifted his gaze and a tiny burst of excitement raced along his spine when he caught her watching his hand.

Releasing her wrists, he gently, reverently, kissed the downy curls. Her fingers threaded through his hair, pulling the long strands over her breasts. He nipped her stomach, then kissed his way up her body until he reached her mouth, and murmured, "Next time you're going to wear those black garters for me." He concentrated on her mouth, trying to burn the warm, sweet taste of her into his memory.

He thrust a finger inside her and her smoky eyes ignited. Her hips rose and fell in rhythm with his hand, her labored breathing more sensuous than any love song he'd ever heard. Gasping, she pressed herself against his hand, then pulled away—her body and mind opposing forces, battling toward completion. He ached to see her shatter in his arms like a million falling stars, then to soar into the heavens with her.

"I can't." She pushed against his shoulders. "It's too much, JD."

He threw a leg over her thigh to keep her still beneath him and clutched a fistful of her hair. "Josie."

Her eyes bright with pleasure-pain begged for relief.

"Let yourself go, honey. I'll keep you safe in my arms." He swallowed the thickness in his throat as he watched the struggle wage in her blue eyes. He wouldn't ask, but by her reaction moments ago, he assumed she'd never had an orgasm. He didn't have a whole lot to offer this woman, but if she'd allow him, he would set free the secrets of her body. Concentrating on her breasts, he loved them with his mouth, lips, tongue. "Please, baby. Trust me."

Curling her arms around his neck, she coaxed him up her body until he lay completely on top of her. She kissed him with such urgency his heart raced and his muscles shook with the effort to keep from plunging into her and ending his torment. While his mouth kept her lips busy, his hands went back to work, unleashing the treasure hidden between her thighs.

She gasped for breath, panted in his face, moaned in her throat. "I can't, I can't."

"Yes," he breathed into her mouth. His fingers moved in circles around the swollen nub until his hand ached. "You." He touched her very core. "Can."

He swallowed her choked cry, his fingers still moving, drawing out every last tremor and aftershock quivering through her body. He rested his head on her breasts, savoring the sensation of her heart thundering beneath his ear. If *this* was as far as things ever went between them, he'd consider himself a blessed man. Never in his life had he shared a moment this intimate, this fulfilling, with a woman. Never had he cared to.

Why now? Why Josie?

Rolling to his back, he pulled her close. She studied him, her face glowing with warmth and something he yearned to call love but didn't dare. Then she rested her head on his shoulder and stretched lazily atop his body. With one fingernail, she traced designs on his stomach and along his upper thigh, sending little jolts through his nervous system. His body throbbed painfully, but he was too choked up to do anything about it.

Damn. This woman tore him up inside. He wanted to tell her how much her trust meant to him but didn't for fear he'd say something stupid or embarrassing.

She placed a tender kiss on the underside of his jaw. "Thank you."

He nuzzled her hair. "For what?"

"For not listening to me."

He chuckled. "I'll have to try that more often."

He felt her smile against his skin. "Only in bed." Her hand roamed around his waist, across his stomach, then hovered over his erection. He tensed, anticipating her touch.

"Is that my ribbon?" With an elbow in his gut, she shoved herself into a sitting position, knocking the air from his lungs. She snatched the ribbon sticking out of his pant's pocket and dangled it in front of his face.

Stunned, he could do little more than stare at the flimsy piece of fluff inches above his nose. "You left it behind."

She pressed the piece of lace to her heart. "You carried this around in your pocket while I was gone?" The awe in her question made him squirm. Then she turned her back to him, but not before he caught the mischievous smile tugging the corners of her mouth. An instant later he jerked—a specific part of his body, that is—when she dragged the ribbon over his erection.

"Mmm. Feels good?"

He couldn't breathe, let alone speak. He nodded dumbly as she trailed the silky lace over his sensitized flesh. Hell, he was so aroused she could drag an emery board across his skin and he wouldn't complain.

"All done."

He stared down his body, then groaned. *Brat.*

"My very own gift-wrapped man." Her eyes sparkled with humor and JD didn't have the heart to object to the fancy bow she'd tied at the base of his erection. He grabbed her by the arms and flipped her under him, surprised and pleased to discover Josephine had a playful side in bed.

"Time to see how your present works, honey." He reached behind him and dug through his jeans until his fingers came in contact with the condom he'd brought along. He reached for the ribbon.

"No. Leave it."

He started to protest, then she tongue kissed him and he decided…what the hell? He rolled on the condom and nudged her thighs apart. He checked to make sure she was ready for him, and his fingers came away glistening with her heat.

As she guided him into her body, he clenched his teeth at the unexpected tightness of her. That she wasn't experienced filled him with a surge of possessiveness.

Inch by inch, he moved deeper. Her hips thrust forward. *Easy, babe.* With his knee, he spread her thighs wider, then buried himself inside her. He exhaled loudly and shuddered. His arms trembled from holding himself above her and beads of sweat popped out across his forehead. The wonder on Josephine's face made every painful sensation bearable as he battled to control his body.

Her eager moan floated past his ear, and she wiggled her hips beneath him. He started out slow, his movements gentle, controlled. But then she went a little wild, and he gave in to the urge to pump into her, stroke after stroke, until his stomach tensed and he felt the burning heat along his inner thighs. Her body tightened around him as she struggled to keep pace. He couldn't hold out much longer, so he reached between their bodies and touched her at the same time he latched on to her nipple.

Her back arched off the blanket, and she came apart in his arms as he exploded inside her.

"Josie. Ah, Josie."

HE'D REALLY SCREWED up. Big time.

JD absently stroked Josephine's bare hip, then adjusted her leg to fit more snugly between his thighs. Holding her felt so right and so wrong at the same time.

Stupidly, he'd believed one bout of hot-and-heavy sex would exorcise Josephine from his system. He hadn't counted on her breaking through his defenses and slipping under his skin. *Way under.* But she had. All of her, from the top of her silky head to the bottom of her painted toenails and every inch in between, tangled his insides in knots.

This wasn't sex. For the first time in his life he'd made love to a woman, connected with her on a level he'd never felt. His explosive climax had been so powerful that for one infinitesimal second he'd left his body and gone into Josephine's to become one person with her.

Thinking about the encounter brought a lump to his throat. To have felt so deeply with a woman he couldn't have was pure hell.

They were from different worlds, brought together because of a small boy. If Bobby had never existed and he and Josephine had met under different circumstances, she wouldn't have given him a second glance, much less a second thought.

She was upper-crust society, intelligent. She had places to go, things to see, business worlds to conquer. He wished with all his being he had something to offer a woman of her caliber.

His chest ached with bitterness. He couldn't offer her a damn thing but a good lay. When he contemplated her returning to Chicago his lungs seized up and quit working. *Love.* He tossed the word around his brain a bit but refused to call what he shared with Josie love. No use getting excited over something he knew so little about. Besides, once he put a label on what he felt for her, he'd never be the same man again. Best to concentrate on the other things he felt for this woman.

He admired Josie. Respected her. Even feared her.

Feared what she made him feel. Until tonight, until Josie, he realized he hadn't dealt with his parents' abandonment. His entire life he'd shoved the hurt and anger to the farthest corner of his heart, locked the pain away and buried the key.

The passionate, giving woman in his arms had finagled a way into his heart, found the secret room and bulldozed the door down, making him realize how badly he still yearned to feel worthy, important.

She sprawled on top of him, crossed her arms over his chest and rested her chin on top of her hands. Then stared him in the eye. "Got everything figured out?"

One hand stroked her back; the other, tangled in her hair. "No, but I'm working on it."

"Maybe I can help." Josephine kissed his nipple, then flashed a sexy smile, hoping to chase away whatever troubling notions had invaded JD's mind after their lovemaking.

"You can't help." His mouth curved up at the corners. "You're the problem." He rolled out from under her, disposed of the condom, then gathered her in his arms again. "When are you heading back to Chicago?"

Her heart lurched. Did he regret making love to her?

Desperate to change the conversation, she kissed him. Poured her heart and soul into the act. When at last he relaxed beneath her, she released his mouth, tracing his slightly swollen lips with her fingertip.

When he began kissing a path straight to her breasts, she scrambled away.

Lips twitching, he crossed his arms behind his head. "Something on your mind?"

She wrinkled her nose. "We should talk about what just happened."

A tormented groan rumbled through his chest. "Don't get emotional on me. We shared some great sex, Josephine. Nothing more. Just sex."

Josephine? What happened to Josie?

She searched his face for the truth and caught a glimpse of such hunger, such yearning, that her breath stalled in her chest. *Liar.* What they'd shared together had been more than mind-blowing sex. He'd felt the connection, the intimacy, the oneness she'd also experienced. He was just too scared to admit he might be falling for her.

Wrapping both arms around her, he kissed her cheek. Sometimes the big, macho, arrogant cowboy could bring her to tears with his tenderness.

He cleared his throat. "Tell me how the visit with your folks went."

She considered saying something flippant, making up a lie, but JD deserved the truth. He'd trusted her enough to allow her to take Bobby back to Chicago to meet his grandparents. In turn, she had to trust him. Trust him to understand and forgive her motives. "The trip didn't go well."

After a long pause, he expelled a harsh breath across the top of her head. "What happened?"

Burrowing her face between his neck and shoulder, she prayed for the right words. "Please believe me when I tell you I had good intentions. Even though I saw for myself how content Bobby was at the ranch, what a good father you were, part of me still believed my nephew deserved better."

Wanting his kiss, his reassurance, she moved her mouth toward his, but he turned his head and her lips skimmed his jaw. In one smooth motion, he lifted her from him, deposited her on the blanket, then sat with his back to her. He drew his legs up and clasped his arms around his knees. "Go on."

Feeling chilly and lost without his touch, Josephine hugged herself. "I believed Bobby deserved the things my parents had given me and Cassandra. A great education, travel opportunities, cultural experiences. But first, I had to be sure my parents were capable of loving Bobby the right way."

"The right way?" He glanced over his shoulder and his confused expression encouraged her to continue.

Her need to touch him outweighed her fear of rejection as she inched forward and pressed her cheek to his shoulder. She couldn't say for sure if the unsettling trip home or this man, whom she'd unintentionally hurt, caused the ache around her heart. A little of both, she supposed.

The brush of his hand on the back of her head made her eyes water. "I wanted to be sure my parents were capable of loving Bobby for who he is and not for who they want him to be."

"And..."

"The trip was a bust." She cringed when her voice cracked.

JD pulled her around him and set her in his lap, holding her as if she were a child suffering from a hellish nightmare.

"Everything makes sense now." She sniffed. "I understand why Cassandra ran away from the family."

"Why did your sister leave Chicago and never return?"

"Because she'd always wanted to be an actress but my parents dismissed her dream as childish. If they'd supported her wish to become an actress she probably wouldn't have ended up doing porn movies."

"I still don't understand why she didn't tell your family about Bobby."

"She knew our parents were too controlling and didn't want that for her son."

"What about you, Josie? What do you want from your parents?"

She blinked back the hot tears clinging to her lashes. "Love. I just wanted to be loved, JD."

"Ah, darlin'." He hugged her close, then kissed the top of her head.

"I'm not sure my parents are capable of unconditional love." She pushed away from JD's chest. "My father wants to enroll Bobby in a boys' military school in Maine."

"What?" JD popped off the blanket so fast Josephine tumbled from his lap and landed in a heap at his feet.

"I told them Bobby was happy at the ranch. I insisted you and he had a great relationship. They wouldn't listen."

Grasping her upper arms, he hauled her to her feet. "Tell me the truth. What kind of chance does your father have of gaining custody of Bobby?"

She ached at the fear shadowing his features. "He has a lot of influence, JD. A lot of money."

He whipped away, his hair flying up in the air before settling across his shoulders. "That's illegal. He can't use influence and money to buy his grandson."

She tugged his arm until he faced her. "I think they can." She touched the nerve pulsing along the right side of his jaw. "If not soon, then later. My father won't give up."

"Why, Josie? Why?"

"Because my father's a competitor. You tell him he can't have something, and he'll do everything he can to prove you wrong."

"This is all a game to him?"

"No. In some twisted way my father really does believe he can offer Bobby a better life."

"Tell me what to do." JD's rusty voice sliced through her.

Even if the judge decided in favor of JD, her parents would continue to fight. After spending a few years in her father's company, she was well aware he didn't raise the white flag willingly.

JD grasped her face between his hands, the pleading expression in his eyes almost bringing her to her knees. "Tell me how to fight your father."

"I know of only one solution to prevent my father from gaining custody of Bobby."

His fingers bit into her flesh. "I'll do anything to keep my son."

"Marry me."

What?

"Marry me."

She's serious. Speechless, JD dropped his hands from her face, cringing at the red imprint his fingers left on her skin.

"You're Bobby's father, JD. He deserves to be raised by *you.*"

"But marriage?"

"The courts will frown upon you not having a wife and Bobby not having a mother."

"Bobby has me. He can survive without a mother." He had to glance away before Josie read the truth in his eyes—that his son did deserve a nurturing female in his life. JD hadn't been blind to the way Bobby had attached himself to his aunt. Basked in her smiles, her touches. Her attention. Stupidly, he'd believed he'd always be enough for the boy—admitting he wasn't hurt like hell.

"What better person to be Bobby's mother than his biological aunt?"

"Josephine—"

"Don't call me that!"

Shocked at her outburst, he frowned. "Call you what?"

"Josephine."

"Huh?"

She stamped her foot like a stubborn child. "I like Josie better."

When her blue eyes welled with tears, he stifled a curse and caressed the fading marks he'd left on her skin. He'd hurt her with his less-than-warm response to her marriage proposal. "Josie. I realize what you're trying to do, and I appreciate the hell out of the gesture, but you can't be serious."

A tear rolled down her cheek and pooled against his finger. "Why not?"

He wished he could make her hurt disappear. "What we did, Josie…being with you…" *Crap.* "I think you're confusing great sex with—"

She jerked as if he'd slapped her. "Is that all I was—a great lay?"

He ignored her crass question and gestured around him. "Don't you understand? This isn't the life for you."

She hauled her bare foot back and he braced himself for the blow. He deserved it. Her toes connected with his shin and he winced.

"No kidding. I don't know of any woman who wants to live in a cave."

He smothered a grin behind his hand. She had a habit of knocking him sideways when he least expected. He had to make her see sense. "You're smart, well educated, a successful career woman. What the hell are you going to do stuck on a ranch with a cowboy the rest of your life?"

Her face softened. When she opened her mouth to answer, he cut her off. "This way of life is new. Different. But after six months, maybe a year, you'll be antsy, in need of excitement." He pulled her into his arms. "I want you to understand how much your generosity means to me."

"Generosity be damned." She pushed away from him. "Have you considered what might happen to Bobby if you die?"

He felt the blood drain from his face. "Nothing's going to happen to me."

"Do you have a will?"

"I had one made a few months ago. Blake's agreed to take care of Bobby if anything happens to me."

"I'm not trying to be insensitive, but Blake's over seventy. He's not going to be around forever."

She was trying to scare him. JD bet she was a force to be reckoned with in the boardroom.

"An old man like Blake won't stand a chance in court against my father's hotshot lawyers if something happens to you."

He forced his attention away from her heaving chest. "I'm having a hell of a time carrying on this conversation with both of us butt naked."

"Actually, I'm kind of enjoying our butt nakedness."

He grinned, feeling some of the tension drain out of him. He opened his arms and she flung herself at him. He skimmed his hands up and down her back, memorizing the feel of her curves. Her scent, her softness.

"Let me get this straight," he murmured against her neck. "You're willing to marry me for Bobby's sake?"

Leaning back, she stared up at him. "Yes."

He wanted to ask, his heart ached to know, if she felt anything more than sexual attraction for him. He didn't dare. Because if she answered no, then he could no longer pretend she might one day learn to love him.

"Bobby shouldn't have to suffer through the same childhood Cassandra and I experienced. He deserves better."

Smoothing a strand of hair behind her ear, he asked, "What about your job?"

"I'll figure out something. I can always do consulting work."

"Your parents will fight you all the way."

"They can't win this one."

JD wasn't so sure. Tired of arguing, he kissed her. He meant the kiss to be comforting, but the way she melted against him kindled the fire that hadn't fully extinguished from their previous lovemaking. He pulled her down to the blanket, rolling her underneath him. Wanting to forget everything save this woman. When he moved on top of her, she clamped her thighs shut.

"Answer me first. Will you marry me, JD?"

Chapter Eleven

"Seems things have changed between you and Josephine since she and Bobby returned from Chicago." Blake sauntered up to the corral and propped a boot on the lower rail.

Keeping his gaze on Josie and Bobby riding double inside the fenced circle, JD grinned. "That obvious, huh?"

"Obvious? Heck, boy. If your chest stuck out much more, I'd mistake you for a barnyard cock."

JD didn't mind the razzing. In truth, since he and Josie had returned from their camping excursion a little over a week ago, he couldn't remember a time in his life he'd felt this…good inside. Making love with Josie had touched him deeply. He'd felt things he hadn't known he was capable of feeling.

"She's special, Blake." Right then, Josie flashed a sassy smile, and he wished he could grab her hand and drag her behind the barn, where he'd spend a good hour kissing the daylights out of her.

Blake waved to Bobby. "How long is she stayin'?"

"I'm not sure." He told the truth. Twice, Josie had brought up the subject of her returning to Chicago, but he'd distracted her with kisses, caresses, bold words in her ear, and had even gone as far as making love to her in the barn late one night.

He wasn't ready to let her go. Not yet. Deep in his gut, he feared that when she drove away in the rental car she'd leave a hole in the middle of his heart the size of Texas. Josie's presence at the ranch made time slow to a crawl. The days passed like a lazy creek trickling along in no hurry to get to anywhere.

Although he'd only known Josie a short while, imagining life without her hurt. He didn't want to think about never again watching her hips sway as she listened to the radio while washing dishes. Never again sitting together on the porch swing, enjoying the sunset. Never again catching one of her meet-me-in-the-barn smiles across the supper table.

He'd been so certain that if he made love to her as often as he was physically capable of, he'd work this driving need for her out of his system. The plan had backfired. Making love to Josie was like a drug addiction—the more he did…the more he wanted…the more he had to have her.

Will you marry me?

Her proposal had knocked his legs right out from under him. His throat had swelled and his eyes had burned as though he'd stared at the sun too long. For the first time in his life he'd felt joy. But the feeling had lasted only a few moments. Until he'd realized she hadn't uttered a word about marrying him because she'd loved him.

Josie was willing to marry him for Bobby's sake.

The fact that he loved his son more than life itself eased some of the sting of her unprofessed feelings for him. At night, after they'd made love, he'd hold her and wait for her to say the words. To tell him how she really felt about him. They never came. Not that love *mattered.* He'd survived an important part of his life without the emotion; he could do it again, easy.

He contented himself with the belief Josie felt *something* for him. She wasn't the kind of woman to jump in the sack with any slick Mick. And he understood enough about life to realize love didn't always guarantee a successful marriage.

As a couple, they had other things going for them. They cared about each other. They both loved Bobby and sought to do what was in the boy's best interest. And he and Josie were great in bed together. All things considered, they had a decent shot at making a nice family.

But how long would their *nice family* last?

A month. Maybe a year. Again, the same questions came: how long before Josie became bored with him and ranch life? How long before she realized she missed her career, or the fast pace of city life? Fancy restaurants?

How long before she walks out on you and Bobby?

Blake nudged his arm. "Ask her to stay."

"Josie knows she's welcome for as long as..." *Forever.*

Old eyes studied JD. "About time you stop running from yourself."

His insides froze. In all the years he'd lived with the rancher, Blake had never spoken so boldly.

"I took you in. Put a roof over your head. Tried showin' you I care." Blake poked a finger in JD's chest. "But you won't let no one in."

JD stared down at the knobby finger, intense anguish sweeping through him.

"That little gal—" he motioned toward Josie with his head "—is the only person you've allowed to get close to you. You're a fool if you let her slip away." He pulled his finger out of JD's chest. "I'm headin' into town. I'll take Bobby along and get him lunch at the café. Should be gone most of the afternoon."

Swallowing hard, JD searched for the words Blake deserved to hear. Words that had been in JD's heart for a long time but had never found their way past his lips.

Clasping the younger man's shoulder, Blake nodded in understanding. "I know, son. I know." He ambled toward the pickup parked down by the barn. "I'm leavin' in ten minutes."

JD had Bobby ready in five. He and Josie waved as the truck disappeared from sight.

She wrinkled her nose at him. "I suppose you have chores?"

Taking a step closer, he fingered the collar of her emerald-green T-shirt. "Yeah. I have a chore that needs my immediate attention."

Fluttering her lashes, she asked, "Can it wait until later?"

He inched closer, his thigh bumping her hip. "Nope. Have to do it right now."

Stepping out of reach, she lifted her chin. "Let me guess. You need my help."

"Oh, babe, do I ever."

She spun, her loose hair slapping him across the face, and sprinted toward the house, laughter trailing in her wake.

He stood grinning like a fool, amazed how this bright, intelligent little dynamo had turned his days upside down and his nights inside out. Every moment with her made him realize how much she'd wormed her way into his day-to-day existence.

Excitement pumped through his blood as he headed for the side of the house like a hound chasing the scent of a fox. His strides ate up the distance between them, but he hung back, content to watch her rounded fanny wiggle-waggle up the porch steps. His fingertips brushed the material of her shirt as she opened the screen door and scrambled inside the utility porch.

Grasping her by the elbow, he hauled her against his chest, enjoying the sound of her laughter as they both struggled to catch their breath.

Fingers tracing the outline of his mouth, she murmured, "You have a beautiful smile."

"Ah, Josie," he growled, grinding his hips against her. His body acted as if months, not hours, had passed since he'd last made love to her. "I can't get enough of you." He swooped down for a quick kiss, but she opened her mouth and moved her tongue against his in a way that threatened to send him to his knees. He clutched her waist and pulled her along as he walked backward into the kitchen, stopping only when the counter got in the way. He spread his thighs, and she squirmed between them, fitting their bodies nice and snug together.

"Upstairs."

She shook her head. "Here. Now."

Her words inflamed him. He figured he had about ten seconds to get out of his pants and inside Josie before he exploded. He swung her around and set her on the counter. Four hands clawed and tugged at clothing. Within seconds they had all the necessary body parts exposed.

He slapped his wallet down on the counter, then nuzzled her neck as he rubbed himself against the downy curls between her thighs. "I'm busy. Get a condom."

"A little distracted, are we?" She giggled, then moaned when his hand got into the action between her thighs. "Hurry," she panted, handing him the packet.

He snatched the condom and sheathed himself in record time, then grabbed a fistful of her hair and tugged until her face was inches from his. He loved watching her as he sank into her…her sweet breath puffing against his face, her chest quivering under his hands.

Their joining wasn't pretty or tender. When he and Josie came together the chemistry between them bordered on explosive.

Maybe when they were craggy old folks using walkers their lovemaking would soften and slow down. But an image of himself in a motorized scooter, chasing Josie around the backyard, entered his mind, and he chuckled against her mouth. He'd always lust after her as if she were the only woman on earth for him.

Legs wrapped around his waist, she clung to him, offering herself up, allowing him the freedom to take her the way he desired. Urgent, hard. Wild.

Had ten seconds passed? Man, he hadn't been kidding. He couldn't hang on anymore. He flung his head back and came apart inside her, shouting his release into the air. Chest still heaving, he grinned. "Your turn." He withdrew, removed the condom and dropped it in the trash, then tugged up his jeans.

Lifting Josie off the counter, he flung her over his shoulder and carried her upstairs, her naked bottom sticking up in the air. She protested and he gave her fanny a playful whack.

When she whispered in his ear that he could swat her fanny anytime, he almost lost his footing. He stumbled through the bedroom door, then dumped her in the middle of the bed. He planned to love her until she was so sore she'd have to soak in the tub for a week.

Funny, but JD ended up being the one sore. An hour later, after their third playful romp on the king-size bed, they sat in a tub of cooling water. He cradled Josie back against his chest, her bottom snuggled between his thighs. She rolled her head on his shoulder, her sigh skimming across his neck. "You still haven't given me an answer."

Hugging her, he kissed the moist skin at her temple. He knew exactly what answer Josie was waiting for—an answer to her marriage proposal.

"Well…?"

Damn pushy woman. But the idea that she found something desirable, something worthwhile, in him made him want to slay her dragons and hand her a fistful of stars from the sky.

He cupped her breast, then lifted the lush mound out of the water and flicked his thumb across the pert nipple. "I'm tempted, Josie." He rubbed his hand over her rounded stomach, then dipped his fingers below the water surface.

Her back arched and her body shuddered.

Distracting her with sex was…wrong. She deserved better from him. Besides, he wanted her to understand how honored her offer to marry him made him feel.

He lifted her face until their mouths were inches apart. "I'd be a happy man, honey, if I could spend the rest of my life loving you."

"I sense a but coming." Her breath fluttered across his neck.

But you aren't in love with me. Her unselfish offer meant the world to him and he'd be crazy not to accept it. Never before had he cared about love. Until Josie. Did he dare believe she might learn to love him with time? Or were those the thoughts of a disillusioned fool? "I can see what Bobby and I get out of the marriage." He sucked in a deep breath and held it until his lungs burned. "But what do you get out of it?"

She opened her mouth, but he touched a finger against her lips. "I'm a simple man. Compared with other guys…nothing exciting or special about me. I work hard, make a decent wage, live an ordinary life. Thousands of men have more to offer you than I do."

One by one, his muscles tensed as he watched for her reaction. Part of him hoped she'd retract the marriage proposal and spare him the agony of waiting for the day she'd walk out of his life. The other part hoped she'd insist he was a one-in-a-million guy, and she was sticking to him like pinesap for the rest of her life.

Rolling, she sent a wave of water over the side of the tub. Her breasts flattened against his chest as she curled her arms around his neck. Her kiss was different from the others she'd given him over the past several days. He tasted desperation and maybe even anger in the hard press of her mouth. She drew back, her face tight with frustration. "I don't want my pick of a thousand men. I want *you.*"

He ached to believe her. Hell, who was he to demand her love when he couldn't say for sure if what he felt for her was the real thing?

If he married Josie, then the feelings he did have for her would grow, mature, evolve, become more entangled. When she eventually left him, Bobby would not only suffer the loss of a mother figure, but he'd also be left with a father who was nothing more than a shell of a man.

Bang. Bang. Bang.

"What the heck?" The sound of someone pounding the knocker against the front door carried up the stairs and into the bathroom. JD started to rise from the tub, but Josie's hand pushed against his chest.

"Don't answer it." She licked a drop of water from his chin. "If it's important they'll come back."

"Honey, when someone drives clear out to the ranch and knocks on the door, they've got a reason." He hoisted himself out of the tub and snatched the towel from the hook on the back of the door, as another round of impatient banging echoed through the house. "Hold on, will you!"

Josie's lower lip jutted in a sexy pout. "Hurry back. I'm not getting out of the tub until you give me an answer."

The afternoon light creeping through the window danced off her blond head, giving her an angelic appearance. He stood staring, as water ran down his legs and pooled on the floor under his feet. She was the most incredible woman he'd ever met. Whether they ended up having a forever kind of relationship or not, he decided right then he wasn't going to pass up the opportunity to share his life with her. Every second, minute, hour with this woman was worth any pain he might suffer down the road.

And he couldn't forget his son. Josie made Bobby happy—reason enough to risk marrying her.

As soon as he sent the visitor downstairs away, he'd give her the answer she hoped for. Grinning, he promised, "Be right back."

Wearing just the towel, he descended the stairs two at a time. The sooner he got rid of the nuisance at the front door, the sooner he could get back in the tub with Josie.

He flung open the door. "Who the hell are you?" The sight of the fortyish-looking man, sporting a receding hairline and a gray suit, caught JD off guard. No one around these parts dressed in a suit in early August, when the temperature hovered over ninety-eight degrees, unless they were getting married or attending a funeral. Since he hadn't heard of either event happening among the locals, an odd warning bell went off in his brain.

The man gawked at the knotted towel around JD's waist and held out an envelope. "Mr.…JD?"

Automatically, JD accepted the letter. "What's this?"

The man shrugged. "All I'm required to say is *you've been served.*" He turned on his heel, scrambled down the front steps and jogged toward the sedan parked out front.

JD stepped onto the porch as the car disappeared down the gravel driveway. He stared at the white envelope, his stomach clenching with dread, knowing in his gut that the Delaneys had something to do with the message he held in his hand.

He tore the envelope open and unfolded the single sheet of paper.

The date, time and location of DNA testing have been provided for your convenience. Your failure to comply will put you in contempt of court....

Shock froze the air in his lungs as a band of panic tightened around his chest, squeezing painfully. The Delaneys didn't believe he was Bobby's biological father.

He slammed his fist against the side of the house, unaware he'd broken the skin across his knuckles. The pain in his hand was nothing compared with the emotional agony ripping him in two.

"JD? Everything okay?" Josie's shout rolled down the stairs and out the front door.

No, damn it. He stared at the letter. Everything was *not* okay.

He couldn't agree to marry Josie until he knew for a fact he was Bobby's father.

"THE DOCTOR WILL see you now."

JD set the magazine he'd been pretending to read aside and followed the tall brunette down the clinic hallway to the last door on the right.

He entered, surprised to find not an examining room but a physician's office. The nameplate on the desk read Dr. Eugene Samuel Kinnerman. A white-haired gentleman wearing wire-rimmed glasses and a rumpled lab coat sat behind a desk covered with mounds of papers, medical magazines and charts.

His bushy gray eyebrows dipped as he stood and extended his hand. "Gene Kinnerman."

"JD Gonzalez." He gripped the doctor's hand, comforted by the man's warm grip. Which was ridiculous—the geezer wasn't in any position to help him. But JD was so blasted scared that he'd take any reassurance he could get, never mind the source.

"Nice to meet you, JD."

"Have a seat." He motioned to one of the leather chairs in front of the desk. "The chart says you're from Brandt's Corner. Quite a distance from Dallas."

JD sat on the edge of one chair. "Yes, sir."

Kinnerman offered a sympathetic smile. "Before drawing a blood sample from you, I'm willing to answer any questions you have about the process."

A million questions ran loose inside JD's head, but he started with the one that had been on his mind the most. "How accurate is the test?"

"Very. The courts require 99.0 percent as proof of paternity. Our results are ten to one hundred times more accurate."

The doctor gestured to the letter on the desk, a copy of the same letter the court clerk had delivered to JD five days ago. "I see the other party has already submitted a DNA sample to a lab in Chicago."

JD bit the inside of his cheek so hard he tasted the coppery tang of blood. The letter confirmed that a swab of Bobby's cheek cells had been submitted for testing the week Josie had taken him to Chicago. Bobby's grandparents didn't have the legal authority to authorize the test. The fact that the sample had been obtained without JD's permission infuriated him. That Josie had kept the test a secret hurt him more deeply.

"This is the process. I draw blood from you today, then send the sample to the genetic-testing laboratory listed in the letter. The two samples will be compared to determine if DNA patterns exist. You should receive the results in nine working days."

Nine days. He'd learn if he was Bobby's biological father on Friday, August 27—a date that would be forever burned into his memory. The possibility that this blood test would steal his son from him made JD's heart contract painfully.

"Any other questions?"

"No. Let's get this over with."

He followed the doctor into the lab room. The court order had specified his blood be drawn by a doctor, not a nurse or lab technician. After the doctor obtained the sample, he left the room and a nurse came in with a cup of apple juice.

Ten minutes later JD stood outside the clinic, with the late-afternoon sun beating down on him. Traffic whizzed by on the busy street, and he cursed the long drive home. He recalled the lost look on Josie's face when he'd informed her he had business in Dallas, and no, she couldn't go along, and neither could Bobby.

She'd asked if the trip had anything to do with the visitor who'd interrupted their bath several days earlier. He'd taken the easy way out and lied, saying the person at the door had been a salesman who'd needed directions.

After slipping into the sweltering truck cab, he started the engine and flipped the air conditioner to high. He left the parking lot and headed west toward the interstate.

Both tired and hungry, he decided to wait until the outskirts of the city or the next stop for gas to buy something to eat. He'd use the time to think. He hadn't solved any of his problems during the nine-hour drive up to Dallas, and he doubted he'd find the answers during the long trip home.

He navigated the congested downtown area with the radio blaring. The loud noise and merging traffic put a halt to his musings for the time being. Approaching the Interstate 20 exit, he veered west toward Abilene. After another fifteen minutes, traffic thinned out, and his mind wandered over the events of the past few days.

Deep in his gut he knew he'd better get a lawyer. A damn

good one. Even if the genetic test came out positive, the Delaneys wouldn't back off. Sooner or later he'd face them in court. But good lawyers cost mega bucks. He didn't have mega bucks—not after using his savings to buy into the ranch.

Returning to the rodeo circuit was a possibility. He might not be in his prime, but he wasn't dead in the grave, either. He had enough horse sense left in him to make the finals one more time. However, the idea of being away from Bobby for weeks at a time didn't sit well. The Delaneys would insist he was neglecting Bobby. If he took the boy on the road with him, the grandparents would claim their grandson was missing too much school. Either way, JD was screwed.

Josie. Sweet, loving Josie. If he agreed to marry her and the paternity test came back negative, would she change her mind and rescind her marriage proposal? After all, if he wasn't Bobby's father, the Delaneys would automatically gain custody of the boy. No sense giving Josie an answer until he knew for sure whether he was Bobby's father.

God help him if he lost both Bobby and Josie.

The past five days at the ranch had been hell. Each time he'd caught Bobby's smile, had heard his laughter, had watched him act silly, JD's chest had tightened and he'd had to walk away to catch his breath.

He'd read the concern in Josie's questioning gaze and had ached to tell her everything, but had feared he'd embarrass himself and break down in front of her. So he'd played it safe and kept his distance from her…emotionally and physically. Now that the test was over, he wanted to go home and seek refuge in her arms.

Eyes smarting, he pinched the bridge of his nose and cursed. Wallowing in self-pity wouldn't do a bit of good. He cranked the radio louder and pressed on the gas pedal. The sooner he arrived home, the sooner he'd be with Josie and Bobby.

Several hours later he pulled off the interstate. Fatigue

gnawed his insides as he leaned against the truck, watching the numbers flip on the gas pump. He should find a motel for the night. He'd only slept in snatches since he'd received the court order. Like his vehicle, he was running on fumes. But he nixed the idea of bunking down alone in some skuzzy motel. Tonight, he would sleep with Josie by his side.

If he continued driving, he'd be home by two in the morning. Bobby would already be asleep, but JD would settle for tucking the covers around him and kissing his silky blond head.

And Josie. She'd be asleep, too. A sense of urgency swept over him. Nine days until the paternity-test results. Nine days until the truth came out. Nine days to pretend he and Josie had forever. He refused to waste a moment of their time together.

The pump clicked off. He went inside. Paid for the gas, two hot coffees to go and a pack of powdered doughnuts. At 2:10 in the morning, JD pulled into the ranch yard. Thank God, Blake's old hunting hound, Buckus, had died four years ago or the mutt would have barked his fool head off and woken the whole house.

He slipped inside the front door, removed his boots and padded up the stairs. He stopped at Bobby's room. The boy lay sprawled diagonally across the bed, bringing a smile to JD's face. He gently straightened his son, smoothed the sheet over him, then retrieved Rascal from the floor and tucked the bear under the boy's arm. Nausea gripped his stomach as he kissed the little forehead and fled the room.

He ducked into his own bedroom, where he grabbed a pair of clean athletic shorts, then went into the bathroom to take a quick shower. Five minutes later he hovered outside the guest-bedroom door. He breathed slowly, forcing his nerves to settle.

"Everything okay?"

JD flinched at the sound of Blake's voice. The old man stood in the hall, his tank T-shirt and baggy boxers wrinkled and twisted, the lines in his craggy face deep with worry.

The temptation to fib and assure Blake everything was fine appealed to him, but he wouldn't lie to the one man who'd given him a home and raised him like a son. "I'm not sure yet."

Blake nodded, accepting the answer. "I'm here if you want to talk." He slipped inside his room and closed the door. Blake never slept with the door shut. The geezer must have sensed JD's turmoil and need to be with Josie.

After quietly turning the doorknob, he entered the room. A warm breeze floated through the open window. He closed the door and stared at Josie's form, outlined by the slivers of moonlight streaming into the room.

Sometime during the night she'd kicked off the sheet. She wore lime-green panties that left a lot of leg to admire, and a matching top that barely concealed her lush breasts. He lifted a strand of blond hair trailing across the pillow and rubbed the silky softness between his fingers.

Easing down onto the bed next to her, he smoothed his hand up her calf, over her thigh, around her waist and farther still, until he cupped her breast in his palm. He laid his head on her hair and breathed in her scent.

With each concentrated deep breath, the tension drained from his body and the knots in his stomach unraveled. Touching Josie, breathing her in, calmed him as nothing else could.

Several minutes passed and his eyelids grew heavy. He moved closer, spooning her from behind, burying his face in the hollow between her neck and shoulder.

"I missed you."

His eyes popped open, and he thought for a moment he'd imagined hearing her voice. Then she wiggled her hips against him, and her soft sigh floated over his arm, making the hairs rise and quiver.

He kissed the soap-scented skin behind her ear and flicked his thumb over her hardening nipple, rejoicing in the way she pressed herself against his hand.

She rolled toward him. "Love me, JD." The catch in her voice made his breath hitch.

He owed her an explanation for the reason he'd taken off so suddenly. "Josie—"

"Shh," she hushed, gliding a finger across his lips. "Just love me, JD."

He yearned to say the words. With all his being he yearned to confess his feelings for her. But fear clogged his throat.

He couldn't give her the words, but by God he'd show her how much she meant to him with his body.

Chapter Twelve

"Camping's cool, Dad." Bobby's dirt-smudged face grinned up at JD.

Bobby had been calling him Dad for a while now, but JD still couldn't get over the warm feeling that filled him each time his son used the title. After pouring water over the campfire, he scrambled the hot coals with the toe of his boot. "Yeah, I think we make a pretty good camping team."

"Can we go again sometime?"

JD wished he could assure his son there would be another outing soon, but he couldn't. He couldn't promise a damn thing until tomorrow.

Tomorrow the results of the paternity test would be available. Tomorrow would determine the future. Determine whether he and Bobby had a future together.

Since he'd returned from Dallas almost two weeks ago, JD had spent every spare minute with his son—something he should have done the moment Bobby had arrived at the ranch last Christmas. But he'd convinced himself he shouldn't push Bobby. That the boy would come to him when he was ready.

In truth, JD had been the one not ready for a close relationship. Until he'd spent the past several days in constant companionship with Bobby, JD hadn't realized *he'd* been the one afraid to love, afraid to reach out.

"There'll be other camping trips. Would you roll up the beds for me?"

"Okay."

JD had to turn away from the sight of his son folding the blankets. He saw himself in the child—the same eagerness to please anyone who paid attention to him. If only he could make Bobby understand he loved him unconditionally. But how could he *tell* the boy he loved him, when the possibility they would be split apart existed? Bobby would hate him then. For now, he would have to settle for *showing* his son how much he cared.

"I gotta pee."

Pointing to the cavern several yards away, JD suggested, "Why don't you go pee your name on the rock."

Bobby's forehead puckered. "How do I pee my name?"

"Just wiggle it around a little to make your letters." JD knew that Bobby could print his name. He'd seen it scribbled on the drawings the boy had done for Blake.

He finished packing the supplies, grinning when he heard Bobby's laughter float back to him.

"Look, Dad!"

With a serious face, JD ambled over to the rock and nodded. "Mighty fine capital *B*. Where's the *y?*"

"I ran outta pee."

Chuckling, JD ruffled the blond head. "Guess you should have finished all your juice with your lunch. Hustle up now. I want to make it back to the ranch by suppertime." As Bobby scrambled away, JD secretly admitted he was fiercely thankful for the court-ordered paternity test. If not for the threat of losing his son, he might never have risked opening himself up and loving Bobby so completely and honestly. He didn't regret loving the boy. But once again he did regret that he and Bobby had missed out on months of this newfound closeness.

JD had convinced himself he hadn't reached out to Bobby when the boy had arrived at the ranch because he hadn't known what to do with a five-year-old. In a bumbling, fumbling kind of way he'd tried, but making up excuses for not spending time with Bobby had been easier than dealing with the possibility he didn't have the necessary something inside him needed to love another person.

"Dad, are you mad at Aunt Josephine?"

Bending down on one knee, JD helped his son tie the blankets together with a length of rope. "What makes you ask?"

Shrugging, Bobby poked at the dirt with the toe of his miniature cowboy boot. "She doesn't laugh no more."

So the boy wouldn't see how his words affected him, JD averted his face and secured the bedrolls to the back of Warrior's saddle. "I'm not mad at Josie, Bobby. I just…"

A little fist grabbed hold of JD's pant leg. "You still like Aunt Josephine, don't you?"

The hitch in his son's voice shattered JD's self-control. He lifted Bobby into his arms. "Sometimes life gets kind of crazy, son. I've had a lot on my mind lately, and I'm afraid I haven't been good company."

"What's good company?"

JD chuckled. "Fun to be around."

"I think you're fun, Dad."

"You're not so bad yourself, sport." He set Bobby on the ground and finished strapping the rest of their camping gear to the horse's saddle.

"Can Aunt Josephine come camping next time?"

JD's lungs seized up on him and he grabbed the pommel to steady himself. *Ah, Josie.* He'd worked so hard to erect the wall that surrounded and protected his heart. Then Josie had swung into his life with the force of a sledgehammer, turning the wall into a pile of useless rubble, exposing his feelings to the world. Not such a bad thing when life was good and he was happy. But hell when life took a wrong turn and he could no longer conceal his sadness, his agony from those around him.

"We'll see, Bobby." He adjusted the stirrups, then reached

down and lifted the boy onto the saddle. "Almost suppertime, so we'd better head home."

"Dad?"

"What?"

His son leaned over, his skinny arms reaching out. "I love you."

Automatically, JD hugged Bobby to him, slamming his eyes closed against the anguish the simple declaration caused. How could *love* hurt this much? "I love you, too, son." He clamped his mouth shut after hearing the choked sound escape from his throat. But his heart insisted he had more to say. "You're the best son a man could ever have."

"Really?"

"I promise." JD swung up behind Bobby on Warrior and clicked his tongue, determined to savor these last moments together before he and Bobby returned to the house.

"Dad?"

"What?"

"How come Mom didn't tell you about me?"

A twinge pinched JD's side. Bobby didn't talk much about his life with Cassandra. JD figured his son didn't have a lot of warm, fuzzy childhood memories. "I'm not sure. I think you're mother was confused or frightened."

"You wasn't gonna hurt her, were you?"

"No, Bobby, no. What I mean is…maybe your mom had other things going on in her life she was struggling with. Maybe she didn't have anyone to talk to, to get help from." JD stopped himself from rambling. How could he make the boy understand something he himself didn't understand?

"Lots of kids at my day care had dads."

JD pulled Bobby a little closer. His son had spent the first five years of his life without a father; that he might spend the rest of his years without one didn't seem fair. "Who picked you up from day care?"

"The bus."

"Did you like riding the bus?"

He shook his head. "I had to go home last."

A picture of his son sitting alone on a school bus, his face pressed to the glass window, flashed through JD's mind. He wanted so badly to protect Bobby from future hurt and pain, but couldn't promise he'd always be there for the boy. "What did you and your mother do on the weekends?"

"Watched cartoons. Mostly, I played by myself."

"What about friends?"

He shook his head. "You think I'm gonna make friends here when school starts?"

The idea that the boy might go to school at some strict military academy instead of attending the elementary school in Brandt's Corner made JD's body shake with anger. "No matter where you are, Bobby, you'll always make friends."

"Grandma and Grandpa got a boy living next door, but I couldn't play with him."

"Why not?"

"Grandma said he was a bad 'fluence on me."

"Next time you visit your grandparents maybe they'll change their minds."

"Grandpa doesn't read bedtime stories like you do."

JD was fiercely glad he and Bobby had their special time together each night. He'd cherish the memories forever. "Maybe when you're older, he'll teach you golf."

"What's golf?"

"A sport where you use a club to hit a small ball off the ground."

"I don't wanna play golf. I wanna ride horses."

Four hours later, the ranch yard came into view, and JD spotted Josie sitting on the porch swing, gazing off into the distance. He'd kept to himself since the trip to Dallas and knew his behavior hurt her. But he was barely holding himself together and feared that if he tried to explain, he'd make a bigger mess of things. He couldn't afford to open up to Josie and risk losing himself completely in her. He'd keep his distance...until he figured out what the future held for him and Bobby. If he wasn't the boy's real father, then she had no reason to marry him.

The thought of losing Josie was enough to make him physically ill.

JOSEPHINE WAS LOSING HIM.

She sat on the porch swing, staring down the ranch driveway, trying to understand where things had gone wrong between her and JD. He rarely smiled at her, didn't touch her—except at night, when darkness settled over the house and he slipped into her bed.

The nights were...*incredible.* Since their interrupted tryst in the tub two weeks ago, JD's lovemaking held a desperate edge—as if each night might be the last time he held her in his arms. Josephine had assumed he'd been ready to accept her proposal the afternoon the doorbell had rung, disrupting their bath. But something had stopped him cold. In her heart, she believed he cared for her deeply or he wouldn't continue to steal into her room at night. But she couldn't shake the feeling something was terribly wrong.

JD wasn't a man to openly share his concerns or feelings. She'd offered to help, to listen. When and if he needed her, she'd be there for him. But he kept his distance emotionally. The realization that he didn't trust her hurt more than his silence.

Only at night, in his arms, did she feel close to him.

The whinny of a horse caught her attention, and she spotted JD and Bobby coming around the back of the barn.

Since the temperamental cowboy had returned from *wherever* several days ago, he hadn't let Bobby out of his sight except at bedtime. They'd gone fishing, horseback riding, had even camped out last night. And she'd been left behind. Not by choice. Yesterday, Bobby had asked JD if she could go camping with them, but JD had insisted the trip was a "guys only" outing.

When Bobby noticed her on the porch, he waved. His huge grin made her feel petty for envying him. Her nephew had blossomed into a different boy since she'd first arrived at the ranch. More outgoing, he offered his smiles freely and the sound of his laughter filled the house.

The screen door creaked softly as Blake stepped onto the porch. "They just get back?"

"Yes." The dear, old man had pretended not to notice the tension between her and JD, but he knew things weren't right. "Blake, did JD ever tell you where—"

"Didn't say a word, Josie." He stopped next to the swing and gave her shoulder a comforting squeeze.

"I wish he'd talk to someone."

"JD does things his own way. He'll speak up when he's ready." Blake hobbled down the porch steps, toward the corral. After a few words with JD he grabbed Bobby's hand and Warrior's reins, then walked the horse to the barn. JD headed for the porch, his handsome face emotionless, blank.

"How was the campout?" She patted the spot next to her on the swing, hoping he'd stay and talk.

The slight hesitation before he approached hurt, but she hid the pain behind a smile.

He sat down, leaving too much space between them. "We did a little fishing." He grinned. "Taught him how to pee his name on a rock."

She laughed. "Seems like you boys could use a chaperon on your next overnight trip. No telling what trouble you'll get yourselves into."

His boots moved restlessly against the floorboards, as if he was preparing to bolt any second.

"Stay and talk with me." She held her breath, praying he wouldn't turn down the invitation, as he'd done the past few nights when she'd wandered out on the porch to sit in the swing.

The silence went on forever, until Josephine thought she'd scream with frustration. Then unexpectedly he put an arm around her shoulders and pulled her against him. He stared into her eyes for a long moment before leaning down and covering her mouth with his. She cherished the kiss, relished the feel of his lips caressing hers, his tongue hinting at what he'd do later with her in the dark hours before dawn.

"Have you and Blake fixed supper yet?"

Supper? Food was the last thing on her mind right now. "No."

"Why don't the four of us go into town and eat at the café."

Although she sensed JD was trying to avoid a serious discussion with her, she thought they could all use a break from the ranch. "Give me five minutes to freshen up."

A CAR-HORN BLAST filled the air as JD swung the truck into a parking space outside Lovie's café. Bonnie Milner waved madly from the front seat of a passing pickup, while the two cowboys on either side of her grinned from ear to ear. Probably on the way to another Dolly Parton look-alike contest.

At six in the evening, the early-supper crowd was long gone when they entered the restaurant. Susie waved from behind the lunch counter, then pointed to a large booth by the front window. Blake motioned for Josephine to lead the way, but one step was all she took before she came to a screeching halt. There, sitting at a table in front of her, not five feet away, were her parents. The looks on their faces warned Josephine this wasn't a social visit.

Automatically, her hand clasped Bobby's shoulder and she edged closer to JD's side, subtly aware of the way his body tensed. "Father. Mother."

William Delaney pushed his chair back and stood. "Good evening, Josephine." His gaze shifted to his grandson. "Robert."

"What are you doing here?" She waited for an answer, but her parents acted as though she hadn't spoken. Instead, they directed their attention to JD, staring at him with disapproving scowls.

One look at the glowering rage darkening JD's features and panic whirled in Josephine's stomach. Her gaze shifted to her mother, who stood poised behind a chair, hair perfectly coiffed, not a dot of shine on her powdered face—as if supper at the café were equivalent to dining at the country club.

People were beginning to stare. The Peanutty triplets were eating supper with Laura Brannigan at a table close by and all four women laid their forks down and eavesdropped unabashedly.

Josephine could think of nothing to say to diffuse the tension, so she remained silent.

"Your mother and I stopped for a bite to eat before driving out to—" her father's eyes narrowed on JD "—his ranch."

"I don't recall inviting you for a visit."

Before her father could respond, Susie joined the group. "Yer all blockin' the doorway." Her head swiveled between the Delaneys and JD. "I can push some tables together."

JD grabbed Josephine's elbow. "No, thanks, Susie. We were just leaving."

William Delaney removed a folded sheet of paper from the breast pocket of his suit. "The test results are in." He tapped the edge of the white stationery against his palm, his eyes glittering.

A chill raced down Josephine's spine. She'd seen the same cold light in her father's eyes when he went in for the kill during business negotiations. JD edged around her, stopping in front of her father, who took a step back in order not to have to look up at JD. Josephine's heart hammered inside her chest at the undercurrents zinging through the room.

"What test?" she whispered. Her question went unanswered, as both men continued to glare at each other. Frustrated, Josephine tamped her foot against the linoleum floor.

Her mother stared pointedly at Josephine's cowboy boots and pursed her lips in displeasure.

JD snatched the letter from her father. His lips pressed into a thin line as he scanned the contents.

Perching her fists on her hips, Josephine demanded, "Would someone please tell me what in the world is going on?"

Her father glanced around, as if making sure he had everyone's attention in the café. "The results of a court-ordered paternity test."

"Paternity test?" Josephine gasped. Every person in the room froze. The only sound was the lonely wail of a country-western song playing softly on the jukebox at the back of the room.

JD shifted his gaze from the paper to her, and she swallowed a sob at the stricken expression on his face, the bleak emptiness clouding his eyes. JD clasped Bobby's shoulder and drew him close to his side. He tore his gaze from her and blinked several times, then swallowed hard. "We'll wait in the truck."

"But, Dad, we didn't eat nothin," Bobby protested, as he followed his father.

JD didn't answer, and not one person in the café uttered a single word until the door closed behind the pair.

William Delaney cleared his throat. "I had a feeling that man wasn't my grandson's biological father. The paternity test proves that I was right."

Dallas. Josephine's stomach churned. That was the reason JD had taken off without any explanation over two weeks ago. A raw pain sliced through her heart. He hadn't trusted her enough to confide in her. How could he assume she wouldn't wish to go with him and offer her support?

Blake moved to Josephine's side, and she was grateful for his reassuring presence. She stared at her parents' conceited, arrogant faces, her insides clenching with anger, frustration and hurt. "I can't believe you'd stoop so low as to—"

"Watch your tongue, Josephine. You understood from the beginning Robert didn't belong with that man. Now we have proof that this…JD person isn't even his biological father. There's nothing to prevent us from gaining custody of our grandson."

William Delaney lowered his voice and advanced a threatening step. "Robert is a Delaney. He belongs in Chicago, not on a ranch in the middle of *Texas.*" He spit the state name as if it were a swear word. "And no daughter of mine belongs here, either. When are you going to come to your senses and return home?"

Disregarding her father's question, she insisted, "JD is the only father Bobby has ever known. You can't tear them apart."

Her mother sniffed. "The boy's only lived with him a short while. In a matter of weeks, Robert will have forgotten all about that…that cowboy."

Appalled at her mother's comment, Josephine warned, "JD won't hand Bobby over without a fight." She cursed the wobble in her voice.

"I don't remember you ever being this emotional." Her father shook his head, his mouth turning down in disapproval. "You've certainly changed since you've become involved with that man."

Ignoring her father's hurtful words, she said, "I won't let you take Bobby away from JD."

"I don't understand why you're putting up such a fuss, dear. Our lawyer assured us no judge would allow Robert to be raised by a man who isn't the boy's real father, let alone a man of questionable upbringing."

"Hear, hear." Laura Brannigan raised her water glass toward Josephine's mother and smiled.

Josephine glared at the shopkeeper, wishing she'd had the nerve to shove the woman's face into the pile of mashed potatoes on her plate. How dared her mother or anyone else humiliate the man she loved and respected with all her heart? Apparently, money didn't buy class. "JD and I are getting married." Her mother's shocked gasp started a chain reaction. Blake grinned. The Peanutty sisters all started talking at once about wedding plans. Susie sighed and shuffled back to the lunch counter. Laura Brannigan made disgusting snorting sounds.

Ignoring the commotion around him, her father persisted, "Josephine, I'm putting a stop to this childish rebellion of yours right now. I'll drive you out to the ranch to get your things, then you're coming home with us."

Home? After staying only a short time at the Rocking R, experiencing the warmth and love inside Blake's old ranch house, Josephine never wanted to set foot inside her parents' cold, austere mansion again.

"You don't understand, do you? I love JD. He's the man I want to spend the rest of my life with. I won't let him lose his son."

Blake stepped forward. "Folks, I think you best leave before things get said that ain't meant to be said."

Her mother huffed, turned on her heels and marched back toward the ladies' room, Laura Brannigan hot on her heels. Her father's expression darkened. "Be careful, Josephine. You're a worthy adversary, but still no match for your old man."

Josephine clung to Blake's arm for support as they walked out of the café. The adrenaline from her parents' unexpected visit dissipated, leaving her shaky and weak as she stood on the boardwalk outside the restaurant. A second later JD pulled his truck up and Blake helped her get inside.

The ride home was made in silence. Thank goodness the camping trip had worn Bobby out. He fell asleep with his head against Blake's chest before they hit the outskirts of town. The scenery blurred in front of Josephine's eyes. She thought about cautioning JD to slow down but was afraid she'd start bawling if she tried to talk.

As soon as they arrived at the ranch, JD lifted Bobby out of the back seat and disappeared inside the house without a word to anyone. Josephine stared out the windshield, watching his retreating back.

She jumped when Blake reached over the front seat and squeezed her shoulder. "I'll be in the barn."

With a heavy heart, Josephine left the truck. She entered

the house and stood in the front hall, listening to the murmur of voices coming from JD's office. She discovered him sitting behind the desk with her nephew curled in his lap. He cradled the back of Bobby's small head in his palm, his other arm wrapped securely around the boy's bottom. She froze in the doorway, too choked up to speak. Neither male was aware of her presence.

"Dad, is you mad at Grandpa Delaney?"

"No, Bobby. I'm not mad at your grandfather."

"How come we had to go? I'm still hungry."

The corners of JD's mouth curved, but his face remained so sad, so solemn, that Josephine's eyes welled with tears.

"We left because there's something I have to tell you and I wanted us to be alone when I did."

"Okay."

JD brushed a strand of blond hair from Bobby's forehead. "When a man and a woman have a baby together, the child has the same stuff in his blood as his parents."

"I took a test to see if you and I share stuff in our blood." JD's eyes closed as if he couldn't physically look at Bobby any longer. "We don't share the same things in our blood, Bobby. I'm not your real father."

Josephine held her breath until her lungs burned. Bobby sat frozen on JD's lap, making her wonder if he'd understood the significance of what he'd just been told. Then understanding hit the boy with force.

"No!" Bobby shouted, pounding his fists against JD's chest. "You gotta be my dad. You gotta! I don't want no other dad!"

JD gathered Bobby to him and pressed the blond head to his chest. Josephine turned away, unable to stand watching the agony rip through JD, making his entire body shudder. She slipped back into the hallway, sat down on the bottom stair step and gave in to the tears she'd held at bay since learning about the paternity test.

She wasn't sure how long she sat there, but eventually,

she could no longer hear Bobby's sobbing and JD's whispered words of comfort. Wiping her own face, she went back to the office and found her nephew curled asleep against JD's chest.

Even though JD's eyes remained closed, she sensed he felt her presence. He confirmed her suspicions. "God help me, Josie. I can't give Bobby up."

She sniffed. Drat, she didn't want to cry again, but was helpless to stop the tears that dribbled down her cheeks as she moved into the room and wiggled behind the desk. Kneeling on the floor by the side of the chair, she wrapped her arms around the two males who'd stolen her heart. "Why didn't you tell me about the paternity test?"

"I didn't want to worry you." He rested his head on the back of the chair. "No, that's a lie."

She buried her face against the side of his neck.

"I…I couldn't talk about it, Josie."

"The man who showed up at the door last week?"

"Yeah. He delivered the court order."

The tone in JD's voice darkened and Josephine lifted her head, surprised at his lukewarm stare.

"The doctor I went to for the blood test in Dallas verified Bobby had already been tested in Chicago."

"What?" she gasped. "I swear Bobby never went to a doctor when we were in Chicago."

JD's eyes iced over.

"Unless." *Oh, God.* How could she have been so careless? "I left him with the maid one afternoon so I could run into work for some files. It's possible my mother returned home and took him to the doctor. But Bobby never mentioned anything."

"Bobby didn't go to a doctor. Someone used a swab to collect a sample of his cheek cells. He probably assumed he was getting his teeth brushed."

She leaned back until she bumped the leg of the desk. "JD, you have to marry me. It doesn't matter who Bobby's biological father is. He belongs with you." She clutched his forearm, unaware her nails gouged his skin. "*Us.* Bobby belongs with us."

The coldness drained from his eyes, and she detected a ray of hope in his gaze.

"We may never know who Bobby's real father is, JD. Cassandra must have wanted it that way, or she would never have put your name on the birth certificate. She wanted *you* to take care of her son. You have to fight for him." She caressed his whiskered cheek with her fingertips. "Marry me, JD."

Her stomach clenched when he moved his face away from her hand. Then the reason for his silence hit her…hard, fast, blunt.

He doesn't love me.

She scrambled from the floor. Determination and pride kept her from doubling over as sharp pains tore through her midsection. She moved to the window, opposite the desk, and gazed unseeingly at the backyard.

After several deep breaths, the pain lessened and a sense of calm settled over her. Maybe JD didn't love her, but he cared about her. Would *caring* be enough to last a lifetime?

"My nephew deserves better than being raised in a military academy. If we marry we can provide a stable, loving home for Bobby. Chances are, the judge would allow him to remain with us." She faced JD, waiting for a sign he understood the significance of her suggestion, but his masked features gave nothing away. Her resolve faltered until he kissed Bobby's tear-stained cheek. At that moment she decided she'd gladly give up her own happiness if Bobby and JD could be together.

Swallowing hard, she lifted her chin. "After all the dust settles and things return to normal, if you feel our marriage isn't…working…" She struggled to keep her voice even. "If you want out of the marriage, I won't stand in your way."

He scowled. "Pretty damn generous of you."

Generous? She wasn't being generous. She was desperate!

The silence stretched between them. "I need time to think."

She lowered her lashes, hoping he hadn't seen how much his answer stung. He could have shown a little emotion, a little gratitude at her offer. A surge of anger shoved aside the hurt, and she went to the desk, set her hands on the top and leaned forward, pinning him with her gaze. "I suggest you don't waste too much time *considering* my proposal. My father's attorneys will eat you alive in court, JD."

She spun on her boot heels and headed for the door. If she stayed in the room a second longer, she'd break down and beg him to love her, beg him to give her a chance to prove she'd make a great mother, a great helpmate, a great partner…wife…lover.

If he didn't know those things about her by now, would he ever?

PRESSURE—UNYIELDING. Hot. Suffocating.

Sitting on Bobby's bed, JD tightened his arms around his sleeping son and cursed the feeling of helplessness gnawing his insides. He stared at the clock on the nightstand and dragged in a lungful of clammy air seeping into the room from the open window. He cringed when the numbers changed: 2:23 a.m.

Time was the enemy.

The yip of a lonely coyote echoed through the night. A creature calling out to a mate that had either died or moved on to new territory. JD sympathized with the animal's forlorn howl. He felt the same desperate, aching loneliness.

No matter how close he held Bobby, he couldn't shake the feeling his son was slowly slipping away. With all his being, JD wanted to believe marrying Josie would guarantee he and Bobby remained together. She assumed a marriage license would convince her parents to back off. But he'd read the unspoken message in William Delaney's cold, ruthless eyes—the man would stop at nothing to gain custody of his grandson.

Marry a woman who didn't love him in order to keep a child who wasn't his. What a mess.

Bobby.

JD remembered the day he'd first met the blond little boy. Somewhere in the back of his mind, a voice had insisted the child couldn't be his. Yeah, he'd had sex with Bobby's mother, but none of the condoms had broken. Add the obvious fact that Bobby shared none of JD's Hispanic genes and...well, the chances were next to nil he'd fathered the boy.

Regardless, he'd stood on the porch steps next to Blake that cloudy, cold day, staring into the wounded, lonely face of a five-year-old, knowing in his heart he couldn't turn the boy away. JD had lived his whole life with the knowledge his parents hadn't wanted him. When Bobby had landed on his doorstep, JD's need to feel worthy rose to the surface like a volcanic explosion.

Bobby had needed him, and JD had grasped the chance to be his father. To use the boy to fill the aching, empty hole inside him.

Stupidly, he'd believed Bobby would always be his. By the time he'd received the phone call from Josie he'd already had deep feelings for the boy. Yet he'd still counted on everything working out and Bobby remaining with him.

Then the court order for genetic testing had arrived, and he could no longer pretend Bobby would always be by his side.

Maybe he should grab the boy and go on the run. Hundreds of people a year in this country disappeared with their children, fleeing from abusive spouses or relatives. And if the Delaneys found him through private investigators, he'd take Bobby to Mexico. He could easily lose himself among the locals. Hiding a blond-haired boy would be difficult but not impossible.

Bobby mumbled something in his sleep and JD relaxed his hold, allowing the boy to roll away from him.

Heck, they could leave tonight. Pack a bag and be gone without anyone the wiser. What about Josie? How could he steal away with her nephew when she loved the boy as much as he did? And he had Blake to consider. The old man was getting on in years and required someone to look after him. As half owner of the Rocking R Ranch, JD had too much at stake to pick up and run. Rubbing a hand down his face, he grimaced. No matter what he decided, no one would escape the situation unscathed.

He rolled over, got off the bed and wandered to the window. The stars blinked like bright dots in the black sky, reminding him of diamonds, which in turn reminded him of engagement rings and weddings. And Josie.

No matter how many different ways he tried to piece together Josie's marriage proposal, he ended up with the same picture.

Josie offered to marry you solely for Bobby's sake and not because she loves you. All considered, not such a big deal. Josie cared about him. She'd be a wonderful mother to Bobby. And he admitted that having Josie to wake up to each morning for the rest of his life was a hell of a lot more than he deserved. Compared with spending the rest of his life alone, not having Josie's love wasn't such a big thing—now, if only he could convince himself to buy into the idiotic notion.

What a fool he'd been to hope she might actually learn to love him. Didn't make much sense for a gutsy, intelligent, classy lady to hook up with a small-time cattle rancher who had nothing but the dirt under his nails to show for years of backbreaking labor. Both she and Bobby deserved better than that.

He loved the kid like crazy, and if given the chance believed he'd be a damn good father to the boy. But he couldn't give Bobby the same future the Delaneys could—an elite education, cultural experiences, music lessons—all the things JD had never had an opportunity to experience as a child. How could he deny this bright boy the chance to explore everything the world had to offer? As much as he wanted Bobby by his side, he wanted him to learn that life was more than herding cows and castrating cattle.

JD had been a loner all his life. He'd find a way to go on

again after Josie and Bobby left the ranch. He'd cherish the memories of their short time together and hold them close through the darkest, longest hours of the night. And there would be a lot of dark, long nights ahead.

Maybe the Delaneys would be willing to work out a visitation schedule. He knew Josie would bring Bobby out to the ranch for a visit once in a while.

A visit.

A measly weekend or two out of the year. A holiday every two years. Enough time between visits for Bobby to forget JD. Then one day the boy would tell Josie he was too busy with his own life to go visit some man he hardly remembered.

JD cast a last, longing look at the small figure on the bed, then padded down the hall to Josie's room. The door stood open, but he hesitated in the hallway, watching the slow rise and fall of her chest. She lay on her back, her blond hair spread across her shoulders. He inhaled deeply, feeling the heavy tug of arousal as he caught her scent. He must have made a sound, because her lashes fluttered and she turned her head toward him.

Without an invitation, he stepped into the room and closed the door behind him. Neither spoke. Sitting on the edge of the bed, he watched her expressive blue eyes...*Bobby's eyes.* Emotion glittered in the deep sapphire circles, but he held back, studying her features. Trying to memorize every detail of her face, so when he closed his eyes at night, an exact likeness of her image would appear in his mind.

Her fingers worked their way under his T-shirt and slid up his rib cage. He breathed deeply, savoring the feel of her touch and the way her hands made his skin shiver and his body tighten.

Tonight. He had tonight with Josie. In her arms, when his body pulsed inside her, the world would make perfect sense. The world would be right and good again.

She sat up, wrapped her arms around him and nuzzled his neck, his ear, his whiskered chin. "Love me, JD."

I will, Josie. I will.

Somehow he'd find a way to make tonight last forever. Hours of slow-and-easy loving. He'd take all she offered and steal more. Her scent, her taste, her touch. He wanted to absorb all of her into his body. And in return, he'd share himself in a way he'd never done with any other woman. Tonight he'd give Josie his heart.

Three times he turned to her before dawn, his stamina fueled by equal parts desperation, desire and love. Too soon, the first rays of sun peeked above the horizon as the good-morning wail of a rooster sounded off behind the barn.

Placing a last, gentle kiss on her forehead, JD eased away from Josie's warmth. In a trancelike state he headed for the bathroom. After a quick shower he pulled on a pair of work jeans and an old torn shirt. He had cattle to move today. Temporary corrals to set up for branding and inoculating the calves. Watering tanks to clean. Enough work to keep him away from the house for two straight days.

When he entered the kitchen, Blake glanced up from the stove, where he stood frying bacon in a cast-iron skillet. "Coffee be ready in a second."

"Thanks." JD went to the fridge, removed a plastic gallon of water and set the jug by the back door.

Blake motioned to the water. "Where ya headin' today?"

"Out to the line shack. Give the guys a hand in bringing the herd in." JD shoved his feet into his work boots.

Blake frowned. "You plan on coming back tonight?"

Avoiding the coot's questioning gaze, JD tucked his shirt into the waistband of his jeans. "No. I'd planned on staying out there for a couple of days."

"I never figured you for a quitter."

The quiet words slapped the backside of JD's head. The rancher was like a father to him, and he didn't want to lash out and say something hurtful. But damned if he'd let the meddling old fart bully him. "Stay out of it, Blake."

"Stay out of what?"

JD swiveled in the doorway. Josie stood by the table, rubbing sleep from her eyes. Her baby-doll pajamas were wrinkled and twisted, her hair hanging in disarray. Her mouth was still swollen from his kisses. His loving. He almost caved into the temptation to carry her back upstairs and love her all over again. Oh, hell. The sooner she was gone, the sooner he could control this constant yearning he had for her.

"Stay out of my business," JD cautioned Blake, who acknowledged the warning with a grumpy, "Harrumph."

Josie's gaze went back and forth between JD and Blake. "What's going on?"

Blake waved a spatula in the air. "Don't ask me. I ain't the one running you off."

"What's Blake talking about, JD?"

He hated for things to end this way. He'd planned to leave a note on the fridge and be gone by the time Josie woke up. He moved toward her, cringing when she retreated a step. "All things considered, it would be best if you and Bobby went back to Chicago. Today."

Her eyes flashed, brightening her complexion. "Best for whom? You?"

"Josie...you honored me with your marriage proposal—" At her horrified expression he rubbed the back of his neck and grimaced. This wasn't going well at all.

Swallowing hard, he gathered his courage. "No court in this country will allow an uneducated Hispanic man to raise the grandson of a white, wealthy, upper-class society businessman. Blast it, Josie, marrying you won't make a bit of difference. Don't you see, I'm not good enough to be Bobby's father?"

"That's the biggest pile of horse crap I've ever heard," Blake grumbled, then slammed the skillet on the counter, splashing grease against the cupboards.

Josie crossed the room and got right in JD's face. "How

can you think such a thing? Ethnicity has nothing to do with love. You're the only man who's ever been a father to Bobby. You can't abandon him."

Abandon? JD clutched the door frame to steady himself. Was he abandoning Bobby? Did he intend to do the same thing his parents had done to him? *No, damn it! This situation is different.*

Bobby would grow up with advantages JD had only dreamed about. The boy had a chance to be *somebody.* Do *something* important with his life. JD refused to deny Bobby a future, no matter how much he loved him.

Josie studied his face until he squirmed under the intensity of her stare. She tapped a finger against his chest. "This isn't just about ethnicity, is it? You're using that as an excuse. I know you, JD. You're an honorable, proud man. You'd never allow Bobby to think so little of himself if he were you."

"No matter what I decide to do, I'm screwed." His hands shook with the need to pull her close and hold her, but he denied himself. This had to end before he gave Josie the opportunity to change his mind. "I can't fight your father and half the lawyers and judges in Chicago, too. I don't have enough money or friends in high places."

Her chin rose in the air. "I've got money. I'll hire a good lawyer. We'll fight my parents together."

"All the money in the world won't fix this, Josie. I'm *asking* you to take Bobby back to Chicago. Please."

"Are you tossing *me* out, too?" Her chin wobbled and JD had to look away before he did something foolish like kiss her and beg her to forgive him.

"I ain't about to stand here and listen to any more bull." Blake scowled at JD, then left the kitchen and walked out the front door.

JD clenched his jaw until sharp slivers of pain shot through the bone. "Bobby deserves a better life than I can—"

"Oh, sure. So Bobby gets a better life. What about me? I

suppose I'll get the man I deserve?" She held up one hand and counted off each finger. "A man who's rich, white Anglo-Saxon, has a college degree—"

"Stop." He couldn't bear to remember her from this day forward with pain and hurt glistening in her eyes. He had to get out of there before Josie's cruel words brought him to his knees. "Tell your father I'm going to seek visitation rights."

"You think Bobby will *want* to visit you after you've given him up without a fight?"

He winced at the direct hit. But remained silent.

She cursed, the word vulgar, succinct. If he hadn't heard it himself, he wouldn't have believed such an ugly word could have come from such a gorgeous mouth. He hated himself for what he was doing to her.

This had to end before he disgraced himself. Stepping onto the back porch, he grabbed his hat, feeling the heat of her glare burn holes through the back of his shirt. "I said my goodbye to Bobby last night."

He glanced over his shoulder, wanting one last look at Josie's beautiful face. Her image blurred before his eyes, but he held her gaze. He couldn't give Josie what she wanted, what she deserved, but he could let her see how deeply her leaving affected him. He owed her that much. And more.

"I expect you both gone from the ranch by sundown."

Chapter Thirteen

Hell on earth—a mid-September Texas heat wave.

Dead tired from the day's work, JD wiped the sweat from his forehead and headed for the house.

His gaze shifted to the trailer parked under the oak trees by the barn. José, with his wife and daughters in tow, had arrived yesterday to help with the fall roundup. Guilt nagged JD. He hadn't been good company since Josie and Bobby had left, so he'd avoided José and his family.

Three weeks, one day and...he checked his watch...twelve hours ago. Better to keep his distance than to risk jumping down José's throat for no good reason.

If JD had his way, he'd start lassoing cows today—no matter that he rode the fine line between exhaustion and physical collapse. His emotional survival depended on keeping busy every second of every minute of every hour of every day.

Daytime was easiest. Nighttime was hell.

Ten minutes asleep, fifty minutes awake staring out the window. Fifteen asleep, forty-five pacing the hallway in front of Bobby's empty bedroom. Another five asleep, the other fifty-five cleaning already-clean horse stalls.

If he didn't get some decent rest, Blake threatened to call 911 and have his carcass hauled off to a hospital in the middle of the night. But JD couldn't afford to rest. He had to keep moving. Had to stay busy. Deep in his gut he feared if he stopped long enough to think about Josie and Bobby, he'd suffer a breakdown.

Last night he'd had a dream about the orphanage. The gut-wrenching loneliness…afternoons sitting outside on the steps, waiting for his parents to come for him. Always the dream had been the same…until last night, when the boy on the steps had had blond curly hair and blue eyes—*Bobby.*

JD struggled to convince himself he'd done the right thing in sending Bobby back to Chicago. But the echo of Josie's words wouldn't stop ringing through his mind: *You're the only man who's ever been a father to Bobby. You can't abandon him.*

Had he abandoned Bobby? Was he guilty of the same heinous crime his parents had committed against him?

"Boss. You not look good."

At the sound of José's voice, JD stopped in the middle of the ranch yard. He had better things to do than shoot the bull, but he forced himself to speak. "María and the girls get settled?"

"Sí. They went to town with Señor Blake."

José's English had always impressed JD. The migrant worker had never had formal schooling, but JD sensed a keen intelligence behind the kind brown eyes. Aside from being a smart man, he was a good father. No matter how hard José worked during the day, he made sure his evenings were spent with his wife and little girls.

"If you run out of anything, just ask. Blake stocked up on extra supplies and food."

The smaller man nodded. "María say your heart is broken."

María should keep her opinions to herself. José had married the younger woman after his first wife died. The significant age gap—fifteen years—between the couple didn't seem to bother María, and the girls loved their papa.

Witnessing the couple's happiness made JD second-guess his decision to send Josie back to Chicago with Bobby. Josie and María were exact opposites. Josie had led a privileged life.

María had been born into poverty. The Mexican woman didn't know any other way of life. Even if JD had allowed Josie to stay, eventually she would have gotten bored with ranch life…tired of the man who couldn't give her the finer things in life she deserved.

As a successful businesswoman, Josie could afford to buy anything she desired. JD's pride insisted *he* be the one to buy her *things*. He couldn't stand the idea of *her* money paying for a new bull or a new corral, let alone a designer watch or diamond earrings.

Besides, marriage didn't guarantee he and Josie would gain custody of Bobby. The boy still might end up with the elder Delaneys. The knowledge that Josie would live with Bobby in her parents' home comforted JD. At least the boy would have one person by his side to love him and care for him.

"Tell María I'm fine."

"Señor Blake say you send away your *señorita* and little Roberto."

"Yeah, well, Blake shoots his mouth off too damn much." He started to walk away, but José's fingers bit into his arm.

The determined gleam in the smaller man's dark gaze surprised JD. "It is time, *sobrino*."

Nephew? "Time for what?"

José motioned toward the trailer.

JD balked, but something in José's expression stopped him. José disappeared inside the trailer for a minute, then returned with two cans of beer. They sat, side by side, on the metal steps. He waited impatiently for José to speak his mind.

"A long time ago my brother, Tomás, fell in love with an American *niña* named Sara. She come to Mexico with her rich father." José absently rubbed his finger against the condensation on the can. "Tomás and Sara fall in love and wish to marry, but her father, he say no. Soon a baby grow in Sara."

While José finished off the beer, JD squirmed against the hard metal step. A sixth sense told him he had a role in the story. Part of him yearned to hear what had happened to the young couple; the other part of him wanted to run like hell through the wooded area behind the barn.

"Sara's father *muy furiouso.* He tell Sara stay in Mexico, no come back to America. Sara live with Tomás's *familia.* Tomás *mucho* happy." José smiled. "Sara have baby *niño.* Tomás name him Juan Diego."

JD held his breath until his lungs threatened to explode.

"Tomás go to *fiesta* to *celebrar* Juan Diego's birth. He drink too much. *Bandidos* beat him and steal his *dinero.* Tomás not live."

After swallowing several times, JD managed to voice his question. "What happened to Sara?"

"She cry. *Mucho* days, she cry. She leave little Juan with Tío José and disappear. One week. Two weeks. Sara no come back. I go to police. They say Sara dead. *Suicida.* A month go by and Sara's rich father come. He take little Juan. I follow across border. See Sara's father put baby in orphanage."

JD's eyes burned as emotions swirled inside him, making him nauseous. Relief his parents *had* wanted him. Sadness the couple were dead. Anger his mother hadn't been able to see past her grief to raise him. And curiosity about his American grandfather.

"How do you figure into all this, José?"

His uncle smiled. "I ask for you at the orphanage. They say, no! Sara's father pay *mucho dinero* to *padre* to keep little Juan." José hit his chest with his fist. "I say *I* am little Juan's *padrino.*"

José was not only JD's uncle but also his godfather. His uncle's voice wobbled, then he cleared his throat. "They call police. Police say if I take little Juan they arrest me." He smacked his fist against his thigh, as if recalling an event that had happened yesterday instead of more than twenty years ago. "I come again and ask for you. They put me in jail. Three weeks I live in filthy prison. They say if I try to see you, they will hurt you. I believe them."

JD clenched his jaw until the joints cracked and popped under the pressure. He could understand his uncle not being able to get him out of the orphanage, but why had he kept his silence so long?

Damn it, I had a right to know who I was!

After several deep breaths he managed to lower his boiling temper to a simmer. "Why have you waited all these years to tell me, José? How could you let me spend my whole life thinking I was a *nobody* with a borrowed name?"

José jerked as if JD had gut-punched him. "Because I fear for you. I fear Sara's father find you and take you back."

"But what about when I was older. After I turned eighteen? Why didn't you tell me then?"

"Because I think you will try to find your grandfather."

"And why shouldn't I find the man who cares nothing for me? He owes me answers, José. Answers I'll never get now."

"You are my brother's child. My *sobrino*. I fear we would never see you again."

JD bounced up from his seat on the step and paced in front of the trailer. "But I have the right to meet the man who set me aside as if I was...was...nothing but a nuisance." His voice cracked and he prayed he'd make it through their "talk" without falling apart in front of his uncle.

"No matter now."

JD glared. "Meaning?"

"Your *abuelo,* he is dead."

"My grandfather's dead? How?"

José shrugged. "The *padre* at the orphanage, he tell me."

"When?"

"Abril."

Last April. His grandfather had died in April and JD hadn't even been aware the man had existed. He had mixed feelings about the news. Part of him was glad the old bastard was dead. And part of him wished the man had remained alive, so JD could have confronted him. Then again, maybe the answers to his questions were best left buried with the source.

"You made the journey to the Rocking R twice a year."

"I not come for work or money." José pressed a hand over his heart. "I come to see you. *Mi sobrino.*"

JD pinched the bridge of his nose, cursing the moisture pooling in the corners of his eyes. He'd been loved all his life. After several deep breaths, he regained his composure. "How did you convince the orphanage to let me come with you to the Rocking R?"

"When the first *padre* die…papers, records…" José waved his hand in the air. "They disappear."

JD didn't care to learn how those records disappeared or who made them disappear. As a matter of fact, he didn't want to know how the first *padre* had died.

"I tell new *padre* we are family. He not care if I take you. I bring you here. Señor Blake is a good man. He say you can stay."

JD stepped in front of José and clasped his shoulder, unaware his hand shook like a drunk on the wagon after five days without booze. "Thank you for telling me."

His godfather shrugged off JD's touch. "I say these things for your *señorita* and little Roberto." He went inside and shut the door in JD's face.

For Josie and Bobby? Bewildered, JD collapsed on the steps, too numb to move. Sending Josie and Bobby away, using the excuse he couldn't provide them the kind of life they deserved, had been easier than facing his greatest fear—that he felt unworthy of their love.

After learning the truth about his past, his fear seemed senseless, unfounded. All these years afraid he'd had something wrong with him. Afraid something inside him was bad. All those agonizingly lonely years wasted because of a senseless fear made him angry as hell. His uncle had held the key to his nephew's self-worth, yet had waited until JD's grandfather had died before unlocking the door to JD's past and setting him free.

He wasn't sure how much time had passed when Blake drove into the ranch yard. María and the girls piled out of the pickup, chattering in Spanish.

He headed in their direction, feeling…different now that he knew they were his family. "Did the *señoritas* have fun in town?"

María nodded. "*Si, señor.*" The two little girls giggled, then raced away calling, "Papa," María right on their heels.

After all three females entered the trailer, JD turned to Blake. "How long have you known?"

"Known what?"

"That José is my uncle."

"Your uncle!"

"Are you really surprised he's my uncle?"

"Heck, yes. Why, ain't that somethin'." Blake grinned. "Explains a lot, though."

"What do you mean?"

"The summer José asked me to keep you. He claimed you were being mistreated in the orphanage, and figured you were on the verge of running away."

The old fear reared its ugly head. JD could barely get the words past his lips. "You kept me as a favor to José?"

"Yes and no. José was a good worker. Good workers are hard to come by. If I watched out for you, he promised he'd return each spring to help with the branding and fall to help with the roundup."

JD stared at the ground. This honesty crap was hell on a man's sense of self-worth. Blake headed toward the house. JD followed.

"And I never had a son of my own. I reckon every man needs a son."

"Some stand-in son I turned out to be," JD grumbled.

Blake stopped by the back door. "Except for once in your

life, JD, you're a man any father would be proud to call son. I've never regretted—"

JD waved his hand, cutting Blake off. "Except for once?"

The old rancher studied JD with sad eyes. "The only time you disappointed me, that I felt I'd failed you, was the day you kicked Josie and Bobby off the ranch."

Blake went into the house, leaving JD standing slack-jawed in the grass.

JD HATED FEELING. Hated emotions.

Sitting on the porch swing in the dark, he wished the night would swallow him up.

Before Bobby and Josie had dropped into his life, he hadn't felt much of anything. Life was a heck of a lot less complicated as a loner. Over the years he'd numbed up inside and avoided life's little entanglements…like relationships.

Where was the numbness now when he needed it most?

Inside a week of coming to the ranch, Bobby had wormed a tunnel straight through to JD's heart. They'd connected on a level deeper than genetics.

And you sent him away. Booted him off the ranch.

JD rubbed the hot, achy knot in the center of his chest. The pain of missing Bobby, of feeling he'd betrayed the boy, damn near crippled him. He struggled to convince himself he had the boy's best interest at heart. That the Delaney money would indeed offer Bobby a better life. A better education. A chance to reach his potential. All good reasons…but not one of them came close to the real reason he'd sent Bobby away.

In a moment of weakness he'd convinced himself the boy deserved better than a half Mexican-half American orphan, has-been-rodeo-cowboy-turned-rancher for a father.

Learning the truth about his parents created a flurry of confusion inside JD. Add missing Josie to the mix, and no wonder he could barely hold himself together.

He reached under the swing and fished another beer from

the cooler. Twisted the top off and downed the amber liquid in several long swallows. He lined up the empty bottle on the porch rail with the other three longnecks. How many beers would he have to drink before the pain disappeared?

He wished Josie were sitting beside him, the night breeze blowing her hair against his face. He had so much to tell her. He ached to share the news about his parents, about discovering he'd been loved by both his mother and father. He wanted Josie to meet his newfound family—José, María and the girls. He thought of the long trip his uncle made twice a year to the Rocking R. If fate hadn't stepped in and taken JD's parents from him, José would never have worked for Blake, and JD would be living somewhere in Mexico instead of Texas.

The boot of his toe dug into the porch floor, and the swing came to a jarring halt. His chest tightened, and he opened his mouth to breathe but couldn't get any air.

Fate.

Fate had killed his father, caused his mother to commit suicide. Fate had landed JD in an orphanage, then at the Rocking R with Blake. Fate had sent him to a motel room with Cassandra Delaney. Fate had brought Bobby to the ranch, and Josie in the boy's wake.

Josie and Bobby had shown JD the meaning of love.

And *he,* not fate, had sent them away. He had only himself to blame for the ache crushing his heart.

Shame filled JD. He had hurt the two people he loved most in life. He could still picture in his mind the fury in Josie's eyes as she'd stood defiantly in the kitchen, her wild mane of hair falling around her shoulders, as she challenged him to be man enough to ask for what he wanted. Brave enough to reach out and take what he deserved.

But she hadn't said the words he'd yearned to hear. After witnessing the confrontation between Josie and her father a few weeks ago, JD believed that Josie, too, was afraid of rejection. Afraid that if she confessed her love for him he'd throw it back in her face. Why hadn't he picked up on this sooner?

Because you're a coward.

But learning about his past from José had helped him realize his self-worth as a human being. He was entitled to happiness and love as much as anyone else. For the first time in his life, he felt free to reach out and grasp happiness. Free to love Josephine. Free to fight for Bobby.

"You gonna sit out here all night and drink yourself stupid?"

"Maybe." JD scowled at Blake as the old man joined him on the porch.

"Drinkin' never fixed nothin'."

Chalk up a point for the old man. JD had slammed back four beers and still hadn't figured out how to fix everything he'd screwed up.

"Josie called a while ago."

His fingers clenched the bottle. "Why didn't you get me?"

"She didn't ask to talk to you."

Well, damn, that stung.

"Said a custody hearing is scheduled for the second Monday in October."

"So," JD snorted, angry at the idea of the Delaneys raising Bobby. Hating the sense of helplessness filling him.

"Josie's suing her parents for custody."

As the words sank in, JD frowned. "*She's* suing for custody?"

"Yep, that's what she said."

"But she's not married—"

"Single women get custody of kids all the time."

"But her parents have money—"

"She's got money, too."

"Why would she—"

"She loves Bobby as much—maybe more—than you do."

"More than me? Wait a minute—" JD popped off the swing, then grabbed the chain to keep from pitching forward.

"Sit down before you fall flat on your face."

Head swimming, JD obeyed.

"You listen to me, young man. Josie loves Bobby as if the boy were her own son, and she loves you, too. Although if she saw your sorry, drunken hide, I reckon she'd change her mind. You get your ornery back end up to Chicago and help her fight for Bobby." Blake stomped into the house, slamming the door hard enough to rattle the shutters.

JD glared at the remaining beer in the cooler, then kicked the plastic container across the porch, the bottles rolling out along the way.

After several long minutes he reached into the front pocket of his jeans and pulled out Josie's pink hair ribbon.

Two days after he'd kicked Josie and Bobby off the ranch, he'd returned to the house and had collapsed on his bed, emotionally and physically exhausted. When he'd awoken several hours later, he'd spotted the hair ribbon lying on the pillow next to his head.

He'd stared at the ribbon for a long…long…time.

"ALL RISE. The Honorable Judge Virginia Gray presiding."

Josephine stood beside her lawyer, watching the regal-looking judge enter the courtroom. The woman wore her salt-and-pepper hair piled high on her head, bright red lipstick and oversize glasses. Josephine guessed her age to be around fifty. She seated herself in the plush, brown leather chair, then banged the gavel, jarring Josephine's already taut nerves.

The judge studied both sets of counsel, lifting an eyebrow at the four lawyers and two assistant attorneys flanking William Delaney.

Her lawyer, touted as the best custody lawyer in the Chicago area, cost a small fortune. His sleek Armani suit and crocodile leather briefcase might impress some judges, but not Judge Gray, given the impassive expression on her face.

While the judge flipped through a stack of court documents, Josephine sneaked a peek at her parents. Her mother turned her head from side to side, offering a sickeningly sweet Madonnalike smile for anyone who bothered to notice. Her father remained calm—only the grim line of his mouth indicated he was losing patience with the whole proceeding. He tapped his watch with the end of a pencil eraser and stared at the members of his legal team.

"Mr. Delaney." Judge Gray motioned to the pencil in his hand. "Are we keeping you from something more pressing?"

Josephine nibbled her lower lip to keep from smiling.

"No, Your Honor," William Delaney answered.

"Well, then. Let's get started, shall we?" The judge removed her large glasses and sat back in the chair. "I'm going to do things a little differently today. I'm not in the mood for opening statements. I've read both custody petitions—"

Josephine's lawyer stood. "If I may, Your Honor?"

"You may not, Counsel. Sit down." She scowled at both legal teams, daring them to interrupt. "I'll give both parties an opportunity to answer my questions pertaining to one Robert Delaney, age five. William Delaney, you may take the stand first."

The lawyers shuffled papers furiously and flipped through law books on the table, but her father ignored them all and strode to the court clerk, raised his hand and repeated the oath. Seated before the judge, he arrogantly crossed his arms over his chest.

"It says here—" the judge waved a sheet of paper from the file in front of her "—that you hired a private investigator to search for your grandson's biological father."

"Yes, Your Honor. The investigator was not able to uncover any information that might lead to locating the man."

"In other words, Mr. Delaney, for the foreseeable future Robert's biological father is out of the picture."

"That's correct, Your Honor."

"Mr. Delaney. Please tell the court why a man—" Judge

Gray perched her glasses on the end of her nose and perused the open file in front of her "—who's sixty-four is better qualified to raise a five-year-old boy than a twenty-nine-year-old woman."

"Age has nothing to do with the ability to raise a child properly. I have the financial means and resources to provide my grandson with a superior education."

"Do you love your grandson, Mr. Delaney?"

"Of course I love him. He's our daughter's child."

Josephine's chest ached at her father's answer. Love was so cut-and-dried in his mind. He believed just saying the word *love* made it true.

"Currently, Robert is enrolled in a public elementary school. But I see here you have different plans for his education. Why are you enrolling him in a boys' military academy?"

"I want nothing but the best for my grandson. He'll receive a top notch education at the academy and will be taught the proper respect for authority, as well."

"This academy is in Maine, Mr. Delaney."

"Only the best for my grandson."

"When will you see your grandson?"

"I assure you, we'll visit him regularly, and bring him home for the holidays."

Josephine had to bite her tongue to keep from objecting. How could her father have forgotten the numerous times he'd made arrangements to visit her and Cassandra at the private girls' school they'd attended, only to cancel out at the last minute due to business conflicts?

"Who will watch over Robert when he's on vacation from school?"

William Delaney rolled his shoulders. "We will, of course."

"Mr. Delaney, you run a multimillion-dollar investment firm."

He sat straighter in the chair, his chest puffing out. "Yes, Your Honor."

"I imagine you put in long hours each day."

"I do. But my wife will be—"

"I see your wife is involved in several charities and ladies' clubs. Who will watch over your grandson when you're at the office and your wife is volunteering her time and services to the community?"

"We've hired an exceptional nanny to help care for him and oversee his activities."

The judge pinched the bridge of her nose. "Let me get this straight. You seek custody of your grandson so you can ship him off to a military academy or place him in the care of a nanny when he resides in your home. Am I correct?"

Josephine's heart lightened at the dark tone in the judge's voice, and she prayed that beneath the judge's stern demeanor lay a woman with a warm heart and a weakness for children. She glanced at her father's counsel and hope surged through her. Three of the lawyers appeared to have come down with a sudden illness that left them pasty faced. The fourth lawyer was still furiously flipping pages in a law journal.

"Your Honor, with all due respect, the boy requires discipline and guidance. I have the means to provide a stable, structured environment in which he will have every opportunity to succeed in life and make something of himself."

"I think I've heard enough, Mr. Delaney. You may step down. Mrs. Delaney, please take the stand."

Regina Delaney rose from her seat and spent a good fifteen seconds straightening her rust-colored fall suit. As she made her way to the witness stand, the *click-click* of her two-inch heels against the tile floor echoed off the walls like the sound of gunshots. After swearing to tell the truth, she took the witness stand and smiled demurely at the judge.

"What have you to say, Mrs. Delaney? Are you ready to welcome your grandson into your home and assume full care of the boy?"

"Well, Your Honor, I can't replace his mother, bless her

soul. But we would certainly love the child and see he receives all the advantages we provided our daughter Cassandra."

Leaning forward, the judge rested her elbows on the desk. "You didn't answer my question, Mrs. Delaney."

"Oh, dear." Josephine's mother fluttered her fingers in the air. "I must have misunderstood. Could you repeat the question, please?"

"Are you willing to assume full care of your grandson when he's living in your home?"

"I believe my husband already mentioned we've hired a nanny with years of experience."

"What is the nanny's name?"

"Mrs. Celina Naravas."

Celina Naravas was her mother's cook!

Josephine pressed her hand to her stomach, almost sick with the thought of what Bobby's life would be like with a sixty-year-old woman swatting his fingers when he stuck his hand in the cookie jar.

The judge made a note in the file, then asked, "Don't you wish to share in your grandson's childhood experiences, Mrs. Delaney?"

"Of course I do. The academy will keep us informed of Robert's progress on a regular basis."

Shaking her head, the judge tapped a finger against the top of her desk. "What about your grandson's birthday?"

"I will not forget Robert's birthday." Regina Delaney sniffed and pointed her nose in the air. "My assistant keeps track of those things."

"Tell me, Mrs. Delaney, is this how your daughter, Robert's biological mother, would choose to raise her son?"

Josephine's mother straightened in the chair. "Of course, Cassandra would wish for her son to have the same upbringing she'd had."

"Mrs. Delaney, why was your daughter estranged from the family at the time of her death?"

"Estranged? Cassandra wasn't estranged. She was merely spreading her wings."

Did her mother really believe Cassandra would have eventually returned home? A deep sense of regret and sadness filled Josephine as she realized her mother truly hadn't understood either of her daughters.

"That will be all, Mrs. Delaney. You may step down."

Judge Gray scanned the case file once again. Josephine waited, her stomach muscles twisting until her insides felt like a pretzel. A few moments later, the judge's gaze zoomed in on Josephine. "Your turn, Ms. Delaney."

Avoiding eye contact with her parents, Josephine approached the clerk. She set her left hand on the Bible, the leather comforting and warm beneath her fingertips. Raising her right hand, she dutifully swore to tell the truth. The whole truth. Nothing but the truth. No matter who it hurt.

After taking a seat, Josephine struggled not to squirm under the judge's stare. She hadn't felt this nervous since the day she'd presented her first economic forecast to the board members of her father's firm.

"Help me make sense of this, Ms. Delaney. Why are you challenging your parents for the right to raise your sister's child?"

"Your Honor." She cast an apologetic glance at her parents. "I love my mother and father. They mean well. But in all honesty, I don't want my nephew raised the same way his mother and I were raised. He deserves better."

Regina Delaney clutched her throat and gasped as if she'd been mortally wounded. William Delaney sprang from his chair and sputtered, "How dare you criticize—"

"Control yourself, Mr. Delaney or I'll boot you from my courtroom." Judge Gray shifted her attention back to the witness stand. "Ms. Delaney, as a child you lived very affluently, experienced opportunities and privileges associated mainly with the upper class. What exactly was missing from your childhood?"

Heart breaking, Josephine stared at her parents, yearning for the one thing they had withheld all her life. "*Unconditional love,* Your Honor."

The judge studied the older couple, who sat in stunned silence. "Elaborate, please."

"I'm not sure my parents know what unconditional love is." Josephine's voice cracked. "I believe my sister, Bobby's mother, chose to live her life away from the family because she realized she could never be what my parents expected her to be." With a lump in her throat, Josephine choked back a cry when her father's weary face appeared to age right before her eyes.

"Until my sister's death, I hadn't known I had fallen victim to my parents' expectations. All my successes and accomplishments were to please them in the hope of earning their love. I didn't understand that no matter what I did, how successful I became, I would always fall short in their eyes."

Josephine turned to the judge. "I didn't have to earn Bobby's love. He offered it freely. And he accepted my love without conditions." Her heart expanded when she saw the bright sheen in the judge's eyes. "A five-year-old boy showed me what really matters in life. Bobby deserves the same unconditional love and acceptance."

"So you intend to raise your nephew differently from the way your parents raised you?"

"Yes, Your Honor."

"How will you juggle the demands of a full-time job and motherhood?"

Ignoring the heat crawling up her neck, Josephine answered, "Yesterday, Your Honor, I was fired from my position at Delaney Financial Services. As of today, I'm officially a stay-at-home mom."

"Fired, you say?" The judge's forehead disappeared into her hairline as she glared at William Delaney.

"Yes, Your Honor."

"I admire your willingness to sacrifice your career to stay at home and raise your nephew, but who's going to pay the bills?"

"I am, ma'am."

All heads turned at the sound of the husky voice. Stunned, Josephine stared at JD, standing tall and proud at the back of the room. The judge banged her gavel until the courtroom quieted. "Who are you?"

"A cowboy in love, ma'am."

"Well, don't stand there, cowboy, approach the bench."

Handsome in his freshly pressed denim Wranglers and western shirt, he removed his Stetson. Josephine stifled a gasp. He'd cut his hair! As he walked toward the judge's bench with long, determined strides, Josephine's heart ached at the dark circles ringing his brown eyes. He'd lost weight, too. Had he missed her as much as she'd missed him? Or did he just miss Bobby?

He stopped in front of the witness stand and gazed at her with such naked longing in his eyes her throat swelled shut. Turning to the judge, he nodded. "Ma'am."

Judged Gray blushed. "It's 'Your Honor.'"

JD flashed his pearly whites. "Yes, ma'am."

"What's your name, cowboy?"

"Juan Diego Gonzalez."

"Mr. Gonzalez. You say you plan to pay Ms. Delaney and her nephew's living expenses. Pray tell, what does she owe you in return?"

"Marriage." JD grasped Josephine's hands, squeezing tightly. "I love you, Josie. With or without Bobby, I want you by my side for always."

The judge cleared her throat. "You're willing to raise Ms. Delaney's nephew and accept him as your son even though you are not his biological father?"

JD turned back to the judge. "When social services drove Bobby out to the ranch and told me I was his father, I knew in my heart we couldn't be related. Then I looked into his sad face and saw the same loneliness, the same fear of rejection, I'd felt as a child growing up in an orphanage. Right then, I believed with all my heart I was meant to be the boy's father. I may not be Bobby's biological father, but I'm his daddy by choice."

JD inhaled deeply before continuing. "I can't compete with William Delaney's millions. I'm nothing but a simple cowboy, a decent bronc rider and half owner of the Rocking R Ranch." He shoved a hand through his short hair. "Bobby may not have all the advantages and material things he could have if he lived with his grandparents, but I can guarantee one thing, the most important thing, Bobby will be loved... unconditionally."

"I see." The judge sniffed, then discreetly dabbed the corner of one eye with a tissue. "You believe marrying Ms. Delaney solves everyone's problem?"

"Yes, ma'am. Josie's a warm loving woman who puts the needs of others before her own. In all honesty, I'm not good enough for her, but I intend to have her just the same. I'll make sure she never regrets taking a chance on this simple cowboy."

Josephine gave up the battle to hold back the tears and let them flow unheeded down her cheeks. No matter the judge's ruling today, she and JD would do everything in their power to make sure Bobby felt loved and wanted all his life.

"Well, Mr. Gonzalez, lucky for you this case landed in my court. I happen to have a fondness for cowboys and Texas."

When the room erupted in a slew of "Objection, Your Honor", Judge Gray pounded the gavel. "Order in the court! I hearby grant full custody of Robert Delaney to Ms. Josephine Delaney, on the condition she marry Texas cowboy Juan Diego Gonzalez!"

JD grinned. "Done, ma'am."

Josephine laughed as JD lifted her off the witness stand. He hugged her, and she whispered near his ear, "I love you, JD."

"God, Josie, I love you so much. Forgive me for sending you and Bobby away."

She stroked his cheek. "You're forgiven, cowboy."

The judge banged the gavel again and sent them a pointed look. "Get yourselves a marriage license and meet in my chambers in thirty minutes."

JD BROKE OUT in a sweat as he opened the door to the Children's Playhouse Day Care—the extended-day kindergarten program Bobby attended until Josie could pick him up after work each day. He ushered her inside and checked his watch.

He and Josie had been married exactly twenty-three minutes and…thirty-one seconds. They'd pledged their love and said their I dos, then hand in hand they'd sprinted from the courthouse and battled late-afternoon traffic to get to their son.

Bobby.

Anxiety gnawed away at JD's insides as he scanned the play area searching for a blond-headed boy. What if Bobby hated him because he'd sent him away? If he had to, JD would spend the rest of his life making amends for his mistake.

"Dad! Dad!"

JD turned at the sound of his son's voice. A ball of emotion choked his airways as the five-year-old sprinted across the toy-strewn room. JD bent at the waist and scooped up Bobby on the fly. His son's blue eyes sparkled with happiness for a few seconds, then his face clouded with confusion.

A steel band snapped shut around JD's chest, and he stopped breathing. He waited for Bobby to lash out at him, accuse him of abandoning him. He deserved nothing less. The boy glanced at Josie. "Is vacation over, Aunt Josephine?"

Vacation?

Stepping closer, she rubbed Bobby's back. "Yes. Our vacation is officially over."

"But Dad ruined the surprise."

Dad. The band around JD's chest eased a fraction. "What surprise, pardner?"

"We was gonna drive Aunt Josephine's Jeep back on Thanksgiving."

Josie's smile widened.

Confused, he asked, "What Jeep?"

She shrugged. "A Jeep seemed better suited for ranch life than my Mercedes."

JD stared at his wife, feeling lightheaded and weak. A deep, joyous shudder racked his body when he realized she'd intended to return to Texas whether she'd gained custody of Bobby or not. He dragged in a deep breath, and sent up a silent prayer of thanks to every god in the heavens for bringing Josie and Bobby into his life.

Bobby's pudgy hands clamped against the sides of his father's face. "Dad?"

"Yeah?"

"Did you come to drive us home?"

JD's throat threatened to swell shut. Josie hadn't told Bobby his father had sent him away. His son would never learn his father had abandoned him in a moment of self-doubt. He gazed at Josie, hoping his eyes reflected his love for her, his promise never to doubt himself or their love again. "Yes, Bobby. I came to take you home."

Right then JD vowed to spend the rest of his life proving to the two people he loved more than anything else in the world he'd never abandon them; instead, would love them forever, no matter what the future held.

"Guess what, sport?" Josie grinned. "You can't call me Aunt Josephine anymore."

Bobby frowned. "I can't?"

JD chuckled at the pucker forming across the bridge of his son's nose. Damned if the kid didn't take after Josie more and more every day.

"Nope. You have to call her Mom."

"Mom? Why?"

"Because JD and I just got married. I'm officially your mother and JD is officially your father and we're officially a family."

Bobby's eyes rounded, and he whispered, "You're really my dad?"

JD's smile wobbled. "Forever."

"There's something else I have to tell you guys."

"What?" Both JD and Bobby spoke at once.

"There's going to be a new baby brother or sister next May."

"Cool. I gotta go tell Jimmy. He's my new friend." Bobby wiggled out of his father's arms and ran back to the play area, as if the bomb Josie had just dropped had had the impact of a popgun going off, instead of a cannon blast.

Heart ready to burst, JD pulled Josie into his arms and buried his face in her neck, needing her warmth, her reassurance. Cupping the back of her head, he held her close, almost afraid of the intense joy filling him. "When?" he whispered near her ear.

"The bathtub."

He chuckled. Shifting slightly away from her, he gently set his palm over her stomach and looked into her beautiful blue eyes. Her love surrounded him and he bowed his head, giving thanks to this woman, who made him feel whole again, made him feel worthy; who gave him a family to love, a family of his own to belong to.

Epilogue

Josephine sat on the porch swing, watching the setting sun paint the sky a reddish-orange. At 9:00 p.m., the late-June heat hovered at tolerable. Practically a full year had passed since the day she'd arrived in Texas, intent on bringing her nephew back to Chicago.

José, María and the girls had shown up three weeks ago, having decided to spend the summer at the ranch when JD had told them about the baby. Josie loved watching JD and Bobby enjoy their newly found family.

She turned her attention to the banging coming from the shed behind the barn. As soon as Bobby had gone to bed tonight, Blake had headed for the shed, where he was secretly building Bobby a go-cart. Josephine smiled as she listened to the racket. After she and Bobby had returned to the ranch last October, Blake had officially announced his retirement and turned over the day-to-day running of the ranch to JD. Now Blake spent his days playing grandpa.

JD's new breeding program had gotten off to a great start last fall. Word was getting around that the Rocking R Ranch had some of the best bulls' calves in the area. Josephine had had to do some hard negotiating, but she'd finally convinced JD to update his computer system and purchase several new software programs.

She'd spent hours creating spreadsheets and tracking not

only profit and expenditures, but also each animal's breeding history. He'd taken one look at her efforts and had appointed her official financial manager for the Rocking R.

Life on the ranch was darn near perfect. And Josephine's relationship with her parents was slowly but surely improving, also. She smiled as she recalled the letter from her father she'd received yesterday.

He'd informed her of the trust fund he'd started so his grandchildren could attend Harvard Business School one day. Bobby might very well be the first true-blue cowboy to attend Harvard. She could imagine all the girls swooning when the blue-eyed, blond-haired cowboy strolled across campus in boots and a Stetson.

With JD's encouragement, she'd invited her parents to the ranch last Thanksgiving and then again at Christmas, but they'd declined. Not long after New Year's, her father had begun phoning every week, with the excuse of seeking her business advice. Inevitably, the conversation would turn personal, and he'd inquire about her pregnancy and her health. Then he'd ask to speak to Bobby for a few minutes. Both sides were trying. That was enough for now.

The front door opened and JD stepped onto the porch, his jeans barely clinging to his slim hips, his face tight with worry and his arms full of his squalling daughter.

"Something's wrong with Sara, Josie. She won't stop crying."

Josephine held out her arms for the five-week-old baby and swallowed a laugh at the utter relief in JD's expression when he handed over the dark-headed bundle. "She's probably hungry."

Her daughter's face turned purple with frustration and her tiny lungs gasped for breath. Josephine was positive Sara had her father's temperament. JD believed the sun rose and set on his little princess, but wait until the two of them went head-to-head for the first time. Josephine would insist on a front-row seat for that one.

With José's help and a trip back to JD's birthplace, El Porvenir, Mexico, her husband had begun the slow, often painful journey of making peace with his past. Wanting to name his daughter Sara, in memory of his mother, had been a huge healing step for JD.

She unbuttoned her top and placed Sara at her breast. Her daughter calmed as soon as she latched on.

JD expelled a rough breath and sank down on the swing. He laid his head back and rubbed his face. "God, Josie, I don't think I'm cut out for this father stuff. I keep making mistakes."

Josephine's throat tightened. She wished JD would stop being so hard on himself.

"I'm always saying the wrongs things, doing the wrong things. Bobby's still mad at me because I flushed the fish down the toilet, instead of burying it in the backyard with a grave marker."

Josephine adjusted Sara in her arms, then snuggled closer to JD's side. His arm came around her, and he kissed the top of her head.

"You're the only one who isn't mad at me." He nibbled her earlobe, then moved his lips to hers and spent a long time loving her mouth.

JD was trying so hard to make amends for sending her and Bobby away from the ranch last August. No matter how many times she told him she loved him, he worried he might do or say something to make them want to leave.

Time. If needed, she'd spend the rest of her life standing by her man and showing him every way she knew how that she loved him. "Parents aren't perfect. We'll make our share of mistakes, but our love will make up for the blunders."

"Do you think we'll ever learn why Cassandra put my name on Bobby's birth certificate?"

"I believe she saw into your heart that night she was with you. Saw your goodness, your honor and integrity. She wanted you to raise her son because she believed you would love him unconditionally."

"But what if—"

Josephine pressed a finger to JD's mouth. She understood he worried about Bobby's biological father showing up at the ranch and trying to take Bobby away. She wished she could ease JD's fears. "If the time comes, we'll stand side by side and fight for Bobby together."

JD opened his mouth to speak, then closed it and glanced away. Josephine ached for her husband. Every so often JD would ask her if she had any regrets about marrying him and having to move to the ranch and adapt to a whole new way of life.

Lifting her face, she kissed the underside of his whiskered jaw. "Nothing you could do or say will make me stop loving you, JD. You're my destiny. I'm right where I was meant to be…by your side."

He rested his forehead against hers. "You're the best thing that's ever happened to me, Josie." Cupping the back of Sara's head, he kissed his daughter's inky mop of hair. "I love our family so much."

"I know, honey. We love you, too."

Turn the page for excerpts
from next month's four lively and delightful books
from American Romance!

Archer's Angels by Tina Leonard
(American Romance #1053)

Archer Jefferson—he's brother number eight in Tina's COWBOYS BY THE DOZEN miniseries. Enjoy this popular author's high-energy writing, quirky characters and outrageous situations. And in June, come back for more with *Belonging to Bandera!*
Available in February 2005.

Clove Penmire looked around as she got off the bus in Lonely Hearts Station, Texas. For all her fascination with cowboys and the lure of the dusty state she'd read so much about, she had to admit that small-town Texas was nothing like her homeland of Australia.

A horse broke free from the barn across the street, walking itself nonchalantly between the two sides of the old-time town. A cowboy sprinted out of the barn and ran after his horse, but he was laughing as he caught up to it.

Clove smiled. From the back she couldn't tell if the man was handsome, but he was dressed in Wranglers and a hat, and as far as she could tell, this cowboy was the real thing.

And she had traveled to Texas for the *real thing.*

That sentiment would have sounded preposterous, even to Clove, just a month ago. Until she'd learned that her sister, Lucy, couldn't have a baby. Of course, people all over the world couldn't always conceive when they wanted to. They adopted, or pursued other means of happiness. She hadn't been too worried—until Lucy had confessed that she thought her husband might leave her for a woman who could bear children.

Clove's thoughts then took a decidedly new trajectory, one that included fantasies of tossing her brother-in-law into the ocean.

Now the cowboy caught her interested gaze, holding it for just a second before he looked back at his horse. The man was extremely handsome. Breathtakingly so. Not the cowboy for her, considering her mission, and the fact that she was what people politely referred to as…a girl with a good personality.

She sighed. If Lucy had gotten all the beauty, their mother always said with a gentle smile, then Clove had gotten all the bravery. Which was likely how she'd ended up as a stuntwoman.

She watched the cowboy brush his horse's back with one hand, and fan a fly away from its lovely flame-marked face. He was still talking to it; she could hear low murmuring that sounded very sexy, especially since she'd never heard a man murmur in a husky voice to *her.*

"Archer Jefferson!" someone yelled from inside the barn. "Get that cotton-pickin', apple-stealin', dog-faced Appaloosa in here!"

"Insult the man, but not the sexy beast!" he yelled back.

Clove gasped. Archer Jefferson! The man she'd traveled several time zones to see! Her TexasArcher of two years' worth of e-mail correspondence!

He was all cowboy, more cowboy than she'd come mentally prepared to corral. "Whoa," she murmured to herself.

Okay, a man that drool-worthy did not lack female friends. Why had he spent two years writing to a woman he'd never meet? She wrinkled her nose, pushed her thick glasses up on her nose and studied him further. Tight jeans, dirty boots. Long, black hair under a black felt hat—he'd never mentioned long hair in their correspondence. Deep voice. Piercing blue eyes, she noted as he turned around, catching her still staring at him. She jumped, he laughed and then he tipped his hat to her as he swung up onto the "dog-faced" Appaloosa, riding it into the barn in a manner the stuntwoman in her appreciated.

Just how difficult would it be to entice that cowboy into her bed? Archer had put ideas about his virility in her mind, with his Texas-size bragging about his manliness and the babies popping out all over Malfunction Junction ranch.

Seeing him, however, made her think that perhaps he hadn't been bragging as much as stating fact. Her heart beat faster. He'd said he wasn't in the relationship market.

But a baby, just *one* baby…

Her Secret Valentine by Cathy Gillen Thacker
(American Romance #1054)

This is the entertaining and emotional fifth installment in Cathy's series, THE BRIDES OF HOLLY SPRINGS. With a little help from Cupid—and the close-knit Hart clan—a long-distance couple has a Valentine's Day reunion they'll never forget! You'll be captivated by Cathy's trademark charm, but you'll also identify with the real issues explored in this book—the tough choices faced by a two-career couple in today's world.
Available in February 2005.

"How long is this situation between you and Ashley going to go on?" Mac Hart asked.

Cal tensed. He thought he'd been invited over to his brother Mac's house to watch playoff football with the rest of the men in the family. Now, suddenly, it was looking more like an intervention. He leaned forward to help himself to some of the nachos on the coffee table in front of the sofa. "I don't know what you mean."

"Then let us spell it out for you," Cal's brother-in-law, Thad Lantz, said with his usual coachlike efficiency.

Joe continued. "She missed Janey's wedding to Thad in August, as well as Fletcher's marriage to Lily in October, and Dylan and Hannah's wedding in November."

Cal bristled. They all knew Ashley was busy completing

her OB/GYN fellowship in Honolulu. "She wanted to be here but since the flight from Honolulu to Raleigh is at least twelve hours, it's too far to go for a weekend trip. Not that she has many full weekends off in any case." Nor did he. Hence, their habit of rendezvousing in San Francisco, since it was a six- or seven-hour flight for each of them.

More skeptical looks. "She didn't make it back to Carolina for Thanksgiving or Christmas or New Year's this year, either," Dylan observed.

Cal shrugged and centered his attention on the TV, where a log of pregame nonsense was taking place. "She had to work all three holidays." He wished the game would hurry up and start. Because the sooner it did, the sooner this conversation would be over.

"'Had to,' or volunteered?" Fletcher murmured with a questioning lift of his dark eyebrows.

Uneasiness settled on Cal. He'd had many of the same questions himself. Still, Ashley was his wife, and he felt honor-bound to defend her. "I saw her in November in San Francisco. We celebrated all our holidays then." In one passion-filled weekend that had, oddly enough, left him feeling lonelier and more uncertain of their union than ever.

Concerned looks were exchanged all around. Cal knew the guys in the family all felt sorry for him, which just made the situation worse.

Dylan dipped a tortilla chip into the chili-cheese sauce. "So when's Ashley coming home?" he asked curiously.

That was just it—Cal didn't know. Ashley didn't want to talk about it. "Soon," he fibbed.

All eyes turned to him. Cal waited expectantly, knowing from the silence that there was more. Finally, Joe cleared his throat. "The women in the family are all upset. You've been married nearly three years now, and most of that time you and Ashley have been living apart."

"So?" Cal prodded.

"So, they're tired of seeing you unhappy." Dylan took over where Cal had left off. "They're giving you and Ashley till Valentine's Day—"

Their wedding anniversary.

"—to make things right."

"And if that doesn't happen?" Cal demanded.

Fletcher scowled. "Then the women in the family are stepping in."

Cupid and the Cowboy by Carol Finch
(American Romance #1055)

Carol Finch is a widely published author making her debut in American Romance—and we're delighted to welcome her! She writes with genuine wit and charm, and she brings you characters you'll like instantly—not to mention a wonderful and vivid sense of place. You'll soon discover that Moon Valley, Texas, is your kind of town....
Available February 2005.

"Damn, here she comes again."

Third time this week that Erika Dunn had shown up uninvited at his ranch house. She was making it difficult for Judd to settle into his self-imposed role as a recluse.

Judd Foster peered through the dusty slats of the miniblinds and heavy, outdated drapes that covered his living room window. She had the kind of unadvertised and understated beauty that intrigued a man who'd been trained to look beyond surface appearances. The woman didn't just *walk* to his house; she practically floated. She was too vibrant, too energized. He didn't want her coming around, spreading good cheer and flashing that infectious smile.

He just wanted to be left alone.

His attention shifted to the covered dish in her hand. Judd's mouth watered involuntarily. He wondered what delicious culinary temptation she had delivered this time. More of that melt-in-your-mouth smoked chicken that had been marinated in pineapple juice and coated with her secret concoction of herbs and spices? Or something equally delectable? Apparently, Erika figured the most effective way to coax a man out of his property was to sabotage his taste buds and his stomach.

Judd focused on Erika's face. Her face was wholesome and animated and her eyes reminded him of a cloudless sky. Her ivory skin, dotted with freckles on her upturned nose, made her look fragile and delicate—a blatant contrast to her assertive, bubbly personality. She was part bombshell-in-hiding and part girl-next-door. A woman of interesting contrasts and potential.

Judd watched Erika balance the covered plate in one hand while she hammered on the front door with the other. He knew she wouldn't give up and go away, so he opened the door before she pounded a hole in it. "Now what?" he demanded.

Erika beamed an enthusiastic greeting as she sailed, uninvited, into his house.

The instant Judd felt himself leaning impulsively toward her, he withdrew and stiffened his resistance. "The answer is still no," he said right off.

Might as well beat her to the punch and hope she'd give up her ongoing crusade to buy his property. He didn't want her to sweet-talk him into signing over the old barn that held fond childhood memories. He didn't want to salivate like Pavlov's dogs when the aromatic smoked meat, piled beneath a layer of aluminum foil, whetted his appetite.

Undaunted, Erika thrust the heaping plate at him and smiled radiantly. "No what? *No,* you won't do me a favor by taking this extra food off my hands? *No,* you've decided to stop eating altogether?"

She glanced around the gloomy living room, shook her head in disapproval, then strode to the west window. "Really, Judd, it should be a criminal offense to keep this grand old house enshrouded in darkness. It looks like vampire headquarters."

Leaving him holding the plate, she threw open the drapes, jerked up the blinds and opened all three living room windows. Fresh air poured into the room, carrying her scent to him. Judd winced when blinding sunbeams speared into the room, spotlighting Erika's alluring profile—as if he needed another reminder of how well proportioned she was.

He didn't. Furthermore, he didn't want to deal with the lusty thoughts her appearance provoked. He didn't want to like anything about Erika Dunn. Erika was too attractive, too optimistic. Too *everything* for a man who'd become cynical and world-weary after years of belly-crawling around hell-holes in Third World countries.

He wondered what it was going to take to discourage Erika from waltzing in here as if she owned the place and trying to befriend a man who was completely unworthy of friendship. He hadn't been able to protect the one true friend he'd had in the past decade and that tormented him. He didn't want anyone to depend on him or expect anything from him.

Emergency Engagement by Michele Dunaway
(American Romance #1056)

In this emotional story by Michele Dunaway, you'll find a classic plot—the "engagement of convenience"—and a group of very contemporary characters. Michele is known for this appealing combination of enduring themes and likable characters who live up-to-the-minute lives!
Available February 2005.

He wasn't supposed to be there. It wasn't his night; in fact, this week he wasn't supposed to deal with any emergencies unless they occurred during normal office hours.

But because of a wedding, there'd been a shortage of pediatricians to staff the pediatric emergency floor. So, when his partner had asked, Quinton had agreed to take Bart's shift. Even though it was a Friday night, Quinton had nothing better to do.

Which, when he stopped to think about it, was pathetic. He, Dr. Quinton Searle, pediatric specialist, *should* have something to do. At thirty-five, he should have some woman to date, some place to be, something.

But the truth was that he didn't, which was why, when the call came through, he was in the wrong place at the right time. He turned to Elaine. He liked working with her. At fifty-something she'd seen it all, and was a model of brisk efficiency, the most reliable nurse in any crisis. "What have I got?" he asked.

"Four-year-old child. Poison Control just called. The kid ate the mother's cold medicine. Thought it was green candy."

He frowned as he contemplated the situation. "How many?"

Elaine checked her notes. "The mother thinks it was only two tablets, but she isn't sure. The container's empty."

Great, Quinton thought. He hated variables. "Is she here yet?"

Elaine shook her head. "Any minute. She's on her way. Downstairs knows to buzz me immediately so we can bring the kid right up."

Quinton nodded. "Downstairs" was slang for the main emergency room. As part of the Chicago Presbyterian Hospital's patient care plan, a separate emergency floor had been set up especially for children. Children were triaged in the main E.R., and then sent up to the pediatric E.R. He shoved his hand into the pocket of his white doctor's coat. "Let me know the minute you get the buzz."